Alpha's Frost Bound Fate

A Shifter Paranormal Romance

Ruby Brinks

Contents

CHAPTER 1

GAVIN

Power shouldn't be handed down from generation to generation. It should be given to the strongest member of the family. It should be mine.

"They're weak," I growl, fighting the same old fight I've battled so many times before.

"That's enough, Gavin! We've already had this conversation," my father replies without even looking up from the pile of documents scattered across his desk.

"Garren doesn't even know how to manipulate the simplest of shadows," I continue, a part of me hoping to make him see reason. "The only time he actually enjoys the darkness is when he's in the confines of his own room, surrounded by a horde of prostitutes."

"Gavin," my father warns, his eyes narrowing as he finally looks up.

"It's true," I insist. "Did you know that the idiot named his dick Claw? He's constantly blabbering about how many women he has clawed. Don't you see it? Our very own crown Prince is bringing disgrace to our family name."

"Your brother is my responsibility," my father tells me, but the slight twitch of his mouth confirms to me that he didn't know the extent of Garren's exploits.

"When?" I challenge. "His official ascension has already begun. He has no military experience and no respect inside or outside this court. He'll be the end of our family."

Father leans into his chair, making himself comfortable. Even though we've had this conversation ever since I returned from the front lines, he still has a never-ending amount of patience for me. I suppose after dealing with Garren day after day, I must be a breeze of fresh air.

"Since you're so smart and full of suggestions, go on and enlighten me. What would you want me to do?" he asks, raising his brow in question.

It's the first time that he's actually willing to entertain my idea. Taking a deep breath, I move forward and sit on the other side of the desk. I need to tread carefully and present my position clearly. It's my only chance to ascend to the throne, surpassing not one, but all three, of my older brothers.

"Out of the four of us, I'm the only one who pursued military training and has been given the command of a pack. You have to admit that being an Alpha speaks in my favor all by itself," I start, proud to be given the highest status that a military officer can have. "Thanks to my travels, I've also gained diplomatic experience and forged connections with other royal families."

"What else?" Father asks, giving me an encouraging nod.

My lips curl up in a small smile, my instincts telling me that this is my chance to shine. My inner wolf stirs in satisfaction. We're finally being heard and treated with the respect we deserve.

"I'm the only one who knows the real situation out there," I continue, playing up my advantages. "I've been on the ground and seen it with my own eyes. The witches are determined to exterminate our bloodlines, one by one. Young pups were murdered in cold blood, their decapitated bodies left behind to rot next to the ashes of their burned heads. Now, more than ever, we need a strong and ruthless leader. We need someone who fills the souls of our wolves with fear and respect. Now's not the time to be a fucking laughingstock left and right, leaving weak-blooded pups behind."

I shake my head, unable to hide the disgust on my face. My lips curl up in a snarl as I spit the words out, "Rumors are going around that Garren's been caught, on more than one occasion, with human women in his bed, leaving in their bellies half-blooded and impure pups. A black spot on our family's good name that could never be wiped away, but don't worry, Father. I made sure to squash them along with their origin. No evidence and no witnesses will ever be found."

"You've made your point, boy," Father tells me when I'm done speaking.

I suppress a low growl at being referred to in such a simple and demeaning way. The condescending manner in which he looks at me and talks to me is a clear enough indication that I haven't achieved anything.

Father leans forward and rests his elbows on the desk. His eyes lock on mine, the powers inside us eager to come out, but we push them back down into the furthest and darkest depths of our inner wolf.

"You claim you want to save our family, but let me tell you what would happen if I were to give you the Crown," he says and slightly lifts his chin, which only makes him look more regal. "Skipping the line of succession is what would weaken us. There's a reason why our ancestors forbid that the Crown could be inherited by the most powerful member of the family. There were too many fights, and too many bloodlines came close to extinction."

I grit my teeth, remembering how, not even two centuries ago, my family's bloodline was one of the ones that almost disappeared. When brothers started killing brothers, fighting to the death, until only the strongest and the most powerful one survived. The Crown's not worth much if there's no one left alive to bow to it.

"Garren will be the King and then his kids. You're well aware that even if something is to happen to Garren, there are still Grayden and Graham ahead of you," my father tells me with a subtle warning in his tone, reminding me of the deeply drilled beliefs and traditions that families should stick together.

"I would never dream of hurting any of my brothers," I say fiercely, meaning every word of it.

"Good, because it would be too big of a coincidence if you were the one to end up on the throne," he comments, then leans back in his chair and runs his fingers through his hair, brushing it back. When he speaks next, his tone is much more relaxed with a hint of amusement, "If you really want the Crown so much, Gavin, there's only one way for you to get it."

"Yes, Father," I say, knowing what he's referring to.

He gives me a slight nod before returning his attention to the big pile of documents. Recognizing the dismissal, I get up and bow my head in respect. He might not acknowledge it, but I've learned from experience the consequences of not following the court's etiquette.

There's only one place for me to be right now. I need to blow off some steam, process the anger that I harbor for my brother, and calm the frustration caused by a set of stupid ancient rules that prevent the youngest sibling from ascending.

"Little brother."

My whole body comes to a stop, my muscles tensing upon hearing the voice of one person who would be best to stay away from me. Despite my inner turmoil, I understand how the hierarchy inside the court works, so I push it all deep, deep down, leaving nothing but a blank mask of indifference on my face.

"Garren," I greet my brother, taking in his half-undone shirt. "You've missed a couple of buttons."

"Did I?" he asks and absentmindedly glances down. "Oh, yes, you're right."

Standing still, I watch him as his fingers fumble with the buttons. After he fails for the third time, I let out a long breath that turns into a low growl. Garren doesn't notice; his attention is still on the shirt.

"For fuck's sake, come here," I say through gritted teeth.

Startled, Garren looks up, the corners of his lips slowly curling into a big grin. He lets his arms drop to his side and lifts his chin, trustingly exposing his neck.

It would be so easy.

When I step closer to him, a musty and sour scent fills my nostrils, making me recoil, but not before I cover my face with my hand.

"Fucking hell, Garren!" I exclaim angrily, surprised that I didn't notice it sooner. I must've been more distracted than I thought. "You're drunk."

Garren tilts his head to the side and furrows his brow in confusion. "Am I? I would've thought that was yesterday, but I suppose I did have a glass of single malt scotch with my breakfast."

"It's not even eleven in the morning," I say firmly, ashamed not only because he's my brother, but also the heir apparent. Taking a deep breath, I approach him again to fix his buttons. "You should at least act like you care."

"Oh, you mean like you do?" Garren asks, his eyes darkening. "Don't fool yourself, little brother. I know all about your conversation with Father. The sooner you accept your place, the better our lives will get."

It would be so easy, my wolf inside gently reminds me again.

My index finger hovers at Garren's Adam's apple, my nail extending into a claw so sharp that it would cut his throat open before he'd even realize what was happening.

With an effort, I pull back and make a fist to hide the subtle shift, digging my claw into the palm of my hand and breaking the skin. Locking my black eyes with my brother's slightly lighter ones, I let him see the power in them. We don't need to fight to find out who's stronger. All we'd have to do is compare the colors, and everyone would know that my irises are several shades darker than his.

"Keep going like that, and you won't have a kingdom to rule," I reply, then click my heels together and give him a slight neck bow. "Brother."

Without waiting for his dismissal, I leave him standing with his brows furrowed in confusion. He doesn't call after me nor does he move.

The moment that I'm out of his view, I stop and inspect the palm of my hand. The wound is deep, but nothing that my wolf wouldn't be able to recover us from in a couple of minutes.

It should've been him, my wolf says matter-of-factly.

We're not committing a fratricide, I tell him with forced firmness.

Furrowing my brows in concentration, I focus my intense and unwavering stare on the wound to speed up the healing process. The shadowy tentacles sew the two sides of the wound together, leaving only a pale line behind, which will fade away with time.

I leave the Grey Manor before my wolf can change my mind and actually convince me to take what, if not by right, then by hard work and effort, belongs to me. I'd prefer to run to the barracks, but it's the middle of the day, and humans have already been reporting too many sightings of wolves. Seeing a wolf running around the countryside doesn't raise as many questions as it does in the heart of New York City.

James stands to attention when I approach the car. I give him a nod and climb in the backseat.

"Where to, Your Highness?" James asks, locking his eyes with mine through the rearview mirror.

"The barracks," I reply, then pull out my phone to catch up on the world's affairs.

Florida's royalty, the Farrells, have welcomed a new heir into the family. My lips curl up into the smallest of smiles as I think of how happy my mother must be to find out that she has a great nephew. Happiness isn't shared across the whole family, especially the second-born son who's dropping lower in the line of succession.

He's still higher than you, my wolf tells me, and even though I want to shut him up, I can't ignore the rightness of his statement. I will have the Crown one day, and I will find a way to get it without murdering my brothers.

James follows the old train tracks until the very end, then stops the car before we can descend into the underground tunnels. Despite the heavy shields and protections, the magic inside the barracks is too unpredictable to risk a perfectly nice car. With young pups discovering their limits, the elements uncontrollably fly left and right.

"You can take a break," I say to James, my eyes fixed on the entrance to the underground. "I'll be at least two hours."

"As you wish, Your Highness," James replies and waits for me to disappear into the tunnels before driving off.

The trick to finding loyal servants is to get to them when they're on rock bottom and lift them up, step by step. When I came across James, he was a starving young pup, stealing from humans whatever little food he could. He wasn't even aware of the dormant wolf inside him, suppressed by trauma far too great for someone his age.

It took him years of hard work to strengthen his body, and while he's still not fully in control of his wolf-given abilities, he's come a long way. I've even asked one of my two Betas to give him private lessons to help him improve faster.

"Alpha on site!" someone calls when I enter the tunnels.

Everyone stops what they are doing, stands up, and straightens their backs to attention. The barracks are the only place where I'm treated according to the status I've earned, not the one I've been born with.

"At ease," I say, and even though my voice is barely audible, the most experienced wolves hear my words with clarity.

As the packs resume their exercises, I go to the furthest and darkest end of the tunnel where my Shadows gather and practice. My Betas approach me, sensing me long before I come into view.

"Your Highness," they greet me in unison.

"Tiana, Jay," I acknowledge them, then stop by their side to observe the training session. "How's it going?"

As the second Beta, Jay returns to run the Shadows through the drills specifically designed to work and improve their power of darkness. Tiana remains back, watching the pack with me.

"Bobby almost mastered Umbrakinesis," my first Beta replies, pointing at the teenager in the far corner. "He can manipulate the shadows to a certain degree, but he's not fully in control yet."

"Work harder with him. If he can't master the basics, there's no place for him with the Shadows," I reply calmly. "The last thing we need is the untrained pup running around, chasing shadows."

"His Night Vision is better than even Jay's," Tiana tells me, jumping to his defense.

I look at her from the corner of my eye and take a moment to consider her words. Umbrakinesis is a very useful and quite powerful ability, but Night Vision also has its advantages. However, if the wielder isn't strong enough to summon the darkness in the middle of the day, then the Night Vision immediately becomes useless.

"He needs to master Umbrakinesis," I reply with a tone of finality. "If I don't see some progress in three weeks, we'll replace him."

"As you say, Your Highness," Tiana acknowledges with a slight bow of her head.

"Anything else I should know about?" I ask, looking around at the pack with watchful eyes for telltale signs of just about anything that could bring shame to the unit.

"Gracie's developed a new ability," Tiana informs me, gesturing at the raven-haired girl half my size. "She's been animating Molly's shadow all week."

"It's too dangerous to practice on each other," I reply firmly, not showing just how impressed I am with the fact that a scrawny little girl wields so much power. "Don't we have any humans in the dungeons?"

"We do," Tiana confirms, then turns to the pack. "Molly, take a break. Oliver, fetch one human trash from the dungeons for Gracie to practice on."

"Good," I say approvingly, then turn to my Beta. "How about you, Tiana? Have you been keeping your abilities in shape?"

Tiana grins, the stretched claw scar across her face making her look utterly wicked and monstrous. "I might not be able to kick your Royal ass, but I can certainly make you sweat for it."

The corners of my lips twitch in amusement, but they never fully curl up. As the ghost of a smile remains on my face, I grab my tie and undo it with one sharp pull, then throw it across a chair. I treat my jacket with more care and gently fold it, careful not to wrinkle it. Considering all the servants running around and tending to my every need, the worry about ruining my clothes is ridiculous, but also something that my brothers don't share. Serving in the military left a bigger mark on me than anyone might think.

When I'm shirtless, my powerful torso exposed, and my carved muscles tensed in anticipation of a fight, I turn to Tiana. "I've had a shitty day, so you better bring it on."

"Don't worry about me, Grey," she teases, stretching her neck left and right until it makes a cracking sound. "While you've been keeping your ass warm inside that shiny manor of yours, I've been working on something special."

A wolfish smile spreads on my lips, making me look more sinister than anything else. I'm the apex predator, and while her powers aren't anywhere near mine, she's stubborn and resourceful. A street wolf.

Tipping my head backward, I close my eyes and let out a loud roar. The primitive call wakes up the deepest parts of me, inviting my wolf out to play.

Kill her. Kill them all, my wolf snarls.

Suppressing the most basic and primal urge for the blood of the challenger, I open my even darker eyes as I'm now fully channeling my wolf. While I didn't shift, we're now one and the same, more than ever.

Tiana responds to my roar with her own, albeit hers is much quieter and weaker. Her eyes are a couple of shades brighter than mine, and she didn't fully suppress the shift, allowing her nails to extend into sharp claws and her teeth to grow into long canines. It's actually quite impressive when the shift can be contained to only certain parts of the body. Most of the time during the shift, my wolf's body takes over ours, turning us into the dangerous four-legged creature of the night.

Bring forth the darkness, my wolf tells me, instructing me on something that has been drilled deep into me since before I could even walk and comes as easily as taking a breath.

My eyes narrow ever so slightly as the thick tentacles of darkness respond to my call. There are some murmurs of complaint as the lights are rendered useless, and only the wielders of darkness have the ability to develop Night Vision.

As my pupils dilate and adapt to the lack of light, my brows cock in surprise when Tiana's not standing where I had last seen her. It's impossible for her to move without me noticing at all. It's then that it hits me.

Shadow Mimicry, my wolf tells me, recognizing the special new ability she was referring to.

"Becoming a shadow is an impressive skill," I say under my breath in approval, knowing that she'll hear me. "The real question is, how long can you keep it up before you tire yourself out?"

"Long enough to do this," she growls, materializing behind me with a hand lifted to claw at me.

With the ease of a skilled fighter, I turn on my heel and catch her wrist before it could be a threat. My other hand clutches her neck, slowly tightening the grip and preventing her lungs from filling with fresh air.

Her little trick would work on lesser wolves, but I don't need to see her to know where her shadow is. I've played along, sensing her slip around me, and waited for her to strike.

The thick, shadowy tentacles restrain her from using her other hand. There's no escape for her, and she knows it.

As her lungs begin to burn and her face turns a darker shade of red, her pupils flash with panic. The wolf inside her is dying, slipping away into the depths of unconsciousness that she might not be able to awaken it from if it goes too far. Having your inner wolf in a coma, knowing it's there but being unable to reach it, it's the worst kind of hell for a shifter.

Tiana's on the verge of it, the panic in her eyes absolute. Her lips move, making inaudible sounds as she tries to beg not only for the wolf's life but her own too.

Finish them, my wolf roars and pushes his influence through me, shifting my nails into claws that break Tiana's skin, drawing blood.

It's the metallic scent of the life liquid that brings me back to my senses, and I loosen my grip. Tiana falls to the floor, caressing her neck and gasping for air. As I release the hold on the darkness, the shadows thin out, and the light returns to the room.

Tiana's eyes are wide and fearful. The teasing smile she carried with ease is long gone. With her hand still on her neck as if willing for the blood to stay in, she shifts her body until she's on her knees and bows low until her forehead touches the ground.

I lift my chin higher, taking in the respect she's show-ing me. My eyes dart around as, one by one, the Shadows follow her lead, lowering themselves to their knees. I bury my surprise when the other packs do the same. It's not uncommon for the Shadows to express deference to their Alpha, but having other packs, along with their Alphas, bowing to me is unheard of.

All hail Gavin Grey, the most powerful King that ever lived, my wolf purrs, giving voice to the blasphemy that could cost us everything. A wolf that was part of a pack his whole life can't all of a sudden become a lone animal. The exile would be the end of us, and yet, the call of power is too strong not to answer.

CHAPTER 2

LEIA

Chin up and smile.

I have to bedazzle them not only with my brain but with my looks as well. No one wants to donate their money to a frowning clown.

"Miss Leia," the paparazzi call one over another, their cameras and flashes going ballistic when I step out of the vehicle.

Disrespectful trash, my inner wolf sneers.

They don't know who I am, I remind her with a polite and happy smile on my face as I walk down the red carpet, waving at the cameras.

We should show them. They should be put in their place.

I send a gentle wave of coldness toward the deepest part of my soul where my wolf rests. She grunts in displeasure, then shuts up as the warning sets in.

"What are your hopes and feelings about tonight?" one of the paparazzi asks, aiming his camera at me.

With an absentminded movement, I tuck a stray ashen-white curl behind my ear and look at the human who posed a question. Despite the flashing lights, I manage to locate him and smile.

"There are so many families who can't afford to buy the most basic necessities, and I really hope that tonight we'll gather enough funds to at least give the kids proper clothes and food. This charity is very close to my heart, and I'll do everything in my power to help it," I tell him, meaning every word of it. With a quick gesture around me, I continue, "I'm loving the outcome. People really want to help, it's just that sometimes they need a bit of guidance on how to do it. That's what we're here to give. Thank you."

The paparazzi go wild, calling my name, asking questions one over another, but I just smile and keep walking. I'd love to answer them all, explain everything in detail, but I don't have the time.

Not that he has much of a choice, but my father can barely tolerate me mixing with humans on the best of days. Considering that tonight's fundraiser is highly publicized, he's driving everyone crazy, claiming that I'm tarnishing the family's good name.

Humans and wolves don't mix, my wolf gives voice to my thoughts.

The fundraiser's going great, my speech was a success, but my two hours are up. Like Cinderella, I need to slip away before my father sends a pack after me.

"You're late," my father tells me when I enter the grand foyer.

I jerk my head in his direction, startled by his presence. When I recover from the initial shock, I frown. "I'm five minutes early."

He growls in disagreement but doesn't push his point further, which only confirms that I'm right.

Encouraged by his unexpected retreat, I lift my chin up and foolishly challenge him. "How dare you wait up for me?"

"You're my daughter, and I'll do whatever I please," he replies without missing a beat. The sharpness in his voice diminishes my arrogance, but his face softens ever so slightly as he gestures toward the direction of his office. "I need to talk to you."

"Now?" I ask, raising my brow in question. "Can't it wait for tomorrow? It's been a long day, and I'm rather tired."

"Now, Leia," he replies and starts walking toward the office without bothering to see if I follow.

Not wanting to push him even more than I usually do, I hurry after him, my heels clinking against the marble floors. The rest of the family's already in their respective rooms and the housekeepers away from view. We're as alone as royals can be.

"Sit down," he says, taking a seat on one of the sofas himself.

On the small table across from it, a tray with two glasses and a bottle of Old Rip Van Winkle has been prepared. That particular bourbon cost more than fifty grand per bottle, and he only drank it when he was tackling a serious topic. For some reason, I couldn't shake the feeling that I won't like what he has to say.

Knowing that I can't refuse to sit down with him, I join him on the other side of the same red velvet sofa he picked, while putting as much distance between us as I can. I might be able to reject my father, but I can't allow myself to disrespect my king.

"Everything okay?" I ask, tilting my head to the side and waiting for him to give me any type of indication of what's going on.

He doesn't reply immediately, but instead leans toward the table and pours a generous amount of bourbon into the two glasses. Even though he knows that I'm not a big fan of alcohol, he still hands me a glass and clinks his with mine. Not wanting to offend him, I follow his lead and take a sip.

My face contorts into a grimace as the expensive liquid burns its way down my throat. Closing my eyes, I urge the coldness to spread over my body, tending to the fire left behind.

"You're ruining it," my father tells me.

I open my eyes, noticing an amused expression on his face. "What do you mean?"

"The ice," he explains, referring to our abilities. "You should allow yourself to feel what Van Winkle was made to make you feel."

"Maybe I prefer not to feel," I reply, not letting his small talk derail my thoughts.

"An ice queen through and through," he says with a hint of pride in his voice.

I allow myself a small smile, but it's wiped away as soon as he opens his mouth again.

"Speaking of," Father continues, finally getting to the reason he wanted to talk to me. "It's time for you to start acting like one."

"Excuse me?" I ask, my eyebrows rising up in disbelief. "With all due respect, Father, but I don't understand what you mean. I attend all the events you ask me to, I nurture good relations with the members of other royal families, and I make sure to follow your rules even though some are rather ridiculous. I mean, would it really make that much difference if I'd stayed another couple of hours at the charity fundraiser? My team and I were doing a really good job. We raised a lot of money, and I'm sure if I could've stayed until the end of the night, I could've squeezed out even more from some of the older gents."

"That's exactly what I'm talking about," my father replies, then takes another sip of the bourbon. "You care more about the filthy human trash than you do of your own kind."

"I never understood the hate our species harbors towards humans," I say, giving my head a sad shake. "The wolves originated from them. We can't even call it evolution because it was a curse, and you know it."

"It doesn't change the fact that, compared to them, we're a lot stronger and practically indestructible," he replies, giving me the usual argument. "You're right, it started with the curse, but our elemental abilities came much later. That was through evolution. We are a superior species, and we shouldn't dilute our blood with theirs."

"As the superior species, it's our responsibility to do everything in our power to take care of the weaker ones," I say, going through the same steps of the never changing discussion we've had ever since my opinion started to differ from his. "Besides, I never said that we should make half-bloods. They'd never fully belong anywhere, and their suffering would be too great."

"At least we agree on that," my father says, then surprises me when he changes our usual direction of conversation and moves on to a different topic. "I'll say this as clearly as possible, so you'll understand exactly what I mean."

A chill goes down my spine, but not of the cold, comfortable variety. My muscles tense in anticipation of receiving an order that I won't like but also won't be able to refuse. Not when my king is the one doing the asking.

"You can continue doing your charity work even though it's pointless. Humans will always steal and cheat from each other, but hey, you do whatever you want in your free time," he tells me, and although it's not as bad as I expected, I suspect that he's not finished.

Adjusting my posture, I sit up straight to my full seated height. My face is a cold, icy mask, showing no emotions as I brace myself for the continuation of his speech that he must've prepared and practiced for a while now.

"I'll allow you to go ahead with this stupidity as long as you start doing your duty properly," my father says, dropping the other shoe with a firm tone of finality. "It's time for you to get married and start the ascension process. I want you to attend the meetings, the councils, and the dinners. For every charity event you go to, you need to do two for the crown. If you fail to do any of that, I'll freeze your assets and cancel your credit cards until you are married and start pulling your weight."

My mouth falls open in shock. Out of all the things that I've thought he'd want to talk about, marriage wasn't one of them. I haven't even considered getting married for at least three more years. I'm still too young.

"I'm not even twenty-five," I breathe, weakly focusing on the only thing that comes to mind. "I can't get married."

"You can, and you will," he tells me. "Your mother and I weren't much older than you when we got married."

"But those were different times," I argue. "Father, please. Don't make me do this. You can't."

"You're right, I can't," he agrees, and I release a relieved breath. It doesn't last long because he continues, "If you refuse to marry, I'll turn your life into a living hell until you'll beg me to find you a match."

A lone tear finds its way down my cheek, turning into ice before it can reach my chin. The wolves consider themselves to be so much better than humans, but when it comes to governing our species, we abide by archaic rules of monarchy. As a human, I'd have more freedom to choose what to do with my life than I do as a princess.

"How do you suggest we go about it?" I ask, knowing that there's no point in arguing with him. My fate was sealed a long time ago, so I might at least try to get the best out of it before I completely piss him off.

"We'll organize a dinner party with all the eligible suitors," he starts in a way that makes it clear that he spent a lot of time thinking about it and probably even talked it through with his advisors. "We'll invite all the second or lower-born sons of royal families to present themselves."

"Will you at least let me be the one to pick?" I ask with a surprisingly solid voice while I'm struggling to keep my lower lip from trembling.

My father's face softens, the hard edges smoothening up and making him look several years younger. He reaches over and takes my hand in his, rubbing his thumb over the top in gentle, soothing motions.

"Of course, you'll be the one to pick, Leia," he says with a voice so kind and warm that I actually have to look into his bright yes, which are identical to mine, just to make sure it's the same person. "I'm not a monster, you know. I just want what's best for you and our family. You'll be the one to spend the rest of your life with your future husband, so it's only right that you pick. I pray to all the wolf gods that you might find a mate."

My heart skips a beat when he mentions the bond. Not everyone's lucky enough to find a mate in their lifetime. The other half of my wolf, the two pieces fitting together in the most perfect of ways. I've been dreaming of having one ever since I was a kid, but as I grew older, I also got to meet a lot of people. When nothing changed, nothing clicked, and nothing settled inside me, I gave up on believing the bond even existed.

"Thank you," I say, appreciating the little bit of freedom he's giving me. I'm well aware that he could've picked someone and sent us to the altar without me even knowing the wolf's name.

"That will be all," he tells me, politely dismissing me. "Go and get some rest."

"Thank you, Father," I echo my previous words, too shocked at the sudden turn of events to come up with anything else.

As calmly as I can, I get on my slightly wobbly feet and walk toward the door. I'm aching to be in my room already and to allow myself to fully process what just happened and what it means for me.

"One more thing," my father calls from behind me, stopping me in my tracks.

Forcing my body to turn around to not seem disrespectful, I look him in the eyes. He has a glass in his hand again and a smug, celebratory expression on his face.

"Don't leave the manor tomorrow," he says with a gleam in his eye that I can't decipher. When I furrow my brows in confusion, he explains, "I want you to be the one to receive the suitors."

My ice-cold blood boils in my veins when I realize that I've been set up. With effort, I keep a neutral if not even an indifferent mask on my face, and only give my father a slight nod in acknowledgment. If he noticed the unusual rosy color on my cheeks, he didn't comment and I'm glad, because I don't think I could've handled him gloating.

The next thing I remember, I'm sitting on my bed with my shaking hands in my lap. I have no recollection of how I got here, but that doesn't matter because all I want to do is cry. In the privacy of my room, tears run freely down my cheeks, but they turn into little droplets of ice and fall on the floor like a miniature hailstorm.

I mourn the life that will never be mine, the person that I'll never become, and the perfect mate that doesn't exist. I mourn the little girl who was born a princess but wouldn't mind being human if it meant being happy and free.

I say a silent, tearful goodbye to one of the last nights that I'll get to spend alone. After I pick a suitor, he'll not only immediately move into the manor, but also into my bed.

Stupid archaic rules, my wolf sympathizes with me before letting out a long, high-pitched howl reminding me that we'll always be together.

My heart shatters all over again as the guilt consumes me. My wolf was always there for me, but I never fully accepted who I was. My father's right and I've been walking the line between the two worlds for far too long. Maybe it's time for me to finally accept who I am and embrace my inner wolf with open arms the same way that she has always loved me.

CHAPTER 3

GAVIN

We can do it at least two more times, my inner wolf growls in encouragement.

Drops of sweat trail the well-marked path down my back. My hair sticks to my forehead, making me look like a wet dog. The muscles in my arms burn, but I welcome it, letting the pain fuel me.

With a loud groan, I pull myself up the salmon ladder, completing another rung before moving the bar up to the next one, and then higher again. I've already done three rounds, but my wolf insists we can do two more, so I guess we're aiming for five.

My core muscles are working hard right now, and my breathing's coming faster. My whole body aches, but it's the only way I can shut out my mind. It's the only time my thoughts don't run rampant.

You would be in your right to kill her. She challenged you, my wolf reminds me.

While I know he speaks the truth, I'm also aware that the ability to be able to stay in control of our actions is what makes us different from following the primal instincts of our inner apex predators. Mine is louder and more powerful than most, but that only means that I need to have double the strength and the discipline than any other wolf would.

The gym door opens, and I don't need to look to know it's James. As an unofficial member of my pack, I can smell him from miles away.

"I'm sorry to interrupt, Your Highness," James starts, but doesn't continue as he usually would, which only tells me that whatever he came to say must be important.

Either way, I don't let it get in-between my workout session, so I calmly finish my last round of the salmon ladder, before jumping down and landing gracefully on my feet. James hands me a towel and a bottle of water, giving me a second to recover.

"What's the matter, James?" I ask when I catch my breath.

"Your father asked to see you," he replies. My eyebrows furrow ever so slightly, giving away the only hint that I've been caught by surprise. James clears his throat. "You and your brothers."

I purse my lips together and nod. "Bring me a suit while I take a shower."

I can count on the fingers of one hand the occasions that my father has called to see me and my brothers at the same time. It was never to share good news.

Being late to my father's summons isn't ideal, but it's much better than showing up anything less than perfect, which meant putting on an expensive suit and being clean. He always says that royals present the standard everyone wants to aspire to. We either are the crown or represent it. The nobility and the commoners need to be filled with jealousy and envy when in our presence. We are perfect, we are invincible, and we are powerful.

Even if darkness hadn't been my ability, black would still be my color. Every piece of my outfit is black, although not in the exact same shade. My fingers swiftly button the shirt all the way up to my collar before making a quick work with the tie.

"Grayden and Graham are already in the private meeting room," James informs me.

"Garren will be late as usual," I comment. "With a brother like him, I'm never the last one to arrive to anything."

James cracks a small smile. "Hard to be a black sheep."

"I'm not a sheep, James. I'll never be a sheep," I tell him, locking my eyes on his. "I'm a pureblooded wolf."

James bows his head at the neck as I pass, then follows me at an acceptable distance. As I cross the courtyard separating the gym from the manor, the clouds gather, releasing a drizzle of rain. Keeping the idea of arriving without a hair out of place, I clench my fist and summon shadows around my body, thick enough to prevent the drops from touching me.

By the time we get inside the manor, James excuses himself and rushes to his room to clean up. If I wanted to, I could've protected him from the rain, but quite frankly, the thought didn't even occur to me. Not that I would've done things any differently if it had.

I don't bother knocking or asking for permission when entering my father's private meeting room. Considering that he summoned me, he's expecting me anyway.

"Nice of you to join us, Gavin," my father says by way of greeting, his eyes taking in my impeccable attire. Since he doesn't make a comment, it must mean he approves, although when he continues, his tone is reprimanding. "You're late."

I make a point to look around the room, my eyes landing first on Grayden before moving on to Graham, and then back to my father.

"Garren isn't here yet," I say as a matter of fact.

"This meeting doesn't concern him," my father replies.

I narrow my eyes when I realize my eldest brother wasn't invited at all, and I've left my father waiting when I could've been ready a lot earlier. Not wanting to dig myself a deeper hole, I quietly take my seat and pay attention to what he's about to say.

"Now that we're all finally gathered," my father says, shooting me a look that I do my best to ignore.

The wolf in me stirs up, eager to show him who's the true Alpha, but I send a wave of darkness deep into my soul, lulling it back into hibernation. Even though

I'm more powerful than my father, we both know that there's nothing I can do about it. If I demand the throne on power claims, I risk exile. The rules are deeply integrated into our community. It's what makes us a society, separating us from the wildness of animals.

"A letter has arrived concerning the three of you," my father continues.

While Grayden and Graham exchange their looks, surprise evident on their faces, I remain expressionless and even go so far as to fold my arms across my chest to feign boredom.

"It's an invitation to the dinner party at The Lafayette Manor," my father goes on, sharing the contents of the letter. "It would seem that Lucas wants Leia to marry, so he's inviting all the eligible suitors to present themselves for her to choose from."

"If that's true, then why isn't Garren here?" Graham asks, his brows furrowing in confusion.

"Because Garren already has a kingdom to rule," my father replies with infinite amount of patience. "He wouldn't be able to marry Leia because the kingdoms can't merge. Princess Leia has to choose her future husband out of the second or lower born sons of royal heritage."

"Does that mean that I could be a king?" Grayden asks, his eyes wide.

"If you're the one she chooses, then yes, you can," my father tells him, but his eyes are on mine when he continues, "You have to understand that if you decide to follow that path, you will need to leave everything that connects you to this family behind. For example, if you are an Alpha of the pack, you'll have to resign. You can't be a part of Lafayette Royalty and command Grey's Army."

It was a warning to me. I'm the only one with military ties and the only one who has a history of being a very good friend with Leia. My father's aware that if I decide to throw my hat in the ring, there's a very real chance that I'll get picked.

The problem is that I'm not entirely sure what he wants. He made it sound like he wants us to attend the dinner party, but at the same time he highlighted the consequences of leaving the family.

Grayden and Graham are completely oblivious to it. They don't realize there's an underlying non-verbal communication exchanged between Father and me. His black eyes are fixed on me, watching my every move, looking for any change in my expression as I weigh his words.

As easily one of the most powerful wolves of our generation, he's eager to keep me in the fold. He'd probably like me to stay in charge of the Shadows and fight my brother's battles.

Not even two full days have passed since I confronted him about wanting the throne. He was the one who told me that if I ever had a chance of getting one, I'd have to look outside of the family. As if the wolf gods themselves have heard our argument, they sent us an opportunity with the solution.

I want this more than anything. A throne of my own and a kingdom to rule. I would prefer not to give up my own name for it. I've always been a Grey and can't imagine myself becoming a Lafayette.

Gavin Lafayette, my wolf chuckles sleepily in amusement.

The funny thing is that cutting all ties with my family wouldn't be the hardest thing I'd have to do. It's the thought of giving up the Shadows that hurts me. I started this pack from zero. I traveled through towns and villages, testing young pups and searching for any signs that they can manipulate darkness. I'm not only their Alpha, but also their creator.

Something must've shown on my face because my father smirks. If I hadn't been so convinced about attending the dinner party before, now I have it clear.

"I'm going," I announce, and even though I haven't spoken loudly, my voice carries, getting everyone's attention.

A shadow fell on my father's face, his brows furrowing in anger. He can't do anything to keep me from going. I'm in my right to attend the dinner and even marry Leia.

My thoughts suddenly turn to her as I try to remember how she looked the last time we saw each other. It must've been six years ago or something like that. As soon as I was eighteen years old, I enlisted in the army and hadn't returned for another couple of years. During my diplomatic travels, I did visit the Lafayette Manor, but Leia had been away at the Academy.

"Are you sure that's something you want to do?" my father asks, playing his last hand to convince me against it. "Don't forget that she's a human lover."

His words hit their marks with Grayden and Graham as their faces suddenly contort with disgust. My reaction isn't anything like theirs. While I also dislike human trash, I did hear the rumors of Princess Leia trying to save them by raising money for several different lost causes.

"Would marrying the Ice Princess be worth bringing such a stain to the family name?" my father challenges, making his first mistake because he used a wrong argument on me.

"What family name?" I ask, keeping my voice low and casual. "If I marry her, the only family name that can be stained is the Lafayette's, so you have nothing to worry about."

My father narrows his eyes at me but says nothing. I'm right, and he knows it.

"Besides, at least she isn't fucking around with them," I add with a smirk, probably pushing it a bit too far. "Unlike our dear brother who's been known to."

My father's face contorts with anger, and I sense it before I see it when he slams his fist against the table, releasing a wave of darkness that blows everything in its near vicinity away, Grayden and Graham included. Not me. I'm no stranger to reacting on the spot, and

I managed to throw my shield up moments before the darkness was summoned.

When he regains control and banishes the darkness, the room's a mess as if a small hurricane went through it. Grayden groans and lifts himself up on his feet. Graham has a cut on the side of his head that disappears into his hairline, but he's sitting up and seems alert.

My father's furious eyes land on me. I'm still sitting on the chair, my arms folded across my chest in the very same position they were before he threw a powerful temper tantrum. I'm in impeccable condition, unharmed, untouched, and without even a hair out of place.

"Get out," my father hisses under his breath.

Graham and Grayden struggle to get on their feet, then leave before Father could summon darkness again.

"Get out," Father repeats, talking to me, his eyes locked on mine.

Without wanting to, I smirk and stand up. If he wanted to prove how powerful he is, it severely backfired. I'm the one who's left standing, without needing to catch my breath. He looks more disheveled than I've ever seen him. A king that's losing control. A king that will lose a kingdom if he gives it to the wrong brother. That future is set in stone, and there's nothing anyone can do to change it.

Putting the last nail in my symbolic coffin, I turn my back on my father, breaking court etiquette. Now more than ever, I need to convince Leia to marry me. If I fail to do so, my father will have the right to punish me for insubordination.

As I'm on my way to my room, my mother crosses my path.

"Gavin," she says, her voice gentle and kind.

My lips curl up into a loving smile that only comes out in her presence. "Mother," I greet her and lean down to kiss her on the cheek. "Are you well?"

"My plants could've done with a bit more sun, but I should've known better when I married into the family wielding darkness," she muses, talking about the greenhouse where she spends most of her time. It was my father's wedding gift for her, welcoming the first Earth elemental into the Grey line.

"Even with all those high-intensity discharge lamps that you keep turned on day and night?" I tease and offer her my arm. She hooks hers through mine and lets me guide her as we walk without destination in mind around the big manor.

"Even with those," she replies lightheartedly. Her smile fades as a more serious expression settles on her beautiful face. She glances at me from the side and tightens her grip on my arm. "Is it true?"

"Is what true?" I ask, my brows furrowing in confusion.

"Do you plan on leaving?" she elaborates, her voice barely audible. She already knows the answer, but still wants me to confirm it.

"I need to, Mother," I reply with a sad sigh. "You know that I'd love nothing more than to stay here and be a part of this family. I would do anything, but it's just not in the cards. As the fourth born son, I'm forced to go out there and make my own way."

"I knew this would happen from the moment you were born," she tells me with a voice that's full of sadness but also understanding. "I think that's why I always kept you so close to me. Don't tell your brothers, but you're definitely my favorite."

A low chuckle escapes me, and I shake my head in amusement. "I don't think that was ever a secret, Mother," I say, remembering all the extra hugs and kisses she gave me when I was a kid.

"I always knew you would achieve a lot," she continues and while she sounds nostalgic, she's also serious. "I honestly don't know what we did wrong with Garren. I fear it's too late to set him straight."

"Sooner or later, Father will have to do something about Garren and his wild escapades," I comment.

"Grayden seems to be following his older brother's footsteps more and more," my mother says with a sigh. "With every day he comes home at a later hour. I don't know where he is or what he does, and I'm too afraid to ask."

"You don't need to worry about him just yet," I assure her.

A long time ago, I put eyes on my brothers for safety reasons. What started as protection, turned into a well-oiled machine of diggers. Since I came back from military service, I had a group of people on payroll that managed to bury all the bones that could hurt our family. Garren especially gave them a lot of work.

"It's true that Grayden's been out a lot, but I think it's because there's a girl he likes," I say in a low whisper, with a wink.

Her face lights up, the creases on the corners of her eyes gone as worry smooths away. She covers her mouth with her hand, then bites her lower lip to keep herself from squealing in excitement.

"What about Graham?" she asks when she calms down a bit.

I frown and look for words that would explain my brother best. When I can't find them, I settle on trying to share my view of him, even though I'm fairly sure that she's already aware of all that.

"Graham's a loner," I start, my brows furrowing in concentration as I gather my thoughts. "He spends a lot of his time in his room working on some secret project that no one knows about. I'm not entirely sure what's going on there, but he does spend a lot of time on his computer. Either way, I much prefer him being a nerd to a drunk."

"Isn't that the truth," my mother agrees.

We walk a bit further in a comfortable silence. As I take in the Grey Manor's beautiful gardens, the very same ones that she planted and nurtured, I realize that if Leia picks me as her future husband, I'm going to miss it.

"You're doing the right thing," my mother tells me, breaking me out of my reverie. I glance at her, cocking my brow in question. "You deserve a lot more than this. You're meant for greater things than servitude. Just promise me one thing."

"Anything," I breathe, meaning it. There's nothing that I'd deny her.

"It's a thin line between being feared and loved," she starts, sounding serious as she shares with me one last life lesson. "Make sure that you earn respect walking in the middle of it. That's the one that'll hold until the end of days."

I'm not completely sure I understand what she's trying to tell me, but I'll have plenty of time to figure it out. Her brown eyes are looking at me expectantly, waiting for me to give her my word right at this very moment.

"I promise," I tell her, hoping to know what she meant by it before I accidentally let her down.

"You'll be a great king, Gavin," she says, gives my hand a comforting squeeze, then leaves me alone while she goes to tend to the gardens.

I stare at her retreating figure, sending a silent prayer to the wolf gods that Leia picks me. My life might depend on it, in more ways than one.

CHAPTER 4

LEIA

The Ice Queen, my wolf remarks in satisfaction when I take in my appearance in the mirror.

The regal white dress, adorned with pale blue colors on the sides, tastefully highlights my curves. Transparent glass heels make me look several inches taller than I really am. My ashen-white hair has been pulled back into a loose ponytail, with two stray curls to frame my face.

The lipstick is too much, don't you think? I ask my wolf, second-guessing rubbing the icy blue color over my plump lips.

Don't hide it, embrace it, she tells me.

"Might as well go all in," I mutter under my breath, finishing the last bit of makeup that I've left.

"Leia, Leia, they're coming!"

The twins' voices reach me before they come running into my room. They're excited to have their boredom broken by a party. When they crash through the door, they freeze in their spots, standing still. Their eyes are fixated on me and their mouths open, but there're no sounds coming out.

"That bad, huh?" I ask with a small smile.

Lily recovers first, and she forcefully shakes her head. "I don't think I've ever seen you so beautiful."

"Stunning," Levi adds, nodding to Lily's words.

"Thank you, guys," I say and wave them in. Some part of me is glad that the dinner party's been organized before the twins leave for the Academy in a couple of days. Having their silent and unyielding support by my side will make the whole ordeal a lot more bearable.

"Do you have any candidates in mind?" Lily asks as she sits on the bed, waiting for me to share some juicy gossip with her.

I roll my eyes and chuckle. "I don't even know who's coming," I reply, hoping that she won't notice that I avoided the question.

"Pretty much everyone," Levi supplies. "I saw Mother sort through RSVPs with the staff, and holy shit, there were a lot of them."

"Have you seen what she did with the dining room?" Lily asks, the tone of her voice turning higher the more excited she gets. "It's breathtaking. Like seriously, if your engagement is so beautiful, I honestly can't wait to see how your wedding will be."

My smile falters, but I have it fixed before the twins can notice. They think it's all a beautiful fairytale with a happily ever after. I really hope they're right because I'd hate to be forced to marry a monster, then die of lifelong misery.

"I just wish there'd be girls invited, too," Levi complains. "You and Lily will both be flirting your night away while I'll be forced to have husband talks."

"When the opportunity provides itself, you'll get a formidable match of your own," Lily reminds him, sounding more naïve than I would've liked for a young woman of her standing. At least Levi seems more grounded and will look after her while they'll be away.

"Leia, honey," Mother calls, walking up the hallway to my room. "Are you ready? Do you need any help?"

"She's perfect, Mother," Lily comes back, looking at me with hearts in her eyes.

"I guess it's time to go," Levi says, understanding the reason Mother's coming.

He stands up and offers me one of his arms. I hook my hand through it, then smile at Lily, who does the same thing on the other side. Mother comes right on time to see us together and united. She looks at us with a proud smile on her face.

"We're ready," Levi tells her after Lily fixes the blue tie of his white suit that matches his twin's dress.

Mother steps aside to let us pass and informs me, "Some of the guests have arrived. Don't forget to greet them properly when you get down. Keep in mind that even if they're not one of your candidates, they're still sons of kings and should be treated that way."

"It will be okay, Mother," I assure her with more confidence than I feel.

Before we reach the top of the stairs, I let Levi, Lily and Mother go down first. Their appearance will call everyone's attention to the stairs, so by the time I descend, the scene will be all set for the grand and memorable entrance.

The things we do to keep our parents happy, I say to my wolf.

Even though I wasn't always so eager to have the animal inside me and a part of me, right now, I can't deny how grateful I am for her presence. In that way, the twins have it easy. With the wolf or not, they'd never be alone.

The things we do to keep the power, my wolf corrects me, making me briefly wonder if that's the real reason why I'm doing this and not to keep the access to money that can support the charities I'm passionate about.

"Our esteemed guests," my father says, raising his voice to be heard over everyone else. "May I present to you my daughter, Princess Leia Lafayette."

Taking this as my cue, I step forward into everyone's view. Some gasp and some even let out low whistles, but most of them remain silent, open-mouthed, and awe-struck.

I grab the handrail and prepare to descend when a tall figure steps out of the shadows, and I must do everything in my power not to show just how startled I am. The shock momentarily clouds my ability to recognize him, yet my eyes swiftly capture the sight of his broad shoulders, his dashing good looks, the chiseled jawline veiled by dark stubble, and his raven-black hair.

"Gavin," I breathe, when I finally connect the memory of the boy that I used to know with a handsome tall man standing before me now.

A ghost of a smile plays on his lips, his black-as-night eyes taking me in with just as much curiosity as mine did him. When he's satisfied with his primary inspection, he offers me his arm.

"Mind if I escort you?" he asks with his usual voice that got a couple of notes lower and manlier with the passing years.

Caught off guard and not wanting to make a scene, I have no other way but to follow his lead. As I hook my arm through his, I feel his strong muscles that are hiding under his fine black suit.

The Shadow Prince is sexy as hell, my wolf says, unhelpfully pointing out what I've already noticed.

Even when I send an ice beam her way, it doesn't stop her from making another comment.

Maybe his hot ass can melt your icy heart, she says sharply, no doubt angry for getting beamed.

"You okay there?" Gavin asks low enough only for me to hear.

My head jerks his way, unsure of what he's referring to. "What?"

"I said that you look beautiful, and you completely ignored me," he says, giving me an amused look. At least he's not offended because I'd hate to explain to my father that it was my wolf's fault.

"Thank you," I reply, then to fix the slip-up, I add, "You clean up rather well yourself."

"It's been a while, Lafayette," he says with a maddening smirk. "We've both grown and changed."

"Not too much, I hope," I comment before I can stop myself.

"Not too much," he confirms, echoing my words.

He escorts me down the stairs, matching my every step with one of his. When we reach the bottom, he refuses to leave my side and hovers behind my shoulder, much to the dismay of my other suitors.

Even though I'm talking with them, saying polite greetings one after another, my mind's not fully present. A big part of me is too distracted by Gavin and the fact that he had actually presented himself as one of the candidates for marriage. While we were quite close in the past, I've never considered him as marriage material. I've heard that the secret to a happy marriage is to marry a best friend, so in that regard, Gavin would've been the perfect choice many years ago, but right now, he's just another stranger with the ambition of being a king.

"Princess Leia," my next suitor greets me, bowing lower than any other before him.

Gavin scoffs behind me, but the suitor doesn't react, nor does he seem offended. In fact, he's intent on ignoring my brooding shadow.

"Welcome..." I say and trail off, racking my brain for his name.

"Prince Felix Farrell," he offers with an easy smile as he takes my hand in his and kisses my knuckles.

A small gasp escapes me when his burning lips touch my cold skin, sending shivers down my spine. His amber eyes meet mine as he slowly straightens up, pulling himself to his full height, making him nearly as tall as Gavin. While my shadow has black hair, the prince in front of me has been touched by the fire.

"A fire user," I comment, returning his smile.

"And a proud uncle of a newborn heir to the Fire Crown," Gavin adds from behind, throwing a subtle jab at him.

Felix's smile falters for the shortest of moments, but he quickly recovers and bows his head for the tiniest bit. "I'm grateful that my brother and his wife were blessed with a strong and healthy offspring."

Ignoring my rude shadow, I offer Felix another smile. "Congratulations indeed. It's always a happy occasion when our families grow."

Felix's amber eyes sparkle when his meet mine, and his lips curl up in a lopsided smile. "Thank you, Princess. I hope you'll save a dance for me before the night's over."

"Of course," I promise although I really don't know how I'll be able to dance with all the suitors that have arrived. There must be close to a hundred of them and only one of me.

Felix presses another fire kiss against my knuckles and bows deep, before leaving me to greet my other guests. The remnant of his heat stays with me for a long while after he walks away. Even though I'm engaged in a conversation with a different guest every couple of minutes, I can't help but glance at Felix's direction. He always notices when I do and curls his lips up into a small smile, or he winks.

"You're lucky that everything that comes out of you freezes, otherwise you'd be caught drooling," Gavin comments from behind, his hot breath tickling my ear.

I pointedly ignore him and keep my attention on the man in front of me, although I have no idea what he said his name was or the family he belonged to. With Gavin distracting me from behind and Felix from the front, it's a miracle that I don't completely blank out.

Thankfully, my father steps in between me and the next guest. "I think we should move to the dining room and start dinner," he says and as the line of ungreeted suitors grumbles. "If you wanted to assure yourself an audience with Princess Leia, you should've considered showing up earlier."

Felix finds his way to my side just as Gavin steps forward and offers me his arm. The two men stare at each other, the growls of their alpha wolves practically heard on the outside.

"Leia," Gavin says with the casual and comfortable tone only many years of friendship can bring.

My eyes lock onto his black ones just as his unspoken demand to not dare humiliate him in front of his mother's kin comes through. I tilt my head to the side, unable to disguise my surprise at being able to understand him so clearly just by looking at him.

"Princess Leia," Felix calls my name, preventing me from figuring out how exactly Gavin got into my head.

I turn to the Fire Prince, his amber eyes shining with warmth as a kind smile plays on his lips. I'm a bit lost as to what to do with both princes suffocating me on each side.

"Excuse me, Your Highnesses," Levi interrupts, pushing past Felix whose smile is replaced by a sharp look of annoyance. "I'm pretty sure that the choosing part comes after dinner."

Just like that, my little brother offers me his arm and saves the day. Without looking at either of the princes, I allow Levi to walk me to the dining room.

Gavin doesn't miss a beat and follows closely behind us, no doubt wanting to intimidate whoever has dared to claim the seat next to me. His brooding presence is frustrating at best, but I can't deny that it's nice to have a friend by my side.

A very sexy friend, my wolf purrs.

"Remember, you're the one who's in charge," Levi reminds me, giving my hand a comforting squeeze, then leaves me at the head of the table.

Gavin's already scared off the Dubois prince, successfully winning himself a seat on my right side, while Felix seemed to come to an agreement with a scrawny boy on my left. Once again, I find myself caught between the two princes with completely opposite abilities. One full of shadows and the other burning with the hottest flames.

"How was yesterday's fundraising?" Felix asks, catching me off guard by inquiring so directly about my business with humans.

On my right, Gavin stiffens, which is more or less the reaction of everyone who can overhear our conversation. When my eyes meet Felix's, he looks genuinely interested to hear my answer.

"We've raised a nice amount of money and will be able to help a lot of people," I reply, cautious not to say something that would anger my father. I have to admit that judging by the way some of the princes have shed their masks of politeness to show disgust, I'm getting a clearer idea of who I don't want to spend the rest of my life with.

"They're lucky to have you," Felix says with a smile that reaches his eyes.

"Thank you," I say, meaning it. Ever since I got involved with various human charity organizations, I've only been hearing about how I'm letting my family down. It's nice to be appreciated by one of my own kind.

Have you noticed how tight his shirt is? my wolf asks, the question causing my eyes to wander lower. *He's packing a lot of muscles underneath there.*

"Leia has always had a big heart," Gavin says, his sudden involvement in the conversation startling me. "For the future Ice Queen, she's surprisingly warm."

"Gavin Grey," I muse, tilting my head to the side as I smile at him. "If I didn't know you better, I would've thought that you gave me a compliment."

"Maybe you don't know me as well as you think you do," Gavin replies with a wink, then leans closer and whispers, "Give me a chance, and I'll surprise you."

I bet that he has a big surprise, my wolf comments.

My usually pale cheeks turn the lightest shade of pink, but it has nothing to do with Gavin. Well, it does, but not because of anything *he* said.

Stop it, I order my wolf before using my ability to cool down my body temperature. It's unbecoming of the future queen to show her reactions so openly.

Gavin's observant eyes have been on me this whole time, his lips curl up in a playful smile. The dark stubble gives him an intriguing depth that I'd like to explore.

"I liked the speech you gave to the graduation class at the Academy last year," Felix says, smoothly adding himself into the conversation.

"Really?" Gavin asks, speaking directly to him with a challenge in his tone. "What did you like about it?"

Truth time, my wolf announces, sounding way too excited at the prospect of an alpha fight.

Looking at Felix, I'm also curious to see if he's only trying to get on my good side or he's actually telling the truth. Felix purses his lips in a thin line, his eyes narrowed at Gavin, who smirks in an infuriating way. The temperature around the Fire Prince raises several degrees, no doubt he's annoyed by Gavin's presence, who's even more annoying than I remember.

Annoyingly hot, my wolf supplies unhelpfully. *I'd do him.*

Stop it! I direct my thoughts toward her firmly, unable to get rid of the mental picture.

In wolf form, you perv, my wolf chuckles, her good mood and amusement warming my icy soul.

Felix takes a deep breath, regaining his control as he purposefully turns away from the Shadow Prince. A flame burns in his eyes, sparkling as he speaks and moves.

"There were many parts of your speech that I liked," Felix starts, ignoring Gavin scoffing at his general reply. Instead, he lifts his index finger and continues, "But only one truly stayed in my mind and is still with me."

"Oh?" I tilt my head to the side, giving him my full attention.

"Do you know that you're the first royal in a position of true power who has ever suggested that instead of treating humans like they're trash, we should consider working together with them, share ideas and collaborate on possible solutions that could potentially save our planet?" Felix asks, casually highlighting the most important points of my speech.

My eyebrows shoot up, surprise evident on my face. The corners of my mouth turn up into a satisfied smile. I give him an approving nod, impressed by his obvious tone of support.

"What I really want to say is that I agree with everything you've said in your speech," Felix confides, significantly lowering his voice due to the topic being highly sensitive in our circles. "Change needs to start at the top, which is where we come in. We're the ones that need to encourage our bright minds to open up to the ideas offered to us by humans. Just think how much we could achieve by truly and wholeheartedly combining their technologies with our abilities. No one would be able to stop us."

The flames in Felix's eyes burns with fervor, his tone one of passion and excitement. Though I find myself sucked into his narrative, there's something that doesn't seem quite right about it.

"Let me get this straight," Gavin interrupts, his cold and serious voice the complete opposite of Felix's. "Are you actually suggesting that we expose our species to the humans?"

"Yes," Felix confirms, his answer making guests nearest to us gasp in shock, me included. As much as I want to help and work with humans, I've never considered sharing with them the information about us. "If we finally show them who we are and how much more powerful we are than their little guns and blades, we can invite them into our society and put them in their proper place."

"You don't want to work with them, you want to rule them," I clarify, not liking the way this is going.

"That's how it should've been from the start," Felix agrees, not noticing the giant hole he's digging for himself. "We're the superior species. We should be in charge, not them. If they're firmly put in their place, we can all coexist with a lot less contempt between one another."

"Exposing us to them would also mean exposing us to the witches," Gavin reminds him, staying cool and in control throughout the whole exchange. "There are areas where they're openly attacking us, trying to discover our locations and our identities. They don't care to share the world with us in a peaceful manner. All they want is to fix the mistake they made when they cursed us in the first place, thinking that we'll cower and die out."

He's faced them before, my wolf says, also noticing the change in him.

"We can deal with a few witches," Felix replies and waves his hand in dismissal. "They're just a couple of old crones who refuse to die."

"You're a fool, Farrell, you know that?" Gavin says and shakes his head in disbelief. "If that's really what you think, then you should try spending a month on the frontlines to fight them."

"We have people for that," Felix retorts.

"Those same people need a leader," Gavin replies without missing a beat. He cocks his brow, looks him up and down, then scoffs. "I suppose it was for the best that your spoiled ass stayed inside the palace walls. Your foolish arrogance would've gotten you killed on day one."

"How dare you—" Felix hisses, his face an angry shade of red, but falls quiet when Gavin abruptly stands up.

"It appears that I've lost my appetite. Please accept my apologies, Princess," Gavin says, his eyes meeting mine for the shortest of moments before he bows his head. A flicker of emotion crosses his face, but he suppresses it just as quickly as it appears. If I hadn't been watching him, I wouldn't have even noticed the change.

Before I can say anything, he turns on his heel and leaves. Felix looks triumphant and rather off-putting. I can't believe I've actually considered him as a candidate. His opinion is completely different than mine, and I find his methods outrageous.

The dinner comes and goes with Felix keeping a steady flow of conversation. He doesn't seem to notice that most of the time, I don't even bother replying or only making a sound, hoping that he'd finally shut up.

No one dares to sit in Gavin's empty place. My thoughts are with him the whole time as I can't help but wonder what he's been through in the years since we last saw each other. I want to talk to him and ask him, but I'm afraid he might be gone.

"I'm going to the ladies' room," I say before they begin to serve the dessert.

As I push my chair back and stand up, Felix jumps to his feet as well, followed by just about every suitor as they raise themselves up to their feet like a wave that goes from my side of the table to the other. I force a polite smile on my face at their well-mannered display of etiquette.

I don't really need the ladies' room, but it was the only plausible excuse I could think of to get some air. The last thing I want is to offend anyone, and quite frankly, more than once, I've come very close to saying a few sharp words to Felix. Fortunately, he's too self-absorbed to notice that he's been completely dominating the conversation and forcing his beliefs on other suitors.

When I exit to the terrace, I lift my head a bit to let the cool air caress my cheeks. Felix's heat has been suffocating me, fighting with my icy nature. Being away from him is a relief that makes me feel like I can finally breathe.

A sudden sensation spreads around my bicep as it takes my brain a moment to realize that someone has grabbed my arm. I open my mouth to cry out in alarm, but only a muffled sound comes out, the small bits of air that find its way through the hand that's covering half of my face.

My heartbeat speeds up and even though the adrenaline's pumping through my body, there's no gut reaction. I only have one thought, and so does my wolf.

We're going to die.

CHAPTER 5

GAVIN

"Quiet," I hiss sharper than necessary, but I'm starting to lose my patience. She hasn't stopped thrashing around and even tried to bite me at some point. Fortunately, the shadows proved to be an impenetrable shield even for the Ice Queen's teeth.

When she hears my voice, she begins to calm down although the cold air around us doesn't go away. It's the only remaining indication that she's pissed off.

"I'll take my hands off you, okay?" I ask and wait for her confirmation before I do it.

Leia nods, the muscles in her body tense, and she remains ready to strike. I brace myself for the possibility of retaliation, but when I let her go, she jerks away from me, putting distance between us.

"What the fuck, Gavin?" she hisses, struggling to keep her voice down. "Do you understand what you just did? I could have you thrown in the dungeons."

"There's no need to exaggerate," I tell her, but it was the wrong thing to say because she goes on a rampage.

"Exaggerate?!" she exclaims in a low, angry voice. "You've put your hands on the future Lafayette queen in her own home. I can make a scene so big that you won't be able to dig your way out."

"You're right," I agree and slowly lift my hands up as in surrender. "I'm sorry. I shouldn't have done that."

"Then why did you?" she asks and although her lips are still pursed in an angry thin line, she doesn't seem as tense as before. Her reaction must've been from the scare I've given her.

"I don't want to make excuses, but in my defense, I was enjoying some fresh air when you came and interrupted me," I tell her. When she opens her mouth to argue, I quickly continue, "You caught me by surprise and before I could realize what I was doing, I was already one with the shadows. I knew that the moment I manifested myself, I'd scare you, so I foolishly tried to keep you from screaming. Honest mistake."

Leia's blue eyes shine with anger, her breathing coming in shallow and rapid bursts. The ground around us turns to ice as her emotions are getting the better of her. Her fists are clenched together so hard that even her knuckles are turning white.

Calm her down, my wolf warns me.

"Hey, I'm sorry, Princess," I say, genuinely worried about her losing control and shifting. "I'm glad you're here. Can we walk around for a bit? I'd really like to talk to you about something."

Her eyes reflect the wolf inside her, staring at me with hungry anger. As she takes another breath, this time a deeper one that's meant to relax her, the wolf begins to move away and back into her soul. The next time she blinks, her eyes are her own again.

"What do you want, Gavin?" she asks me, but this time there's not even a hint of sharpness in her tone. Instead, she sounds tired and sad.

I offer her my arm and let a question hang in the air, "Walk with me?"

She doesn't reply, but she does hook her arm through mine and matches my small steps with hers. I guess that some things never change because I'm still a whole head taller and towering over her. A smell of fresh, newly fallen snow hangs around her, and I can't help but inhale deeply, enjoying the winter vibes. With her plump lips, piercing blue eyes, pale skin, and ashen-white hair, she's grown into a real natural beauty.

"What do you want?" she asks, echoing her previous question.

"Do you ever think about the time we spent together as friends?" I ask, ignoring her question. "I do, and I miss it. I miss you. You were the only person that really got me, the only one that listened to me and made me feel understood. You were my best friend."

"And then you left," Leia finishes, giving me an accusing look. "You enlisted in the army and left me alone. Do you have any idea how it felt being paraded around like the future queen? I've been gawked at, handed from one disgusting councilman to another to entertain and impress. A long time ago, you promised that you'd be by my side when I had to do this, but you lied. As soon as the first opportunity presented itself, you abandoned me."

My heart aches for her. I had no idea that my actions affected her as much, but she's right. I let her down.

"I know this probably won't make much difference now, but I still want you to know that I'm very sorry," I tell her, meaning every word of it. "I should've been here for you. I know that a lot of time has passed since then, but if it's not too late, I'd like to be here for you now. If you allow me, I'll be your friend."

Leia hesitates for a moment before replying, her voice barely audible, "I'd like that."

"Good," I say, a ghost of a smile playing on my lips. "Well, now that we've got that sorted out, shall we move on to the next topic?"

"I knew that it was too good to be true." Leia sighs, disappointment palpable in the air. "You're being nice to me because you want something. It's the story of my fucking life."

Busted, my wolf remarks.

A wave of guilt washes over me, leaving a bitter taste behind. While I attend the dinner for my own selfish reasons, I can't ignore the feeling of protectiveness that she brings out in me. It's always been like that. It's always been her.

"I won't deny that I want to be king," I tell her, opting for honesty. There's no point in lying to her because she's the only one who has ever really known me and could see right through my bullshit. "I also won't deny that this was the only reason why I even considered coming to the dinner. That was all true until I saw you."

Leia continues walking, her arm still hooked through mine. I'm taking it as a good sign. She's still here with me and didn't imply any of wanting to return inside just yet. It's my one and only chance to explain myself, so I better not fuck it up.

"I don't know if you felt the same, but my heart stopped when I saw you at the top of the stairs," I continue, remembering how even my wolf mocked me for being left speechless. "Being next to you again felt right. Being here with you feels good. It's like I was walking around with only half of myself, and now that I'm here with you, I'm whole again. I had no idea how much I missed you until I saw you. I like to think of myself as a man of few words, and I haven't spoken so many of them in one go since the last time I've talked with you."

Leia's cold skin warmed up a degree or two, giving me the only indication that she likes what I'm saying. I can't expect her to openly display her emotions to me after all this time. That's the level of trust we'll have to build up to again. If only she gives us a chance...

"You're not in love with any of the suitors, and you're afraid of what you have to do next," I continue, finally getting to the point. "I can help you with that."

Leia looks at me, her brows furrowing in confusion. "Oh, yeah?"

"I'll make you a deal that will benefit us both," I say. I stop walking and turn to the side so we're facing each other. Leia's eyes lock on mine, wanting to hear more about what I'm offering. "Pick me as your future husband, and I promise you'll have the freedom you want. I'll take care of our species while you can focus on helping humans. I won't stand in your way, nor will I expect you to let go of doing what you love."

"Why should I believe you?" she asks, her tone defiant. "Why shouldn't I randomly pick someone out of the guests inside? Why should I pick you over Felix, for example?"

"Because no one will dare challenge me," I insist, playing on my power. "You'll need a husband that will be able to keep your kingdom under control and in good shape, so you don't need to worry about it. Felix isn't a good choice for that. Haven't you been listening to him? He told you what he wants to do with humans. He wants to expose us and doesn't care for the risks that the exposure might bring. He doesn't care that the witches are still out there, determined to exterminate us. His head is so high up his ass that he doesn't even know what's truly happening in the world."

"That's a bit harsh," Leia says, but she can't suppress the chuckle that escapes her.

"I'm only speaking the truth," I say with a small smile. "Whatever happens and whatever you decide, I just want you to know that it was really nice to see you. I'm glad we got to spend some time together."

"Do you have to go already?" she asks, cocking her eyebrows in question.

"I don't, but you do," I tell her and nod at the manor. "They're waiting for you."

Leia glances over her shoulder and sighs. Before she leaves, she turns to me again. "Will you be there for the announcement?"

"I'll always be around," I promise her, unsure why I didn't just give her a simple yes or no answer.

When Leia's lips curl up in a shy smile, I'm glad that I overdid it. I use the shadows to give her a gentle push toward the manor. She rolls her eyes, but there's no anger in them.

Did it work? My wolf asks.

I hope so, I reply, although right now I couldn't care less about what happens to me as long as she's happy.

You made her happy once, my

wolf reminds me, conjuring old memories of Leia and I running around the gardens and laughing. I don't bother replying because I don't even know how to respond to that.

I keep an eye on Leia's retreating figure, watching how her dress kisses her curves, making my fingers itch to touch the smooth fabric. I'm convinced that she left the two curls outside of her ponytail with the purpose to drive me mad. The whole time that we were talking, I wanted nothing more but to brush them behind her ears. The absence of her arm through mine left a cold residue that isn't entirely the consequence of her ice power.

The Ice Princess has grown into a Queen.

You'll miss the announcement, my wolf howls at me, bringing me out of my reverie.

With slow but sure steps, I make my way toward the manor, hoping that the shadowy mask of indifference will settle on my face before I enter. The worst thing would be to not be chosen and for my competitors to realize just how important it was to me.

I arrive just as everyone's being gathered in the grand salon. The lesser wolves step aside, giving me plenty of space to pass. They're smart to keep out of my way. As I slowly come to the front, my eyes spot Felix, who's standing right next to Leia's siblings and looking quite smug.

Lily notices me and gives me a little wave. I get a hold of the shadow from behind her to tousle her hair a bit. A loud giggle escapes her, causing everyone's eyes to turn her way. Her cheeks heat up, washing her pale skin with rosy color. She covers her mouth with her hand, her eyes wide and mortified. When she looks at me again, I wink to let her know it was me. Her eyes narrow to angry slits, but she's in no position to retaliate right now, and she knows it.

Surrounded by her parents, Lucas and Valerie, Leia joins us in the salon. She positions herself ahead of Levi and Lily, making the hierarchy clear. Felix reluctantly returns into the crowd, a flicker of annoyance flashing on his face.

It's not over yet, my wolf tells me, confirming what I've also come to realize. Leia hasn't chosen him. It's his arrogance that's making him overplay his hand, which will ultimately also be his downfall.

"My esteemed guests," Leia addresses everyone, her strong and confident voice carrying to the farthest corners of the grand salon. "The time has come for me to choose my future husband."

The room collectively holds a breath, every single one of us believing we could be chosen. Leia gives us a polite and well-trained smile.

"Before I make that announcement, I would like to thank you all for coming on such short notice," she continues in a proper fashion of a politician who knows how to avoid getting to the point.

She's scared, I tell my wolf, who makes a small sound in agreement, before replying, *She didn't choose yet.*

"Some of you, I've known for a long time while others I've met today," she continues, buying herself time. "I tried to talk to all of you, but the ones that I didn't get to, I hope you're not offended. We've had only a couple of hours, after all. I hope you at least managed to talk to one another and make friends. It's events like these when lasting connections are formed."

"Hear, hear," Felix says as he lifts his glass in a toast.

Rude, my wolf mutters, and I let out a low growl in agreement.

While Leia's eyes narrow in annoyance, she brushes it off with a smile. Felix beams as she looks at him, so sure that he'll be the chosen one. Her eyes dart from him to the far left where I'm standing. I give her a curt nod, meaning it more as an encouragement than a reminder of the deal I'm offering.

"It's been a very hard and intense evening, but I've come to a decision and from the bottom of my heart, I believe it's the correct one," Leia continues, raising her voice to be heard over the toasting.

A silence spreads across the room, the tension in the air so palpable, it would be quite easy to cut through it even with the rustiest of blades. Everyone's eyes, including Levi's and Lily's, are locked on the future Ice Queen.

"I choose," Leia starts, then pauses as her voice shakes a bit. She takes a deep breath to gather herself, before announcing, "Gavin Grey!"

Fuck yeah! My wolf exclaims and howls so loud that I can barely hear the applause in the room.

I lift my chin higher and smirk, pretending that I wasn't worried one bit, when in reality I was holding my breath just like everyone else did. I've been clutching my hands into fists, trying really hard to stay in control over my emotions in case this would go the other way.

Leia extends her arm toward me, wordlessly inviting me over. When my eyes lock on hers, I can clearly see the fear in them. Giving her a small, almost secretive smile, I do my best to assure her that she made a good call.

When I reach her, I take her hand in mine and do what I've never done for anyone else but my father. In front of everyone, I lower myself on one knee and bow my head at the neck. It's the highest sign of respect I can show her, while at the same time making it clear to everyone that Leia is the real monarch. I'll be more than happy to fulfill the role of a consort, which will give me more power than being the fourth born prince ever could.

Leia's breath hitches, her hand trembling in mine. Still on my knee, I give her a reassuring squeeze, silently letting her know that she'll never walk alone anymore. Without taking my eyes off hers, I bring her hand to my lips and gently brush them against the knuckles. Her plump lips part open, a blue spark igniting in her eyes.

"All hail Her Royal Highness, Princess Leia Lafayette, and her future husband, His Royal Highness, Prince Gavin Grey!" Lucas roars, lifting his hands in the air summoning the snowflakes over the grand salon as if they were confetti.

I pull myself up on my feet just as the room erupts in cheers. Leia hooks her arm through mine, trusting me not only with her future but also her life.

Standing in front of a purebred Royal crowd and having my name called out and cheered for makes me feel powerful. It's something that I've been working my whole life toward. I deserve this. Having my best friend by my side while living my dream feels right.

"Enough of this fucking shitshow!"

A voice yells, followed by a loud scream as a blast of fire shoots through the air and melts the snowflake confetti.

Some of the suitors cower and crouch while others call on their powers, creating a shield around them. The room is yanked into a wild chaos, the powers summoned and mixed where they shouldn't be.

Leia digs her nails into my arm, her body trembling with fear. Lucas pushes forward at the same time that I shift myself, so I'm positioned in front of Leia, protecting my future queen with my body if I have to.

It's a fire user, my wolf tells, pointing out the ability to make the pool of suspects smaller.

I know who he is, I tell him, knowing that there's only one suitor who's foolish enough to make a scene at quite possibly the biggest event of the year. It's the worst place for it because there are too many enemies that can be made, burning the family's good reputation to ashes.

It's also my family's reputation because, even though my mother gave it all up, the blood doesn't lie. She's his aunt, which officially makes this piece of shit my cousin.

"Felix," I call out, my eyes darting around the crowd in an attempt to spot him.

Lucas is getting the fire under control, but there are still some stray flames dancing on the ceiling. While he has his hands full taking care of that, I'll sort my cousin out.

Smother his flames, my wolf howls in angry encouragement, sending an adrenaline boost through my veins.

"Felix!" I roar, my call being carried through the room louder than any scream.

"Shadow thief," Felix says, his voice coming from my left.

I shift to be turned his way, effectively pushing Leia's body behind me. Her fingers grip at the back of my jacket, looking for comfort from my closeness. I don't shake her off, needing to know her position just as much as she's looking for my protection.

"I haven't stolen anything," I reply, keeping my tone controlled.

"You walked in here with your tricks and false promises," Felix accuses, flames erupting in his hands.

They're blue, my wolf warns me.

He's more powerful than I thought, I note as I carefully take on the hottest type of fire.

"I haven't played any tricks," I reply, wanting to keep him busy to buy time and assess the situation that's on the verge of turning catastrophic. "You know as well as I do that our lives aren't our own. We're all a part of the bigger puzzle, trying to find pieces that fit together while showcasing our intricate skills as politicians. At the end of the day, it's not even about power. Because if it had been, things would be completely different, and you know it. You and I wouldn't be here, giving ourselves up for someone else's crown. Not when we're the most powerful members of our families, and those thrones should be rightfully ours."

"Don't pretend that we're the same," Felix hisses, the fire burning brighter as it spreads from his hands to his elbow. "You have no idea what I've been going through."

"Your brother had a son, which pushed you lower in the line of succession," I say, probably reminding him of the worst possible thing at the moment, but I need it to get the point across. "At least your brother is taking his job seriously, while my brother couldn't care less about the throne or our people. He spends his days whoring around, not even bothering to actively participate in the ascension process."

"We're not the same," Felix repeats, the fire spreading higher up his arms and all the way to his shoulders.

I pull myself to my full height, look him straight in the eyes, and lose the pretense. Trusting my instincts, I lift my chin and smirk, knowing it will piss him off.

Felix plays straight into my hands, reacting exactly the way I expected him to. Lifting his arms up, he sends a blue fire beam my way, but he doesn't realize what's been happening behind him.

Even though I'm confident in the strength of my shadow shield, I still absorb the surrounding light into me to give it extra strength. Blue fire is no joke and I'm in no mood to tend to the third-degree burns that it would leave.

Behind me, Leia's grip on my jacket tightens, and she steps as close as she can, pressing her body against mine. My already near-impenetrable shadow shield gets an icy layer around it. Leia's ice power isn't much against Felix's blue fire, but every little bit of his attack that she takes off me helps.

It also allows me to focus a part of my mind on what I've been doing behind Felix where the shadow around his feet has thickened. I mentally grab on it and yank hard.

Felix cries out as he loses his balance and lands on his back. His hands move with his fall, the fire beam that was previously aimed at me now burns its way above my head and marks the ceiling.

We need to get out! my wolf howls, bringing my attention to the burning disaster around me.

Most of the room has already been emptied. Felix, Leia, Lucas, and I are the only ones that have been left behind. Lucas was too busy trying to salvage the salon, while Leia and I fought Felix.

"We need to go!" I call out, making sure that Lucas hears me.

He shakes his head, adamant to save the manor. "Get her out!"

"Father!" Leia cries, struggling against me when I grab her and hand her through the window to Levi.

Not wanting to leave my future father-in-law behind, but also respecting his decision not to leave, I stay with him and use my shadows to smother out the fire. Lucas is a powerful ice wielder, his ability effectively freezing up the flames. From the safety of the outside, other abilities join us, and together, we eventually manage to save the manor.

When the fire's out, I walk up to Lucas, who's half-kneeling on the ground, too exhausted to stand. He looks up at me, his previously piercing blue eyes now dull since his ability has been spent. I offer him my hand, then pull him up on his feet, half-supporting his weight.

"Where's Felix?" he asks with a weak voice, looking around the mostly burned salon.

I shake my head, only sure of one thing. "He's gone."

CHAPTER 6

GAVIN

"Are you sure about this, Your Highness?" James asks me as he drives through the iron gate of the Lafayette Manor, officially entering their premises.

Even though the engagement has been made official from the moment Leia picked me and I kneeled, I still have a little wiggle room to get out of it, but it will only be there until we spend the night together. After that, we'll be connected with a bond that cannot be broken unless one of us dies. It's like a marriage before the marriage.

"There's no way back for me," I reply, remembering my father's anger, even though my mother tried to tell him that me leaving will ultimately benefit the whole family. With two Grey men on the throne, the New York area won't be divided anymore.

"Can I stay with you?" James asks, his voice barely audible.

My eyes jerk his way, unsure if he's serious. I've taken it for granted that by leaving the Grey name, I'll have to say goodbye to everything that anchors me to my old life. Maybe that's not the case. Maybe James is a loophole.

"I'm not sure how that would be possible," I reply, mentally cursing myself for not informing myself better.

"If I tell you that it is, would you accept me in your servitude?" James asks, his eyes shining with hope as he turns back in the driver's seat to look at me.

"Of course," I assure him without missing a beat.

James' lips twitch, but he regains control over himself, remaining stoic as he continues in a calm but content voice. "Your Highness has found me on the streets and took me in. I've never officially belonged to your family, nor am I related to anyone that serves your family in any way. Therefore, as far as loyalties are concerned, I'm a free wolf who would like to swear myself to you. My life is yours to do with as you bid, Your Highness."

My mouth falls open in surprise as I realize that he's speaking the truth. I've never officially welcomed him into the Shadow pack because he's far too inexperienced and unskilled to be one of them. I mean, I did plan on getting him in, which was why I had my Betas training him on the side, but that doesn't mean anything now.

"You know your laws," I comment with a ghost of a smile.

"I do, Your Highness," he confirms, his expression one of determination. "Will you accept me as your loyal servant?"

"If that is what you desire, then yes," I agree, trying to sound nonchalant to make it look like I'm the one doing him the favor and not the other way around.

"Thank you, sir," James says with a slight tremble in his voice and bows his head at the neck.

"It's show time," I comment when I notice the Lafayette family gathered at the entrance. "Take care of my luggage and then go to collect your stuff. Take everything because I doubt that we'll be allowed to return anytime soon or ever. I'll make sure that by the time you come back, there'll be a room waiting for you."

"Yes, sir," James confirms, then climbs out of the car to open the door for me. I don't really need him to do it, but I'm grateful to have the extra moment to myself before I need to face the circus.

Leaving James behind to do my bidding, I go ahead to meet my new family. Leia's standing in front of everyone with the twins closely behind her, then Lucas and Valerie hovering above everyone on the highest step.

Unsure of what kind of etiquette applies to cases like this, I improvise, figuring that my best bet is to show some respect. Instead of dropping to my knee or making some big display of deference, I simply bow my head, bending my neck at the slightest angle. As the fourth born, I've done my fair share of bowing and bending. If I have any say in it, this will be one of the last times I do so.

"Gavin," Leia greets me, reaching for my arm.

Instead of hooking hers through mine, she takes my hand, intertwining our fingers in a sign of more intimate unity. Lucas raises his brow but doesn't say anything. He actually greets me with a nod, which is more than I expected from him. Saving the grand salon must've meant more to him than I thought.

"Welcome to Lafayette Manor," Valerie says, looking as classy as ever in her knee-length tailored sheath navy blue dress. "And to the family."

"Thank you, Your Majesty," I reply, referring to her in a proper way.

"We don't use formal titles between the close members of the family," she replies, waving off my attempts for propriety. "Shall we have a cup of tea so we can get to know each other a bit better before you settle in?"

I glance at Leia for confirmation, and when she gives me a small smile, followed by a reassuring squeeze of my hand, I turn back to her mother. "I'd like that."

"Splendid," Valerie says with a smile of her own, then turns to her husband and hooks her arm through his, guiding him toward the door. "Follow me."

"When in doubt, remain silent," Levi advises in a low whisper.

Lily nods, giving me a serious look. "They can get anything out of you if you keep talking. It's better to stay quiet."

Before I could ask them what they meant, the twins run up the stairs and disappear inside the manor. With a question in my eyes, I turn to Leia, my brows furrowed in confusion.

"Don't mind them," she tells me with a light chuckle. "They tend to exaggerate."

"Okay," I say slowly, then let her take me to the smaller salon where everyone's already waiting for us to join them.

Leia and I will have plenty of time to catch up and talk later. Right now, we need to go through the second round of screening and get her family's official approval. After we spend the first night together, no one can do or say anything to break off the engagement.

"Sit anywhere you want, Gavin," Valerie tells me, but she says it in a way as if it's a test.

I look around at the variety of sofas. Lucas and Valerie each sit on a throne-like chair of a dark blue velvet, while the twins share a two-seat sofa on their left. The options I've left are the other two throne-like chairs across from Lucas and Valerie, although those two are less regal ones, or I can take the exact same two-seat sofa across from the twins.

If you pick a two-seater, you show that you're submissive, my wolf tells me, giving voice to my thoughts.

Still holding Leia's hand, I lead us to the throne-like chairs. While I want to sit on the right one, I force myself to remember that Leia's the true queen, so I offer it to her, then take a seat on her left as a proper prince consort.

My choice has challenged the current leaders enough as it is, and I don't need them to reject me before I actually get the power. At the moment, all I want is for them to see that they won't be able to push me around.

The corners of Valerie's mouth lift up, and she tilts her head to the side, giving me a barely noticeable nod.

She approves, my wolf concludes.

"Okay, now that you've had your fun, dear wife, I think it's time we have a serious talk about the future of our newly engaged couple," Lucas announces, speaking for the first time.

"Certainly, husband," she says, giving him a smile that reaches all the way to her eyes, then turns to me, "Apologies, Gavin. Sometimes you learn more about the person by the way they act and the choices they make than by the words they say."

"No offense taken," I reply, agreeing with her methods.

"I've held up my end of the bargain, Father," Leia tells him, her voice strong but respectful. "What's next?"

"We're doing this for your own good, Leia," Lucas says, letting out a tired sigh as he leans back in his chair. "The situation out there is worse than we let people believe. Gavin probably knows what I'm talking about, don't you?"

"I wish I didn't, but I do," I reply, feeling the weight of the knowledge resting on my shoulders.

"Care to share?" Leia asks, giving me a look that's a mix of annoyance and impatience.

Geez, who pissed in her cereal this morning? my wolf comments, making me force out a cough to cover a chuckle.

"These things are only shared with the high-ranking officers in the military and the top royals," I say cautiously, waiting for Lucas' lead.

While I'd have no problem telling the truth to Leia who, as the future queen, should've known those things already, I'm less eager to give the information to the twins. If everyone found out, fear and panic would spread like wildfire that'd be impossible to contain. The risk of discovery would jump through the roof, bringing us closer to the danger of extinction.

"The family is only as strong as its weakest member," Lucas says and looks around at his kids. "We've protected you for as long as we could, but now that Leia will undertake the ascension to the throne, she'll need everyone's support. If we keep things from the twins, she'll never be able to rely on them."

"I want to know," Levi says with determination.

Lily nods in agreement and adds, "We won't tell anyone. We know how to keep a secret."

"You heard them," Lucas tells me with a sad smile. "Go ahead."

Another test? my wolf inquires, and while I'm not so sure it's not, I also don't think Lucas would start the topic so openly and then not finish it.

"Okay," I agree, then take a deep breath to collect myself and gather my thoughts. "I'm sure that you're all aware of our origin story, right?"

Leia and the twins nod in confirmation. It's a story that we're all told when we're kids. It teaches us the importance of keeping our species a secret while highlighting some of the reasons why we should stay away from humans. Witches walk freely among them and until they reveal themselves, we're unable to recognize them. Unfortunately, it's easier for them to pinpoint our species. A couple of noticeable temper tantrums and supernatural occurrences help them connect the dots when looking for wolves. It's the hunters that scare us all. Even the fully grown wolves.

"It's also no secret that witches have been hunting us for years," I continue, keeping my voice even and controlled. Now's not the time to show emotion, whether it's fear or anger. "More often than not, our kind gets discovered because some wolves decide to break the rules and lay with humans. A half-blooded baby is like a beacon to them. We're not sure how it works or why those babies are different."

"It leads the witches right to the wolves," Leia concludes.

I nod and continue in a grave voice, "The witches don't kill the wolves right away. They're very good at capturing our species and coaxing out our secrets. When one wolf goes astray, their whole family gets killed. Massacred. Not just their family, their friends too."

"What are you saying?" Levi asks, his eyes wide with fear.

"I'm saying that as long as there're wolves mixing with humans, our lives are in danger," I reply, trying to sound as if I'm simply stating a fact. I don't want Leia to think that I'll stand in her way when she does her charity work.

The more time that she focuses on other things, the bigger influence I'll have over her kingdom.

"When one wolf is found, sooner or later, they'll give up their family and friends. Their family and friends will give up connections of their own, and so on," I explain in case they didn't understand the gravity of the danger we're all in.

"If things were always like that, why should we be even more scared now?" Levi asks, posing a good question. "What changed?"

"I'm not entirely sure," I admit with a shrug. "Maybe the witches have finally decided to eradicate their mistake, or maybe there are too many wolves that mix with humans, and the witches don't like that. They consider themselves as sort of their unofficial protectors, and as you well know, we're all of the firm belief that we're better than them. The human species is beneath us. They're trash."

"Do you believe that?" Lily asks me, her blue eyes just as wide as her brother's.

Careful how you answer, my wolf warns me just as I risk a quick glance at Leia, whose full attention is on me. She's curious about my reply more than both twins combined.

"I don't think that it's any of my business," I say, trying to avoid the topic as much as I can while still giving her a somewhat satisfying answer to get her off my back. "In my ideal world, we would live our own lives and they their own. Our paths would cross only when they must. Of course, in my ideal world, there wouldn't be any witches and we'd all be safe."

Nice save, my wolf growls in approval.

"Let's get back to the point," Lucas says, then gestures for me to continue.

"Right," I agree, wishing that I wouldn't have to be the one to tell this story. I much prefer being informed than doing the informing. I clear my throat before continuing, "While the attacks from the witches have been sporadic in the past, they're becoming more and more frequent. Our losses are high and, as a result of too many premature deaths, our population is rapidly decreasing."

"We're dying out," Leia says, her mouth open in shock.

"Yes," I confirm. "The extinction is coming unless we do something about it."

"What's there to do?" Lily asks, looking from me to her parents.

It's Levi that answers, "We should reproduce more. Make more pups."

"It's not that simple," Valerie says with a kind, sad smile. She reaches for Lucas' hand and locks her eyes with her husband's when she continues, "Once we're married, we fully belong only to our partner. Bastard pups with no proof of their pure bloodline are, in best case scenario, thrown on the streets or, in the worst case, killed long before they take their first breath."

"Stupid archaic rules," Leia mutters in anger. "Humans are a lot more advanced and modern when it comes to these things. Pups born out of wedlock have just as much of a right to live as the ones born to a married couple."

"You'll soon find out that there's more to it than you know right now, Leia," Lucas says calmly, his voice full of patience. "There are different dangers surrounding them and us. We'll talk about that some other time. Finish your story, Gavin."

A bubble of cold air appears around Leia as she quietly wallows in her anger. I hope I won't have to be the one to explain to her why so many innocent pups have to be killed.

You have just as much blood on your hands as anyone else, if not even more, my wolf says, but I ignore him, pushing down the terrible memories his words threaten to conjure.

"A lot of the higher members of the courts are slipping and making big mistakes," I continue and study their faces for any sign that they know Garren's one of those fucked-up royals. "While in the past, only lower classes mixed with the humans and got themselves caught in the process, they didn't have enough knowledge that could bring our society down. If any of the royal members gets caught, it would be the beginning of the end. Just imagine all the secrets we'd reveal if any of us gets tortured by the witches. We know each other's identities, addresses and the ins and outs of each other's abilities. At the end of the day, we're our biggest threat."

They might not know about Garren now, but it's only a matter of time, my wolf tells me.

Garren is my father's problem, I reply even though I know it's not exactly true. If my brother gets caught, we're all fucked.

"That's enough for today," Lucas announces as he gets up. "We should let Gavin settle."

"Thank you, sir," I say, standing up myself.

"Please, call me Lucas," he says and offers me his hand.

Without hesitation, I cross the short distance between us and shake it. Lucas' grip is firm and strong, but his eyes are softening with every second that passes.

"Welcome to the family, Son," Lucas says. "We're happy to have you."

"Thank you," I reply in a controlled voice, swallowing the unexpected emotion bubbling in me at such a warm welcome. I was fully prepared to be a guest in my new home and a stranger in my new family. The reality is completely different as my new pack opens their hearts and minds to accept my shadow wolf.

"If there's anything you need, please don't hesitate to tell us," Valerie says, standing behind Lucas.

"Actually, there is one thing," I tell her, then continue as she raises her brow in question. "I was hoping that one room could be prepared in the servant's quarters for a free wolf that wants to follow me."

"A free wolf, you say?" Lucas echoes, his brows furrowing. "Isn't that just another word for a street wolf?"

"Yes and no," I reply with a shrug. "James' story is a bit more complicated than that, but I can assure you that he's not a half-blood. I wouldn't take that kind of a risk, nor would I willingly associate myself with them."

Lucas narrows his eyes, studying me for the longest of moments before finally nodding. "Very well. Valerie will speak to the staff to have it ready."

"Thank you," I tell him yet again.

Good call on not telling him that James wants to swear loyalty directly to you and not to the family, my wolf comments.

I'm pretty sure that if Lucas knew that about James, he wouldn't let him follow me. There's nothing more dangerous than an already powerful wolf with a direct line of loyal servants. It would have make me a bigger danger to Garren because, compared to him, I was a nobody. Lucas wouldn't have liked it, but it wouldn't carry as much weight because I'm going to be a king, after all.

Leia takes my hand in hers again, her cold fingers intertwining with mine and sending shivers down my spine. I glance down at her, locking my eyes with her piercing blue ones. She's even more beautiful in her casual clothes, showing her natural and everyday beauty, than she is in her formal attire.

"I'll show you to our room," she says, sounding nervous.

If she sleeps in her wolf form, I want to be the one sharing the bed with her, my wolf calls it.

With a quick nod at the direction of her family, I turn and follow my fiancée. When we get to the door, Valerie calls my name. Because of Leia's strong grip on me, I can only half-rotate to look at her mother.

"Out of all the boys that Leia used to hang out with, you were always my favorite," Valerie says with a wink.

"Mother!" Leia exclaims and groans, but the damage is done because I already have an insufferable smirk plastered on my face.

Leia pulls me out of the small salon, but the sound of her mother's laughter follows us up the stairs. She's walking too fast for me to mark a path in my head, but I'll have plenty of time to do that later. The one thing that I do notice is that her room isn't in the same area as her old one.

As soon as Leia ushers me through the door, she lets go of my hand as if I'm carrying some contagious disease.

Rude, my wolf mutters. *It's not like you're the one spending your free time with human trash.*

It's not like that, I say back, swallowing its unjust anger.

"Are you okay?" I ask, my eyes following her as she sits on the edge of the bed.

"I don't know," she says weakly, letting go of all pretenses. "I haven't thought this through. I don't even know what's next."

With slow steps, as if dealing with a scared animal, I approach her and lower myself until our eyes are leveled. I take her hands into mine and give them a comforting squeeze, offering her the same support she gave to me.

"We'll figure it out," I promise, my voice barely a whisper. "We'll take it step by step, okay?"

Her bright blue eyes lock on mine, holding so much hope and trust inside them that it nearly makes me lose my balance. No one has ever looked at me that way before. Not even my pack, whose lives were in my hands more often than not.

"What's our first step?" she asks, her plump lips slightly trembling as the reality of our situation settles over us.

"We have to talk about the sleeping arrangements," I say awkwardly, referring to the fact that there's only one bed in the room.

"What do you mean?" Leia asks, her brows furrowing in confusion. I pointedly look at the bed, watching her as her eyes widen in realization. She quickly shakes off the awkwardness, rolls her eyes and laughs. "We've been best friends since forever, Gavin. It's not like we haven't shared a bed before."

"It's not the same, and you know it," I say with a low growl, annoyed that I'm the only one affected by it.

"I don't see what's so different about it," she replies with a nonchalant shrug. "We're friends who happen to be engaged because of the deal we made that will benefit both of our lives. Simple as that."

"Right," I say slowly, suddenly feeling ridiculous about pointing out just how much our bodies changed during the years we haven't seen each other, how our needs and desires grew, and how our thoughts went in a completely different direction than they used to.

This won't end well, my wolf says with a chuckle, then quickly adds, *Don't forget, her wolf form is mine!*

Shut up, I growl back, mentally preparing myself to share a bed with a girl who's grown into a beautiful woman with curves in all the right places. My cock twitches at the thought of having her only inches away from me with only a thin fabric separating our naked bodies.

"Do you want to go to the bathroom first or can I?" Leia asks, bringing me out of my thoughts.

"I'll go," I tell her, needing an extra cold shower to get me through the night. Something tells me that it will be the longest one yet, which says a lot because I've done my time in the army. The tortures I once feared at the hands of witches pale in comparison to what Leia is doing to me now.

CHAPTER 7

LEIA

I slowly wake up, gradually becoming aware of myself and the daylight entering the bedroom.

The first thing I notice is Gavin and his unexpected closeness, despite the king-size bed. His front's pressing at my back, his arm thrown over me, resting on my breast. His hot breath tickles the back of my neck in a slow and steady rhythm. He's still asleep.

My usually cool body is heating up, and I'm trying to convince myself it's because of Gavin's higher temperature. It's his fault that my hands are starting to sweat and that unexpected wetness pools between my legs. It's also his fault that my stomach feels weird as if someone has released dozens of butterflies in there, allowing them to wreak havoc. I squirm slightly, hoping to regain control of myself.

My tiny movement causes Gavin to stir, pressing himself more tightly against me. I become very aware of something hard pressing against my ass and the back of my thighs. His hand, still until now, gives my breast a gentle squeeze and his fingers timidly circle my nipple, giving me every opportunity to push him away. Its response is immediate as it swells and grows stiff.

I hold my breath, waiting to see what he'll do next. When he doesn't move, I squirm again in another foolish attempt to regain a semblance of control, but I only make it worse because I press further back against Gavin's hardness.

Gavin must've taken this as a sign because he takes a deep breath and begins to massage my breast with a newfound determination. He squeezes a little harder, his fingers rolling my stiffening nipple and pulling gently at it.

The wetness between my thighs only grows, and I have to press them together to resist the urge to completely give myself to him.

Gavin's fully awake now and starts to kiss the back of my neck. The touch of his soft lips sends goosebumps down my spine, turning my insides to jelly and further exciting the flutter of butterflies. I inhale deeply and reach for his hand to press it more firmly to my breast.

While Gavin's kissing my neck, his hot breath tickling me, and massaging my breast, I risk another move and lift my leg ever so slightly, so his hard erection slips between my thighs. Gavin lets out a low groan into the back of my neck, removing his hand from my breast to pull at his boxers, readjusting them to make his cock more comfortable. We're still separated by the thin fabric of his boxers. I'm only wearing a light nightgown and a thong, which doesn't leave much to the imagination anyway.

I'm enjoying the sensations he's causing inside me. I'm ready, wet, and eager for more. In a desperate moment of need and want, I roll over, moving into him and falling into his embrace.

Our mouths meet, exchanging kisses, wet and passionate yet gentle and intimate. He catches my lip between his and gently sucks on it, then releases it and coaxes my tongue out with his, inviting me for a dance with a perfectly synchronized choreography of our lust and desire.

I roll further, forcing him over onto his back and lying on top of him, my breasts pressing against his hard chest.

His strong arms encircle me, one hand grabbing my ass while the other one runs up my back, leaving gentle but maddening scratches in its wake.

My hand travels lower, tracing a line of his uncovered chest. I'm so glad he sleeps wearing nothing but his boxers. My fingers touch every curve of his strong muscles all the way from his broad shoulders to the V-line leading into where I'm planning to go.

Grabbing the hem of his boxers, I lift it just enough to let my hand slip lower and grab his...

"Leia!"

I fall off the bed, the painful impact with the floor darkening my vision. I close my eyes in hopes of clearing it, and when I open them again, I see Gavin standing over me, a towel wrapped around his waist and stray drops of water kissing his skin. His wet hair is thrown messily over his forehead and his stubble freshly groomed.

"What happened?" I ask, looking at him in bewilderment.

"I went for a morning run, took a shower, and when I came back, you were making weird sounds in your sleep. I wasn't sure if you had a nightmare, but I didn't want to risk it, so I decided to wake you up," Gavin replies with a casual shrug.

"Oh," I breath, the heat rising all the way to the tips of my ears, leaving angry red marks in its wake. "Thank you."

Gavin furrows his brows and tilts his head to the side as he gives me a worried look. "Are you sure you're okay?"

"I'm fine," I assure him, avoiding his eyes at all costs. "I need to take a shower too. We have a long day ahead of us."

"Right," Gavin confirms, nodding his head. "I met your father on the way up, and he told me that we're meeting with the advisors today."

"It's a part of the ascension process," I tell him, slowly picking myself up off the floor. "He introduces us to the people vital to running the kingdom. He observes our interactions with them and offers advice. When he's happy with the way we handle everyday tasks, he'll step down and hand us the reigns of the kingdom."

"Easy enough," Gavin comments, but I recognize the subtle layer of the sarcasm. A ghost of a smile on his lips further confirms that he's aware of just how grueling and challenging the ascension could turn out to be.

"We just need to make sure to be on our top game and our best behavior," I say as I go toward the bathroom.

As I pass him, Gavin grabs my arm, stopping me in my tracks. His touch wakes up the remnants of the damn sex dream I've just woken up from, causing the butterflies in my stomach to go wild. My breath hitches and my heart speeds up when he presses his index finger under my chin, applying a slight pressure until I'm looking him in the eyes.

"Are you sure that you're okay?" he asks, his brows creasing with worry.

Even though he's a head taller, his neck is bent and his lips are only inches apart from mine. I'm painfully aware that he isn't wearing anything under his towel, his cock lazily resting against his thigh.

"I need a shower," I mutter and pull away from him before I can do something stupid that would ruin the deal we've made.

"Did I do something?" he calls after me, but I pretend not to hear him, going straight for the shower.

After my mind's cleared and my body cleaned, I'm ready to start the day and forget about the unfortunate dream. Gavin's already having breakfast in the dining room with my parents.

"Good morning," I greet everyone and take a seat across from Gavin, who shoots me a confused look for not choosing the one next to him.

"Good morning," my mother replies and raises her brow. "Productive night?"

A sip of the orange juice goes down the wrong hole, and I go into a coughing fit that has nothing to do with her comment, or so I'm trying to believe. Gavin's reaction is the opposite of mine. He leans back in his chair and smirks, his eyes locked on mine. A wave of heat washes over me, making matters much worse than they are.

"That good, huh?" my mother comments with a chuckle.

"Mother!" I exclaim and look to my father for support, but I should've known better than to expect it. He's having just as much fun with this as my mother.

"Where are the twins?" Gavin asks, gracefully changing the topic.

"At the Academy," my father replies. "It's their last year of schooling, and after that, I'm hoping that they'd be willing to take over a slightly more important role inside the family."

"As the advisors?" Gavin inquires, sounding genuinely interested.

"Perhaps," my father allows and shrugs. "Honestly, I don't care which role they choose, as long as it's for the best of the family. How did that work in yours?"

A shadow flickers across Gavin's face, leaving an impenetrable and expressionless wall behind. While he's still here and polite, he's also holding his cards close to his chest.

"Garren's the heir," Gavin replies, starting with his eldest brother. "I'm not sure what Grayden and Graham do, but I enlisted in the army and served my time there. I got the highest rank of an officer, returned home, and started my own pack under the Grey banners."

"I'm sorry," my father says with sincerity that makes my head jerk his way.

"It is what it is," Gavin replies, seemingly the only one in the know about their conversation.

I give my mother a questioning look and she shakes her head, silently telling me to drop it.

Weird, my wolf mutters, perfectly summing up my thoughts.

I make a mental note to talk to Gavin about it when we have some time for ourselves. I don't have much time to dwell on it now because my father has already called the royal advisors to meet us in the conference room.

"We'll keep it small in the beginning," my father tells us as I'm finishing my piece of toast. "I'll have them bring you up to date on the affairs inside the kingdom, our financial situations, and various businesses. If we have time and aren't too tired, we might talk a bit more about the latest updates from the frontlines."

Gavin nods, his face grim and serious. He's looking sharp in his black suit, his black-as-night faux hawk neatly styled and his stubble groomed to the point that makes it look as if there's a constant shadow on his face.

"Let's go," I say and stand up, taking my coffee with me.

"Take the time to finish your breakfast in peace," my father tells me, giving me a small smile. "If you start doing things on their schedule too fast, they'll expect you to show up as soon as they snap their fingers together. Never forget that you are the queen, and they're the ones that need to adapt to you."

"That's right, honey," my mother agrees. "They're the ones that should wait for you, not the other way around."

"I don't blame you for wanting to get it over with," Gavin comments, giving me a small smile. "I'm also eager to get back to the room."

My eyes widen to comical proportions, my cheeks heating up until they're the color of a ripe tomato. If they plan on making fun of me, I'm going to have to start wearing powder on my face to keep my embarrassment private.

Or you can just fuck him and be done with it, my wolf unhelpfully suggests, causing the heat to reach the tips of my ears.

I empty my cup of coffee in one big gulp and set it on the table with more force than necessary. An icy web spreads around it as my emotions get out of control.

"I think that's enough for today," my mother says, finally noticing my discomfort. But then she goes ahead and ruins it all when she adds, "We can continue teasing Leia tomorrow. Same time, same place."

I'll be there, my wolf promises with a chuckle.

"For fuck's sake," I mutter under my breath.

"Don't get upset," my father tells me. "It's all in good fun."

"Whatever!" I snap like a child and turn on my heels, eager to get some fresh air before facing a group of royal advisors.

"Wait up," Gavin calls, picking up his pace to catch up.

"Leave me alone," I say over my shoulder, but subconsciously slow down, hoping that he won't listen to me. While all of a sudden being alone with him makes me nervous, I'm also craving his company, wanting to hear his thoughts and see his smile.

"Care for a short walk before the meeting?" he asks, offering me his arm like a gentleman.

My lips curl up into a smile, and I roll my eyes, unable to be angry at him. Hooking my arm through his, I half-lean into his strong body as we do a round outside the manor.

"You're being weird today," Gavin comments, looking at me from the corner of his eye.

"I'm always weird," I reply with a low chuckle.

"You're right about that," he agrees with a nod. "I guess I should've been clear. What I meant was that you're being weirder than usual."

"Oh," I breathe, struggling to come up with a reply, but nothing comes to mind. Fortunately, Gavin senses my discomfort and changes the topic.

"Do you know that you snore?" he asks, and though he sounds dead serious, the corners of his mouth are twitching as he struggles to suppress a smile.

"I do not!" I exclaim, my mouth falling open in out-rage.

"You're right, you don't," he agrees, unable to hold back a smile any longer. It softens the hard angles of his face, making him look years younger and a lot more playful.

"Why would you say that?" I inquire, tilting my head to the side and running my fingers across his forearm.

"I wanted to coax a reaction out of you," he replies. "It's been so long since we've really talked, and I guess a lot has changed. We've changed. It's not that easy to jump back into who we were and pick up things from where we left them. I was hoping that starting with a few jokes would help us create a bond similar to the one we once shared."

"I don't think it ever went away," I tell him, touched by his honesty. It's only right that I return the favor, otherwise the deal between us will never survive. "Do you know that for years after you enlisted in the army, I looked for you at every party? I was hoping to get a glimpse of you, even if only from afar."

"I've missed you, too," he says softly, his voice barely a whisper. "Leaving you was the hardest thing I had to do. You were the only bright light in the darkness I grew up in. Your friendship kept my shadows at bay."

"What happened after you left?" I ask, genuinely curious. "Did the shadows come?"

Gavin shakes his head and lets out a low chuckle. "Not exactly. I mean, yeah, they did, but by then, I was ready to welcome them with open arms."

"I've followed your military career or at least the part that was made a public record," I confess, a flicker of surprise appearing on his face. "Someone has redacted a lot of paragraphs, but I got the gist. You've earned your place through sweat and blood, didn't you?"

"Yes," he confirms with barely a whisper, that one word carrying the weight of the world that's threatening to crush his broad shoulders.

I slide my hand forward and take his in mine, intertwining our fingers. With a strong but comforting squeeze, I'm hoping to wordlessly communicate to him everything I feel. He's not alone anymore. We're a team, and I'll carry his burdens that same as he will mine. Our wolves will howl at the moon together, our beasts embracing each other without the slightest hint of judgment. Maybe we're not in love, but at least we have the bond of friendship, and at last, we've found our forever home.

"We should go back in," I say after a while, breaking the comfortable silence.

"After you, my queen," Gavin tells me and gestures ahead.

"No," I say, taking his hand in mine. "We're in this together and as equals."

A spark of emotion that I can't decipher lights up Gavin's eyes, and he nods, a ghost of a smile on his lips.

"As equals," he echoes, matching my step with one of his as we enter the manor and make our way to the conference room.

The four advisors that have been called to the meeting stand up as one and bow their heads at their necks.

"Your Highnesses," they echo, showing us the respect that befits our status.

My father remains seated, but he winks when I look at him. Only when the advisors straighten up, my father finally stands up and gestures toward Gavin.

"Allow me to introduce you to Prince Gavin Grey, soon-to-be Lafayette, our future king," my father presents him, then points at the advisors one by one as he names them, "Duke Jackson Green, Duchess Liberty Crane, Marquess Dylan Wilson, and Countess Hannah Bailey."

"It's a pleasure meeting you all," Gavin says as he takes a seat next to me, but not before he gently pushes my chair closer to the table like a proper gentleman.

"As you all know, it's about time that we start the ascension process, which is why Prince Gavin and Princess Leia will be a part of our meetings from now," my father says, then he opens the top folder from the big pile in front of him. "Shall we start?"

"Certainly, Your Majesty, although, if we may slightly adjust the pile," Duchess Crane says, her aged eyes just as sharp as ever.

"What for?" my father asks, his brows furrowing in confusion. "We always start with the inner affairs concerning our kingdom."

"I'm afraid that some new information has come to light that needs to be discussed as soon as possible," Duchess Crane replies while the other advisors nod in agreement.

"What kind of information?" my father asks, sitting straighter in his chair in alert.

Duke Green pulls a black file from near the bottom of the pile. He gestures to us to do the same, giving us a second to find it before jumping into the explanation.

"We've been dealing with the threats from the frontlines since we can remember, but those were mostly contained to the Canadian borders on the West Coast, so we didn't put more thought into it than necessary," Duke Green says, his voice grave and his expression serious.

I open the file, glancing at the pictures within. My heartbeat speeds up and my breathing turns shallow as I realize what I'm looking at.

"It would appear that a second frontline has been formed, but this one seems to be not too far from us," Duke Green says, lifting one of the pictures up for everyone to see even though we have them in our own files. "A suburban town on the outskirts of New York has been attacked. Young families brutally murdered, the wolves that shifted were torn limb from limb."

"Is it the witches?" Gavin asks, his voice low and controlled.

Duke Green glances at his fellow advisors, before sighing and turning back to Gavin and replying, "We're not sure."

"What do you mean you're not sure?" my father asks with a raised voice. "That town was a part of our kingdom, was it not?"

"It was, Your Majesty," Duke Green confirms.

"Then how did we not know about the attack? What happened to our informants? Did all our channels get blacked out?" my father demands, the temperature in the room decreasing several degrees. "I want answers, and I want them now."

"If I may, Your Majesty," Countess Bailey speaks up, saving Duke Green from responding when my father nods, giving her permission to continue. "Due to the fact that we've had no word on the attack beforehand, we believe that there's a chance it wasn't the work of the witches."

"What are you saying?" I ask, unable to comprehend who else could've been responsible for such terrible atrocities.

"Witches have a different M.O.," Gavin replies, carefully studying the pictures one after another. "They take the wolves for information. They don't go around killing them without getting anything out of it, and they especially don't go around leaving bodies for anyone to find. It's rare that we find the remains of a wolf that's been taken by a witch."

"Prince Grey's right," Duke Green agrees, looking at Gavin with a newfound admiration.

"These wolves haven't been tortured," Gavin continues, not caring that he just earned himself the most important advisor's stamp of approval. "They've been massacred quickly and efficiently. It's clear that whoever did it knew what they were doing."

"That's our belief," Duke Green confirms, agreeing with Gavin once again.

"I don't understand," my father says, running his fingers through his hair in frustration. "Who did it?"

"That's just the thing, Your Majesty," Duke Green says, forcing himself to look my father in the eyes. "We have no idea."

My father's brows fly up his forehead, the icy anger bringing the temperature so low that everyone, except him and I, started shivering.

"I have a theory, but I'd have to get a closer look to confirm it," Gavin says, his eyes still on the pictures as everyone's heads turn his way.

"Speak, boy," my father demands and slams the palm of his hand against the table, freezing the whole surface.

Gavin clenches his jaw, no doubt he's bothered by the manner in which my father addressed him. Not wanting matters to escalate, I reach under the table and rest my hand on his thigh, giving it a gentle squeeze, willing him to drop it just this once. Gavin's muscles relax the slightest bit as he lets out a long exhale and shifts his right hand under the table, intertwining his fingers with mine.

"If you look at the pictures, you'll see in the background areas that various abilities have been used," Gavin says and waits a moment for everyone to check what he's referring to.

"So?" Marquess Wilson challenges. "That's completely normal. The wolves were attacked and tried to protect themselves."

"You're forgetting that most of the wolves there were youngsters with no proper experience," Gavin continues. "Yes, their parents had the experience, which is why they've been killed first, as we can conclude by the fact that they're still in their human forms."

"What are you saying?" my father asks, actually making Gavin spell it out for them.

"This is only a theory, but I firmly believe that these wolves were killed by wolves," Gavin replies and slightly tightens his grip on my hand as the shocking implication takes root.

"That's outrageous!" Duchess Crane exclaims, her eyes wide with horror.

"Wolves don't kill wolves!" Duke Green snaps, even jumping on his feet, momentarily forgetting in whose presence he is.

"Blasphemy! You have no proof of that." Marquess Wilson gasps, wildly shaking his head.

"Everybody shut up," Countess Bailey raises her voice, then looks at my father and bows her head. "I meant no disrespect, Your Majesty."

"Carry on," my father says and waves his hand in encouragement, leaning forward in his chair to hear what she has to say.

"Prince Grey said that he has to get a closer look to confirm it," Countess Bailey continues, her eyes locking with Gavin's. "Why don't we send him and Princess Leia there as royal representatives, assuring people that we're not taking this lightly? Princess Leia is loved and respected, so seeing her in person would undoubtedly bring our people some peace, while at the same time also allowing Prince Grey an opportunity to see the areas of attack by himself."

"I won't risk my daughter's life," my father says, immediately rejecting the idea.

"I'll keep her safe," Gavin tells him with so much confidence that I find myself believing it.

"I think I should go," I say before my father can shut him down. "We need to get ahead of this as soon as possible to get the knowledge that might help us prevent future attacks."

"I don't think it's a good idea," my father says, but his voice lacks his usual authority. He's talking to me like a father, not a king.

"You're the one who wanted me to get more involved in the matters of our kingdom," I tell him, looking him straight in the eyes. "Our people are in danger, and Gavin can help. We can help, but only if you'll let us."

Even before he says it, I know what his decision will be. It's the way the hard edges of his face soften, and his brows furrow ever so slightly. He looks at Gavin, reaching over to touch his forearm.

"I'm trusting you with my most precious treasure," my father tells him. His voice is low and resigned as he pleads, "Protect her with your life."

Gavin meets his eyes and promises, "I will."

CHAPTER 8

GAVIN

"Are we there yet?" Leia asks for the hundredth time since we left the manor.

"Relax," I tell her, taking her hand into mine to offer comfort. "Everything will be okay."

Leia looks at me with wide and fearful eyes. She's more nervous than she's willing to admit but the closer we get the less she's able to hide it.

"Can we go through the plan again?" Leia asks, and I nod, knowing it will help if she feels in control.

"When we reach our destination, we'll walk around town for a bit so I can check it out," I say. Then I lean closer and add in a lower voice, "You can stay back with James. I don't want you to see the state of the area."

"I'll think about it," she promises, and that's enough for me.

"After we're finished there, we'll go to the local gym where they put the survivors for now," I continue, going through the schedule Lucas has given us. "We'll make a speech in front of the crowds, including reporters, assuring them that their kingdom will take care of them. We'll do what royals should do. We'll be there for our people, protect them, and reassure them that everything will be okay."

"You make it sound so easy," Leia muses, her icy blue eyes shining with a hint of admiration.

"It's far from it," I reply, not wanting her to think that today will be a walk to the park. "Facing so much sadness, fear, and destruction all at once can be overwhelming. It's very important that you know that if you feel low or weak, you can always come to find me. I'll be there to step up whenever you need to step down for a minute. Today could very well be one of the hardest days of your life, so lean on me if you have to."

Leia nods and leans her head against my shoulder. "I'm glad you're here with me."

You should tell her the real reason why you're getting up so early to workout, my wolf teases.

Shut up, I mutter back.

Oh, Leia, I want to bask in your light all night long, my wolf mocks with a high-pitched voice.

I send a ball of darkness his way to teach him a lesson, but not strong enough to hurt him. My wolf yelps, then laughs as he retreats into the background, the echoes of his amusement staying behind long after he falls silent.

"We're almost there," James announces from the driver's seat.

Lucas wouldn't let us go just with one bodyguard, especially someone who's on the weaker side of the spectrum like James is, so he insisted that we have two cars of fully trained wolves following us. He basically assigned a whole pack to us, which I'm not happy about, but I didn't argue with him because we both want Leia safe. I can take care of myself, but it's true that it will be easier to focus on the task at hand if I know that Leia's surrounded by Lafayette's strongest pack.

They're not Shadows, my wolf comments with a hint of sadness in his tone.

No, they're not, I agree.

"You can park there," I tell James, pointing at the police barricade.

I'm the first one out of the car, ignoring the two black SUVs parking behind us. Walking to the other side, I open the door and offer Leia my hand. She takes it, leaning on my strength to join me outside.

"Remember what we're here for," I say, talking to both of them. Leia and James nod, each of them knowing what their particular tasks are.

"Where do you want us, Your Highness?" the Alpha of the Lafayette Pack asks Leia, who looks at me for guidance.

I take a step ahead, making it clear that I'm in charge. "What's your name, soldier?"

"Alpha Joseph Jenkins, water user, Your Highness," Alpha Jenkins introduces himself with a military salute. The members of the Lafayette Pack have control over ice and water. The two abilities are similar enough that the training doesn't differ too much.

"I want your pack to create a perimeter around Princess Leia. She's to be protected at all times. I want you running the whole op, while keeping both of your Betas by her side," I order, channeling the authority I have as a prince and the remnants of the status that always stay with the Alpha, even if he doesn't have a pack anymore.

"Right away, Your Highness," Alpha Jenkins confirms and salutes once again before leaving to attend his duties.

I take Leia's hand and walk us to James. "I want you to stay by her side at all times," I tell him, hoping that I'm not being overly protective and paranoid. "If something happens, I trust you to get her out away from the danger while the rest fight. Is that clear?"

"Crystal," James replies and though his answer is lacking the usual military assertiveness, he's just as determined and stubborn to get it done.

When the tasks are distributed, I turn to Leia, whose eyes are even wider and more fearful than before. I put my hands on her cheeks to get her to look at me. Her icy blue eyes dart toward mine, and her lips part open in surprise.

You could kiss her, you know, my wolf comments, using the most opportune moment to point out the lack of distance between us.

"Everything will be okay. No one will come anywhere near you," I promise her, making sure that I sound confident and powerful. "Are you sure you don't want to stay in the car for this first part?"

"I want to be there with you," Leia replies quietly. "For you."

I slowly lean forward and gently rest my forehead against hers. I close my eyes and focus on the parts of our bodies that touch, channeling her strength while lending her mine. My forehead against hers is the closest and most intimate we've been. My hands on her cheeks, creating a semblance of privacy in the midst of the chaos we're about to venture into. Her tiny body seeks comfort in the shadow of my bigger and broader stature.

"Pardon the interruption, Your Highnesses," a woman apologizes, coming from the other side of the police barricade.

The stolen moment over, I pull away from Leia, feeling emptier than ever before. Her absence is as notable as if I was missing a limb.

I don't like that feeling, my wolf comments, finding it just as weird as I do. We've always been independent and self-sufficient, so this is new to us.

"It's okay, we were just getting ready to enter," I reply, taking control of the situation to let Leia stay in the shadows, where she'll be safe and protected.

"You must be Prince Gavin Grey," the woman says, extending her hand and bowing her head at the same time. "Priscilla Powell. I am or...well...was the mayor of this town."

"Nice to meet you, Mayor Powell," I say and shake her hand. "I'm sorry for your loss."

Mayor Powell nods, then goes to Leia, offering a hand and introducing herself in a similar fashion as she did with me. Once we've taken care of the pleasantries, we move on to the part none of us is looking forward to.

Mayor Powell walks us down the street and describes what happened, based on the conclusions of the investigators. While Leia seems to listen to everything Mayor Powell's saying, she doesn't seem to be actively looking around, but instead has her eyes trained on my back. It's better that way. Hopefully, she won't come out of this trip with a new collection of nightmares.

"Everything happened so fast that it must've been coordinated," Mayor Powell says, without a hint of doubt in her voice. "We don't know how many attackers were there, but one thing's for sure, there must've been enough to kill all the senior members at once."

"So they wouldn't fight back," I say, taking the information in. "If the attack came from the witches, they'd do the opposite. In their case, the young pups are useless to them because they don't have the inner knowledge of how the kingdoms work. Most of them don't even know that the Academy exists."

"Correct," Mayor Powell agrees. "As you'll soon see, the survivors are the young pups who've just started to discover their abilities. Some of them don't even know how to shift yet."

"What's your theory, Mayor?" I ask, and when the woman hesitates, I press harder but with an encouraging tone, not wanting her to clam up. "Come on, you must have one. I know I do. I promise to share it after you share yours first."

"It's crazy," Mayor says, reluctant to give voice to what I'm sure is close to what's on my mind.

"Would you be more comfortable if we speak privately?" I ask, and when she nods, I lift my hand toward Leia, inviting her closer while with the other I create a wall of impenetrable shadows, thick enough that not even the sound carries through.

"You can trust us," Leia says, gently touching Mayor Powell's shoulder.

The older woman seems visibly distraught just by the thought of loudly implying the blasphemy that's on everyone's minds.

"We're not here to judge," I assure her. "We just want to help and make sure that something like this never happens again."

Mayor Powell's face crumbles and her lower lip trembles as she lets her façade fall. It's as if she's aged five years in front of our eyes, the weight of the situation hunching her back. She takes a deep breath and clears her throat, gathering the strength to share the town's whispers.

"We believe that the families knew the attackers," she says, her voice gaining strength with every word as the anger takes over. "We believe that the families opened their door to them, inviting them in with open arms. They wouldn't do that for humans. Not that this looks like a witch attack, but witches are humans who know how to tap the Source. They can't disguise themselves to look or smell like anything other than filthy trash."

"Go on," I encourage, wanting her to say it. Leia finds my hand, seeking support. It's not easy on any of us to accuse our own species of the massacre like this.

"After discarding every other option, we were really only left with one," Mayor Powell continues, using way too many words in her attempt to avoid the topic, but no matter how much time she tries to buy herself, Leia and I will wait for her until she says it. She must've realized that because she lets out a sad sigh and averts her eyes to the ground. "We think it must've been wolves. It was no one from the community because everyone's accounted for, either as dead or alive."

"The attack came from the outside," I conclude, taking over to let her breathe and recover. "Whoever did it, knew exactly what they were doing. It was well-planned, well-coordinated, and deadly. I believe they wanted to make some sort of a statement, but it's too soon for us to figure out what."

"Something like that," the mayor agrees, lifting her head to meet my eyes again. "Who could've done something like that?"

"We'll find out," I promise, then let go of the shadows around us. "Let's take a walk."

Leia pulls on my hand, getting my attention. I turn to her with a question in my eyes.

"I think I'll stay back," she says, and I nod, a small wave of relief washing over me. "You'll update me later?"

"Of course," I assure her and lean forward, gently kissing her forehead before realizing what I'm doing.

Not wanting to give too much importance to the gesture that escaped me, I meet James' eyes. "Stay back with the princess."

James nods and moves closer to Leia, offering her his arm to lead her back to the car. Alpha Jenkins has already set up the perimeter to keep her safe, while Mayor Powell and I take a walk down the bloody streets.

With a deep breath, I force myself to move, crossing the police barricade and matching the Mayor's steps. They've set up the barricade a good distance away from the actual horror scene to keep civilians from accidentally seeing it.

We walk in silence, each in our own head, battling with intrusive thoughts. The further we go; the paler Mayor Powell gets. It's as if the blood that drained from her face is now coloring the previously green lawns. There's one thing I must give to the woman, she's tougher than she looks and more stubborn than many other wolves that I've met.

I take in the horrors, but don't really focus on them until we're at the heart of it all. If I were to activate my senses too soon, I'd risk getting overwhelmed. As I've told Leia before, today's agenda holds some of the hardest things we'll have to do in the span of our entire lives.

"Let's stop here," I say, breaking the eerie silence.

Mayor Powell follows my lead, giving me plenty of space to do what I came here to do. I take off my clothes piece by piece, my movements automatic. It's something I've done more times than I can count, but even on the frontlines, I've never been in the heart of so many triggers.

I hope you're ready, I say to my wolf when I'm fully naked. I close my eyes and focus on channeling the animal inside me.

While, to the outside observer, the shift happens in a matter of seconds, the passage inside the mind takes a bit longer. It's the moment where my consciousness meets my wolf's on an equal field, allowing the animal to step up and claim my place in the world while trusting he'll do the same when asked. We are two entities living in symbiosis, and it's very important that we're on good terms most of the time.

The next time that I open my eyes, I'm on all fours, my vision sharper and clearer. Taking a deep breath, I fill my nostrils with the smells of different stages of death. The metallic scent is the one that lingers in the air, followed by one of burned flesh.

My eyes take in the houses, the intricate details on the doors finally making sense. The leaf carved on the green one, the yellow lightning painted on the dark blue one, and the windmill of rainy clouds hanging in front of the door across from me.

Their elemental abilities, I comment to my wolf who lets out a low growl in agreement.

I put my nose against the ground and sniff, further discarding the option of human smells mixing with the ones of wolves.

In my wolf form, I'm a lot faster than I could ever hope to be as a two-legged man. In a matter of minutes, I've run through the attacked streets, my eyes focusing on the little things that my mind finds important enough to dissect on a deeper level.

When I'm satisfied with my investigation, I return to Mayor Powell, who's exactly where I left her. My wolf immediately yields to my request, allowing me to shift back. Mayor Powell politely looks away as she offers my clothes back to me.

Once I'm dressed, I start walking back toward the cars, my pace faster and more urgent than before. Mayor Powell struggles to keep up, but she's too stubborn to fall behind.

"What did you see?" she asks me and when I don't answer, she breaches the etiquette, grabbing me by the arm.

Before I can rein in my wolf, I'm facing her with a shadow expression on my face, my eyes like those of one of the apex predators, stirring in annoyance and itching to scratch the surface.

Mayor Powell recoils, her head bowed in deference as she mutters an apology.

Stand down, I order my wolf, willing him to retract its claws, which he does but with great reluctance.

Once I'm back in control, I take a step toward the scared woman who's witnessed only the smallest extent of my significant power, and yet, she cowered with her tail between her legs.

"I think your theory is on point," I tell her, offering the information as a form of apology.

Mayor Powell looks up without a hint of surprise on her face. I told her exactly what she expected to hear.

"We should get back and talk to the survivors," I say, turning on my heel again to return to Leia. I'm eager to see her, to be in her cooling presence again.

When we reach the police barricade, I send Mayor Powell to one of the SUVs. She can ride with the pack, giving Leia and I privacy to talk.

"What did you see?" Leia asks me the moment I enter the car.

"It's not good," I reply, not bothering to hide our conversation from James as I go on to describe what I sensed in wolf form, skipping the gory details.

"You were right," Leia says when I finish the story. "It was the wolves."

"I'm afraid so," I confirm. "The houses were clearly marked with the elemental abilities of the families that lived in them. I ran the streets, looking for one particular element, but it was nowhere to be found."

"Because no one wielded it," Leia concludes, and I nod.

"Our attackers are the masters of fire," I say, the smell of burned bodies still lingering in my nostrils.

CHAPTER 9

GAVIN

Grieving faces gaze upon us when we enter the local gym. The fear still hangs in the air but now that they're surrounded by fully trained packs to assure their safety, the sadness took over any other emotion.

"I think you should take the lead on this one," I whisper to Leia. "Sympathy and compassion aren't my strong suits."

"You did plenty," she whispers back, then takes a step forward to address the crowd.

Vultures, my wolf hisses, referencing to the reporters with their cameras aimed high as they chase the terrible story.

It's good publicity, I reply in their defense, although I'm just as disgusted by it as the animal inside me.

"Hi," Leia says timidly, her voice echoing around the gym as she speaks into the microphone. "I'm sure that most of you know us, but for ones that don't, I'm Princess Leia Lafayette, and this is my fiancé Prince Gavin Grey."

I give a curt nod in a general direction when she gestures at me.

You could at least smile, my wolf comments, but I don't bother replying because we both know that public displays of emotion aren't something we do.

"We're so glad that you're here with us, surviving the horrible events of the last twenty-four hours," Leia continues and while her voice doesn't shake, a small web of ice spreads around her feet, giving the only indication of the pressure she's under.

"We want you to know that the criminals that did this will be found and brought to justice," Leia announces. Then adds with a firmer voice, putting a special emphasis on one word, "*Our* justice. They will pay based on *our* laws, appropriate to the crime *they* committed. First, they will suffer a fate worse than death, and then, when they beg for us to kill them, we will torture them some more. We'll end them under our terms and when we say enough. We'll take control back in our hands, and we'll never let it go ever again."

The murmurs of agreement spread throughout the young crowd. Leia's telling them exactly what they need to hear, making it clear that their families will be able to rest in peace.

"What will happen to us now?" one of the girls calls, giving voice to a question that's on everyone's mind.

Leia glances back at me, and I nod in encouragement, ready to do whatever she says. We haven't really discussed the fate of the young pups during the meeting with the advisors, but she can't ignore the question. Not when it's been asked in front of everyone, turning every survivor's eye on their princess.

"One thing's for sure," she starts, radiating all the confidence in the world. "You're not alone, and we won't leave you behind. In fact, we'll set up temporary housing for you, and Prince Gavin himself will take over your training."

Oh, no, she didn't, my wolf says with a low chuckle that turns into a growling laughter.

Did she just turn me into a fucking babysitter? I ask my wolf in disbelief, struggling to keep my real emotions hidden behind an expressionless mask.

I think you meant to say puppy-sitter, my wolf roars with laughter, his enjoyment further fueling the anger.

Above me, a light bulb explodes, the sparks flying in every direction. Leia crouches and covers her head. James immediately goes to her side, looking left and right for any attackers. The Lafayette Pack comes into view, scanning the crowd.

I'm the only one who doesn't move, doesn't flinch, doesn't react. My hands are clenched into fists, my breathing heavy as I fight with the darkness within me, forcing it back into the shadows.

"It's okay," I say at last, my voice coming out forced and breathless.

Having power is cool, but not when the emotions turn against me. I've fought many battles, but I've never faced an enemy that'd be a more memorable opponent than the one I've been fighting day after day to keep my abilities in check. It's a battle that doesn't allow me to rest nor let my guard down even an inch.

"It's okay," I repeat louder, sounding stronger and in control again.

Leia looks up at me with a question in her eyes, but I ignore it. Now is neither the time nor the place, so I'll have to deal with her later. She takes my hand and stands up. I gesture for her to continue her speech, since she's already done all the damage she could.

"Everyone okay?" Leia asks, her eyes traveling across the crowd of young pups and the reporters. When she's satisfied that no one's been hurt, she continues, "To end this on a slightly positive note, I want to assure you all that you won't be forgotten. You might've lost your fathers and mothers, your brothers and sisters, your whole families, but that doesn't mean that you'll be cast to the streets as lone wolves. From this day forward, no matter the age, you'll be known as The Pack of Survivors. With time, I want you to wear your scars proudly, to protect the weaker from the injustices that were done to you, and to serve the kingdom that will stand by your side in your lowest moments. We are only as strong as our weakest member. The Pack of Survivors!"

"The Pack of Survivors!" the gym echoes, picking up the cheer. It's the first time that a glimmer of hope appears on the young faces as the pups' future doesn't look so grim anymore.

The Pack of Survivors, my wolf cackles.

Shut up, I mutter, sending a shadow ball his way, but instead of cowering, my wolf inside opens his mouth and swallows it whole.

Yum, he comments and makes a lip-smacking sound.

Dick, I say, then do my best to shut him down.

"How did I do?" Leia asks when she returns to my side. She's actually looking at me with eager hopefulness, fishing for a compliment that I can't give.

"We should do our rounds and get out of here," I say, ignoring a flicker of hurt that flashes across her face as I push past her and toward the horde of young wolves.

They look at me with expectant eyes, waiting for me to say something. My eyes travel from one to the next, taking them all in.

Weak blood, my wolf mutters in disgust.

It's up to us to make warriors out of them, I reply, knowing that I've no other choice. By announcing it in front of everyone, Leia has successfully tied my hands.

"James," I call without taking my eyes off the young pups.

James appears by my side less than a second later. "Your Highness?"

"Take the names of every young pup. I want them accounted for and assessed. Start a file, keeping track of their abilities and the powers they've already started showing," I say, speaking loud enough for everyone to hear. No one will ever be able to claim that I'm not taking my responsibilities seriously. I glance over my shoulder at James and offer him a ghost of a smile as I continue, "Congratulations. You just became my Beta."

Without another word, I exit the gym, leaving Leia and the rest of the entourage behind. I need some air and time away to cool down. Right now, I'd want nothing more than to face the wolves responsible for that horrible massacre and take them down, one by one, with my own bare claws. I'm itching for a fight, I'm in need of a way to release my anger.

You really should have pack up the salmon ladder before moving to the Lafayette Manor, my wolf says, not helping at all.

He might be useless, but he's not wrong. I need to train until I'm too exhausted to stand on my feet. In the past, I would've joined with the Shadows during one of their training sessions, but that's not an option anymore. I'm going to have to find a different solution for it or my vast well of dark energy could put everyone around me in danger.

The ability is only as strong as the person wielding it, my wolf comments, still unhelpful.

I'm not sure how long it takes for Leia to come out, but it has gotten darker, and I don't think it's entirely my doing. I've been pacing back and forth, mentally fighting my inner battles while blacking out on whatever's been going on outside.

"What the fuck, Gavin?!" Leia whispers angrily when she spots me at the car. "Where did you go?"

I open the door for her, not wanting to make a scene for everyone to see. Especially since there are still cameras pointed our way, recording every royal second that could bring them a couple of extra bucks. I refuse to be the one that fills their bank accounts.

"Get in," I say, gesturing with my head at the car.

Leia narrows her eyes at me as if in a staring contest. I grew up with three brothers, so I'm no stranger to it. As predicted, she's the first one to give up, but not without sighing loudly. Fortunately, that's the only sign of a public temper tantrum, but even that could be written off in so many different ways by our royal publicists if the press decides to run with an angle that wouldn't suit our reputation.

"Will you talk to me now?" she asks angrily as soon as I join her in the back.

"Wait," I say, keeping my replies to one word.

She rolls her eyes and groans, but other than that, she does as she's told. James takes the driver's seat, and when we've been in the car for ten minutes, getting far away from the reporters, or the vultures and whatnot, I turn to Leia.

"How dare you?" I ask with a low voice, barely keeping myself in check.

Leia tilts her head to the side and furrows her brows in question. "How dare I what?" she asks, sounding genuinely confused.

"How dare you create a new pack out of nothing and name me an Alpha of it," I hiss, clenching my fists so hard that my nails dig deep into my palms. "Do you know how insulting that is?"

"What?" she asks again, her confusion clearly written all over her innocent face.

"Do you have any idea how packs are created?" I ask and when she shakes her head. I sigh and continue to explain, "The most promising graduating students from the Academy are drafted by Alphas. Do you know what the difference is between those students and the survivors?"

"No," Leia breathes and even though her eyes fill with realization, I push on to make her truly understand what she did.

"If we completely ignore the fact that they're too young to be in a pack, or that some of them haven't even developed their abilities, or that we don't even know how powerful they might be, or that they've probably never even heard of the Academy at all," I say. I take a deep breath before continuing, "So, if we ignore all that, the biggest difference is that the Pack of Survivors will most likely be the only pack in all of the kingdoms that has wolves with mixed abilities. Do you know what that means?"

"No," Leia repeats, the anger completely gone from her body, realizing that mine is more justifiable than hers.

"It means that they'll be very hard to train," I explain, my voice softer as pity for the young pups takes over any other emotion. "They should be among their kind, trained by someone who knows how their abilities work. I don't know how to train an Earth elemental, nor can I show someone how to create light when I'm all about the darkness."

"I fucked up," Leia says, burying her head into her hands. "I tried to help them, but I made it worse. Now I get it. I humiliated you by putting you in charge of the weakest and weirdest pack. I marked them as misfits. I should've let them find their own way."

"If I may, Your Highnesses," James interrupts, and I can't even be mad because it's so unlike him, so instead I simply nod, giving him permission to continue. "What Princess Leia did back there was admirable and inspiring. You think that they'd be better off on their own, but I can assure you, based on my personal experience, that they'd find themselves on the streets, struggling to get through the days. Your Highness gave them hope and a purpose. Your Highness gave their life a new meaning and a promise that, no matter what happens, they'll always be a part of something bigger. They have their own pack now, other wolves to rely on. No matter how you turn it, by starting the Pack of Survivors, Your Highness saved a lot of young lives, and by naming Prince Gavin as Alpha, Your Highness forced the whole world to take them seriously."

"Thank you, James," Leia says, a slight tremble in her voice. She turns to me and takes my hand in hers. "I'm sorry, Gavin. I allowed myself to be swept up by the current. My heart was breaking, seeing so much grief on their young faces. In the last twenty-four hours, they've been through hell and back. Some of them might've even seen their own families killed in front of their eyes. They can probably help us identify the attackers at some point."

She's not wrong about that, my wolf says.

"It's not just them that I wanted to help," Leia continues, her eyes locked on mine. "I thought that I was doing a good thing for you. You had to leave everything behind when you accepted the engagement. You lost your pack, but you've never stopped being an Alpha. It's in your blood. It's who you are. I wanted to give you a new pack, not just because I thought it would be good for you, but also because the pups need a strong role model."

"I'm not fit to be anyone's role model," I tell her and shake my head, unable to comprehend that she actually seems to believe what she's saying.

"But you are," she insists, giving my hand a gentle squeeze that sends a jolt down my spine. "You've always refused to see it, but I won't let you think less of yourself anymore. Oh, Gavin, if only you could see yourself through my eyes, then you would see just how good, kind, and honorable you are. You are loyal and reliable. You have all the best qualities of a wolf."

Don't forget handsome, my wolf adds. *Why didn't she mention handsome?*

"You only see what you want to see," I reply with a harsher tone than intended. "I'm nothing close to what you've described. Quite the opposite actually. I'm cunning, ambitious, and greedy. I'm not above getting my hands dirty if it will get me what I want. The sooner you face it, the easier our life together will be. I'm a killer, Leia."

"Yes, you're ambitious, but there's nothing wrong with that," Leia tells me. "You might be only the fourth in Grey's line of succession, but you're the one that should've been on the top because you're a born leader.

I know that you're a killer, but I also know that you've served in the army, fighting on the frontlines. You're an accomplished commander, a true Alpha. They didn't give you the rank because you were born into royalty. You earned it through your own blood and sweat. It's true that more often than not you can be quite scary, but you're also highly respected. Your wolves love you. You're ruthless when you have to be. Your actions always have a reason because you're fair and honorable. Your ability might be darkness, but your heart is full of light."

"You really think so?" I ask, raising my eyebrows at the idea, making it useless for me to even try to hide my surprise. I had no idea she saw me that way, but I like it. I want to be the man that she sees. I don't want to disappoint her.

"I do," she says, the word barely in a whisper.

It's when her plump lips part open that I realize just how close she is. All I need to do is bend my neck a little to press my mouth against hers. I bet she tastes amazing, like fresh snow.

For fuck's sake, just kiss her already, my wolf snaps, but instead of getting me to do his bidding, he successfully breaks the spell.

I turn to look out of the window, putting some distance between us. It could've been my imagination or just wishful thinking, but I could've sworn that there was a hint of disappointment in Leia's eyes. Maybe I wasn't the only one that wanted this.

How far am I willing to go to be a king?

Could one kiss ruin the deal?

CHAPTER 10

LEIA

"I know that this is important, but I really wish we could skip the dinner with both families," Gavin groans, his fingers fidgeting with his bowtie.

"It will be okay," I tell him and gently swat his hands away before he can make an even bigger mess. "Raise your head."

Without the slightest of hesitation, Gavin does as he's asked, revealing his neck to me. I do a quick work with his bowtie, although it's mostly thanks to the years of practice. Levi never bothered to learn how to tie his. I hold my breath the entire time, conscious of just how close we are standing. If he levels his head with mine, I'd only need to stand on my toes to cross the distance.

"Thank you," Gavin says, bringing me out of the reverie and making me realize that I've done it. I clear my throat and take a step backward.

"As I was saying," I continue, looking away from him to cool down my cheeks and get rid of the ridiculous flush, "the engagement party is a big deal. It's one of the hoops we need to jump through to get what we want."

"I get that, but my brothers will be there," Gavin complains, running his fingers through his hair.

I've never seen him so unnerved, and we've been caught in the burning grand salon together. It's the kind of nervousness that only family members can bring out of us.

"Your father, too," I say, wondering if he's the one that Gavin doesn't want to see.

"Yeah," he confirms, the word coming out as a quiet whisper.

"It will be okay," I say again, this time louder and surer. "Nothing they say or do will change anything between us."

"I don't know, Leia." Gavin sighs and shakes his head. Sitting at the edge of the bed, he's looking at me with his brows furrowed in worry. "Garren's a piece of shit, and my father might tell you some stories about me, the things I've done that I'm not proud of."

I crouch down and look up at him, taking his hand in mine. "We all did things we had to do in order to survive," I tell him with a gentle voice.

"I doubt you were ever forced into doing anything you didn't want," he replies, giving me a pointed look.

"I'm marrying you, aren't I?" I joke, my eyes widening when I realize what I blurted without thinking. The worst part is that it's not even true and Gavin might be offended.

Tilting his head to the side, his brows furrow for the longest of moments before his face softens and the richest laughter that I've ever heard comes out of him, straight from his belly. I raise my brows, surprised by his reaction. When he's done laughing, he shakes his head and smiles.

"That's what I love about you, Leia," he says, gently cupping my chin. "You always know how to make me smile."

He said the L word! my wolf exclaims, pointing out what I've been trying very hard not to obsess over.

"I do what I can," I reply with a forced smile, sounding lame even to my own ears.

Gavin gets up, his face brighter and his whole demeanor a lot more relaxed. He offers me his hand and pulls me up with him.

"Time to face the music, Princess," he says with a ghost of a smile on his lip as he intertwines our fingers and leads us toward the dining room.

You should talk to him, my wolf insists, but I ignore her, not wanting to ruin the fragile bond that Gavin and I have built.

Levi and Lily meet us halfway, their outfits matching through little, ingenious ways such as Lily's broch having the same design as Levi's cufflinks, or the shade of his tie exact same as the color of her shoes. The only way Gavin and I match is thanks to his shirt and the white embroidery on the side of my dress. I'm not upset because the twins have been playing this game a lot longer.

"I'm sorry to be so direct, Gavin, but your brother's an asshole," Levi says while Lily nods to his words.

"Which one?" Gavin asks, not sounding surprised at all.

"Garren," Lily replies, her brows furrowed in angry creases.

"For fuck's sake, the dinner didn't even start yet, and he's already a fucking disaster," Gavin says with a shake of his head. When he speaks to Lily, his voice is earnest with a hint of regret. "What did he do?"

"It's not what he did, it's more what he said," Lily replies and puts her arms around her body as she suppresses a shiver.

"He asked her if she wanted to play with the Claw," Levi continues, his face a vision of anger.

I glance from the twins to Gavin, clearly being the only one who has no idea what they're talking about. While Lily seems traumatized and Levi angry, Gavin is downright furious. His hands clench into fists, and his facial features contort with hatred I've never seen on him before.

Do something, my wolf urges, giving me the push that I need to react before he can.

Tugging on Gavin's arm, I force his attention on me, his eyes clearing ever so slightly when they lock on mine. I shake my head, willing him to see and hear me.

"Now's not the time," I tell him. "It's important that we do this well, or you'll never be rid of them."

"He insulted your sister," Gavin hisses, tentacles of darkness slithering around his feet.

He did? my wolf asks in surprise, also not getting the meaning of the claw joke.

"That doesn't matter now," I say, making a mental promise to myself that he'll pay for it one day. "We need to present a unified front and get this over with."

"Fine, but I can't promise that I won't turn his shadow into my pawn if he turns out to be an even bigger ass than expected," Gavin grumbles and offers me his arm again.

"That's probably the only puppet show I'd be willing to pay good money to watch," Levi jokes, exchanging a smile with Gavin. My heart warms upon seeing their interaction. I want nothing more than for my future husband to be good friends with my siblings.

"I hope you got all the jokes out of your system because it's time to go," I tell them, pulling Gavin after me. "It's not polite for the hosts to make their guests wait."

"Calling them guests is too polite," Gavin whispers. "They're parasites."

"Shh," I hiss back, painfully aware of the heightened wolf hearing.

Gavin makes a face, but mercifully doesn't say anything else as we round the corner and enter the dining room. My parents are already there, keeping Gavin's family entertained until our arrival.

"There they are," my father says proudly as he stands up as we approach.

It's clear that they've already done the introductions between themselves, and since Gavin already officially met my family, I'm the only one left that needs to go through this part.

Without the slightest hint of hesitation, Gavin guides me to the side where his family is seated. His face is a cold, indifferent mask, his eyes black and emotionless. This is what his family brings out of him. They make him put up an invisible shield, a barrier that keeps them on the other side of everything he cares about.

"Princess Leia, please allow me to present to you my father, King Gael, and my mother, Queen Fallon," Gavin says, his voice only warming up when he talks about his mother.

He cares about her, my wolf points out the obvious, but then she has to ruin it by adding a bad joke, *He's either a momma's boy or a boy with mommy issues.*

"It's a pleasure to officially meet you, Your Majesties," I say to both of them.

Gael's eyes darken when he realizes I won't bow, but Fallon's reaction is the complete opposite of his. The corners of her mouth lift up into the warmest smile I've ever received, with so much love and kindness radiating through it.

She's precious, my wolf comments, feeling the same things I am.

"It's such an honor to see you again, Princess," Fallon says, her voice just as warm as everything else about her. "Gavin has always been very fond of you."

I glance at Gavin, a ghost of a smile playing on his lips. His goodness definitely comes from this woman. Gael seems to be a definition of a bully, although not the kind that would physically hit his family. While I'm sure that he's verbally abusing everyone around him, I'm also leaning toward the possibility that he's not against using his dark abilities on them, especially if they're openly disagreeing with him.

Like Gavin, my wolf concludes, and I give her a mental nod. Gavin isn't the type to follow orders he doesn't believe in or if they come from a person that he has zero respect for.

"These are my brothers Prince Garren, Prince Grayden, and Prince Graham," Gavin continues, introducing me to his siblings, but when I try to take a step forward to greet them, he doesn't let me.

"Oh, come on, little brother," Garren chuckles. "Are you afraid she'd change her mind if she gets too close to my claw?"

Gavin lets out a low growl, his eyes locked on his eldest brother. I take his arm and squeeze hard enough for him to notice me.

"Should we have the food brought in?" I ask, eager to get the evening moving. "Is it just me or is anyone else hungry?"

"I'm starving," Fallon says quickly, and I send her a grateful smile. She'll be a big asset throughout the dinner.

Gavin leads us back to the Lafayette side of the table. I don't miss the way his father's eyes narrow when his son sits with my family and across from Garren as his equal now. His brother also doesn't like it, his lips pulled back into a snarl. They really hate each other.

My father and mother observed the whole scene with quiet interest, no doubt making mental notes and measurements of my fiancé's family. Levi and Lily are keeping themselves far away from Garren, sitting across from Grayden and Graham who seem a lot more pleasant.

"Did you two sleep together yet?" Garren asks, biting into a raw carrot and chewing it with his mouth open.

"Garren!" Fallon exclaims, her own cheeks turning red.

"What?" Garren asks, turning to his mother. "It's a good question."

"The boy's right," Gael agrees, his eyes locked on Gavin. "The union needs to be confirmed in every single way for it to be legitimate."

"I won't let you discuss my daughter's sex life so blatantly, and at my dinner table no less," my father jumps in, his eyes burning with cold fire.

"Do you have anything to hide, Lucas?" Gael challenges, tearing his eyes away from his son to look at my father. "Aren't those the kind of things that are confirmed at events such as this?"

"That's enough, Father," Gavin says, his voice firm and full of authority. "You'll do well to remember that you're a guest in King Lafayette's home, and you'll act as one."

"But we're all family now, are we not?" Gael asks with a mocking tone and an innocent smile that disappears when his face darkens. "Be careful how you speak to me, boy. Mind your place."

"I'm aware of my place, Father," Gavin replies calmly. He then looks at me as he continues, "Ever since the engagement was announced, I've officially fallen under King Lafayette's jurisdiction. As one of his subjects, it's up to me to make sure that he or his family aren't disrespected."

"It's disgusting to see how low you've fallen," Gael snarls, venom dripping from his words.

"I haven't fallen. Quite the opposite actually. With no help from you, I've risen through the ranks and will soon be your equal. You're lashing out, trying to bring me down because you know that you've picked the wrong son," Gavin replies, seemingly unaffected by everything his father throws at him.

"You piece of—" Gael snarls, but is interrupted by Fallon, who claps her hands together, breaking the tension.

Fallon smiles and says to my parents, "We really appreciate the dinner invitation. With everything that's been going on recently, it's very hard to take a moment and sit down with the family."

"We're happy to have you here," my mother replies, but it's clear she's only saying it because of the protocol. Neither one of my parents is charmed by Gavin's family.

The first course passes without any other serious altercations, but it's entirely thanks to Fallon, who's filling up what would be an awkward silence with small talk about her garden. Gavin seems quite knowledgeable about it, asking her questions and participating. He has a massive soft spot for her, and I'm not surprised because she's a gem of a woman.

Halfway through the second course, and well into our fourth bottle, we dropped our formal titles and started addressing each other in a casual manner.

"Oh, Leia," Fallon says and looks at me with a big smile on her face. "Do you remember that time at the Academy when you and Gavin had to play the protagonists of our origin story? During Christmas break, you two insisted on being method actors and even went so far as to force us to agree to your sleepovers because you didn't want to break character."

"Even then, they were the perfect couple," my mother adds, joining in with her lips slightly curled up.

"Oh, gosh," I groan and shake my head. "That's so embarrassing."

"You were telling everyone who'd listen that you'd get married one day," my father says with a chuckle. My mother and Fallon nod, laughing at the memory.

"What we can learn from that is that we're very good at keeping our word," Gavin says casually, reaches for my hand, and he gives me a comforting squeeze as he winks.

"I completely forgot about that play though," I comment, returning back to Fallon's story. "Wasn't it canceled? How old were we? Six?"

"Eight," Gael replies, surprising everyone. "That was the year that Garren got to participate in his first hunt, and he became a man."

My back turns rigid at the mention of the hunt and the atrocities it puts humans through. It should be illegal to release a bunch of uncontrolled pups in the wilderness for two hours and count who's torn apart more campers. The human news called it a wild animal attack, but they didn't know better.

"I think it was canceled," Gavin says, replying directly to me and ignoring his father's attempts to rile us up again.

"You two were always very close, and it's nice to see that you've reconnected again," Fallon says, sounding genuinely happy, not only for Gavin, but for me as well.

"Time apart only made us stronger," I comment, my eyes locked on Gavin's.

"Ugh, I can't handle it anymore," Garren groans, all eyes turning on him. "Everyone's saying Gavin this, Gavin that. Well, let me tell you the truth about my darling little brother."

Gavin tenses by my side, his eyes drilling holes into his brother's skull. The hate he nurtures for him is obvious and too big to disguise.

"Careful, Prince Garren," my father says, purposefully addressing Garren by his title as he comes to Gavin's defense, even though it's not necessary nor needed, but it does mean a lot to me, giving me a subtle confirmation that he accepted him as one of us.

"Does anyone here know of a wolf named Tiana?" Garren asks, completely ignoring my father's warning.

Under the table, Gavin's hands clench into fists, the name clearly hitting a sore spot. Gael's eyes flicker with curiosity and he leans forward on the table, looking across Fallon at his son.

"She's one of Gavin's pack," Garren continues, his lips curled up in an arrogant smirk. "Or well, was a part of his pack. You don't have a pack anymore, do you, little brother?"

"Actually, he does," I say, stepping in even though Gavin doesn't need me to defend him. I can't deny the enjoyment that I get from Garren's flicker of surprise and annoyance. "He's the Alpha of a new pack, fighting under the Lafayette name. They've already experienced action and have proven resilient. They're true survivors through and through, and their powers are different than in any other pack."

Nice embellishment, my wolf comments, and while I did skip a lot of important details, I haven't exactly told them anything that's not true.

"Is that true?" Gael asks, his voice low and angry.

"Yes, Father," Gavin replies, taking it better than I thought he would. Or maybe he's just very good at pretending to be in control when needed. "I'm a leader. An accomplished commander. There are many wolves out there who'd sell their own souls for an hour-long training session with me."

"Speaking of training sessions," Garren jumps in, eager to continue his story. "Tiana used to be Gavin's Beta, but now that he's gone, she's more than happy to serve as my Beta."

"You're the Alpha of the Shadows?" Gavin asks, losing control of himself for the first time this evening; the lights above us flicker twice or three times before he regains it.

Garren grins. "It's about time that our most powerful pack gets the strongest Alpha in our kingdom."

"You're only the strongest because I'm not a part of that kingdom anymore," Gavin snarls, letting his inner wolf get the better of him. "Being an Alpha is an honor that's earned, not appointed. They'll never respect you. You'll never be truly accepted."

"They already did," Garren replies with an infuriating smirk. "As soon as I got Tiana to spread her legs for me, they were mine as were the secrets they kept for you. Wolf killer."

A low growl escapes Gavin, and he pushes himself on his feet with so much force that his chair tips over. His facial features contort with hatred, his fangs coming out and straight through his lip, coating his chin with blood.

Gael chuckles and claps, then turns to my father with a condescending smile. "You're more than welcome to keep the black sheep, Lucas. He always thought himself to be better than us, when in reality, he's nothing but trash."

Gavin growls again, this time louder. My father stands up, the aura of his power surrounding him. While he calmly points at the door, his tone is firm and regal, "Get the hell out of my sight."

I hold onto Gavin, making sure that he doesn't pounce on his brother as he passes us. The one I really feel bad for is his mother. She's a good person who's stuck with a monster. If only there was something I could do, but she's under Grey's rule, which leaves me with tied hands.

"I'm sorry, Lucas," Gavin apologizes to my father once his family's gone.

"Don't worry about it," my father tells him, sounding more tired than anything else. "They're a handful, and to be honest, I wanted to shut them up a couple of times myself. If I had done what you did, we'd be dealing with bigger problems. Until you're officially the new Lafayette King, you can still get away with things like that, just make sure that they don't happen too often. Control is important. It's what makes us better than animals."

"Yes, sir," Gavin replies with the slightest bow of his head. "If you'll excuse me, I think I should get some rest."

My father nods in permission, and my mother gives him an actual sympathetic look. It seems like they both understand what it feels like to have a rotten family. The twins wave after Gavin and I make quick apologies, wanting to follow him more than anything.

He's already in the room when I catch up to him, sitting on the carpeted floor at the foot of the bed with his head buried in his hands. Even though he's aware of my arrival, I still keep my steps small and slow as I approach him.

"How are you holding up?" I ask in a tentative voice.

He scoffs and leans his head back against the bed. "I fucked up, didn't I?"

"Quite the opposite," I tell him, meaning it. "Now, more than ever, you have my mother and father on your side. You're a Lafayette in everything but name now."

He turns his head toward me, our faces leveled. His soulful black eyes are locked on mine in a hypnotic gaze. His chiseled jaw, covered with a perfectly groomed five o'clock shadow, moves as he gives me a small, genuine smile.

"I don't know what I'd do without you," he tells me with a low voice that makes my heart skip a beat. "I'm so lucky to have you back in my life. I was such an idiot to let you go in the first place."

"We both followed the paths that were laid in front of us," I reply, not wanting to admit that I've often wondered what would happen between us if we hadn't lost touch so long ago. "What matters is that we're here now."

"You're absolutely right," he whispers, then catches me completely off guard as he does the unexpected.

Gavin reaches over with his right hand, puts it on my cheek and closes the distance between us, softly pressing his lips against mine. It takes me a moment to process it, to realize what's happening. By the time I do, and the shock wears off, allowing me to reciprocate, he's already gone, leaving behind the phantom feeling of his soft lips.

His eyes are wide with horror and his face drains of all color. He shakes his head, looking regretful.

"I'm so sorry, Leia," he says, sounding genuinely distressed. "I shouldn't have crossed this line. I didn't mean to disrespect you."

"It's okay," I tell him, wanting him to know that I wanted it too, that I liked it, but the right words don't come.

"I'm sorry," he repeats, running his fingers through his black faux hawk. "It was an accident. I was upset and wanted to feel something different. I shouldn't have used you to suppress my anger."

"Don't worry, Gavin," I say this time with a firmer voice to make sure he hears me. "We're good."

He meets my eyes for the shortest of seconds, as if to check that I'm telling the truth. Whatever he sees on my face must be confirmation enough because he nods to himself and mutters something about taking a shower.

There goes your chance, flying full speed out of the window, my wolf teases, but I'm not in the mood for her jokes.

The reality is that this was my chance to bring our relationship to the next step, but I screwed up. It took me too long to fucking recover, and now Gavin probably thinks that I didn't want to kiss him.

If only he'd known that ever since that dream, kissing him is all I can think about.

CHAPTER 11

GAVIN

"Set them in line," I say to James when I arrive to watch the Survivors' training session.

James has been working with the pack for a week now, helping them move into one of Lafayette's smaller manors. He's been staying there with them as well, practically acting as their guardian. They're mostly kids who have seen way too much in their short lives already, but if I don't set them in order now, some of them might end up in a ditch later on with a needle in their arm. Trauma's a bitch, and there's more than one way to address it, but as it happens to be, strict discipline and rigorous training happens to be my best.

"Attention, Survivors. Your Alpha has arrived," James calls out.

A bunch of kids come running down the stairs, pushing one over another to reach the bottom first. I have to take several deep breaths to keep my cool. They're not soldiers. Some of them aren't even older than fifteen. This is ridiculous.

This is beneath us, my wolf hisses, just as annoyed with the outcome.

It's for Leia, I remind both of us. *She trusts us to do this.*

My wolf growls in response then falls quiet and retreats in the background again.

It takes way too long for the kids to form a line, but James is doing his best, especially considering that he's barely twenty-two years old himself.

"Quiet," I say with a low voice, but underline it with power so it carries.

The kids fall silent, their wide, fearful eyes locked on me. I walk the line, up and down, nodding in approval at the name tags on their chests.

"John Harvey, thirteen," I read his name and age, starting with the first kid. "What's your power?"

"I don't know, Alpha," he replies quietly.

"Have you shifted yet?" I ask even though I already know the answer.

"No," he says, confirming what I know.

"Alright," I say with a sigh, then glance at the whole line again. "Let's start again. Everyone who hasn't shifted, take a step forward."

Five kids move to the front, most of them on the younger side, as I predicted, except one. I walk up to the taller red-headed girl.

"Olivia White, sixteen," I read her tag out loud before meeting her brown eyes. "You haven't shifted yet?"

She shakes her head, her lower lip trembling.

The fear is suppressing the wolf in her, my own wolf tells me, diagnosing her at first glance.

"Okay, you guys are group B," I announce, not wanting to put even more pressure on the non-shifters. I nod at James, giving him a sign to pick up a pen to mark it down as I read him their names. "John Harvey, thirteen. Kayden Barker, fourteen. Olivia White, sixteen. Yasmin Murphy, fifteen. Bella Hopkins, fourteen."

If five of them are non-shifters, that means that I'm left with seven shifters, who might have possible first signs of power developments. I'm walking into foreign territory and will have to tread carefully. Those kids deserve to have someone that will help them develop their abilities to their fullest potential. Before I call in a couple of favors, I need to discover how those powers will manifest.

"Group B," I call again to get their attention. "I want you to do five laps around the manor. Go."

After a couple of groans and muttered complaints, they pile out of the line and start their run. With them gone, I can put my attention on the rest of the kids.

"Step forward, one after another, announce your name, your age, and your ability," I say and fold my arms across my chest.

"Zak Reynolds, Alpha," the first kid says way too loudly, but I appreciate his enthusiasm. "Fifteen years old, Water ability."

"Cameron Lewis, Earth," the second kid says, speaking too fast and too quietly. Compared to the first one, he's quite shy.

"Age," James asks, glancing up from his notebook.

"Fifteen," the kid replies, his face turning a bright shade of red.

"Sebastian Griffiths, sixteen," the raven-haired kid says, looks me straight in the eyes and smirks. "Darkness."

Interesting, my wolf comments.

The kid might be a fellow dark wielder, but I can already tell that he's an insufferably arrogant little prick. If I want to teach him how to control darkness, I'm going to have to humble him first. If he doesn't get himself in check, his power could overwhelm him.

"Scarlett Hudson, fourteen. I don't know what my power is," the next girl says, and I'm half tempted to send her running with the other kids, but I remind myself at the last possible moment that she's just a kid. They might be a part of my new pack now, my soldiers, but that doesn't mean that I should fully treat them like ones. Not yet at least.

"Jodie Turner, seventeen," the white-haired girl with eerie white eyes says. There's a unique kind of beauty about her, and she knows it. She looks me in the eyes, nibbles on her lower lip as she gives me a seductive smile. "I'll bring the light to your dark any time you want, baby."

I'd be offended if it wasn't funny, my wolf chuckles.

She's a child, I tell him.

Stop acting like an old man. You're not even twenty-five years old yet, my wolf reminds me.

I'm promised to Leia, I snap back.

Good, my wolf makes a sound in approval. *And don't you ever forget it.*

"On the ground," I say and while my voice is low, it's clear that I'm giving her an order. "You better hope you can do twenty push-ups, or you'll sleep in the dungeon."

The girl's creepy white eyes widen, and she looks like she wants to complain, but thinks better of it. She lowers herself to the ground and starts doing push-ups. I nod at James to take over, while I move on. If my attention's what she wants, she'll get the opposite of it.

"Next," I say and step up to the girl with orange hair and brown eyes that she's hiding behind square-framed glasses.

"Tina Waibel, seventeen, Fire elemental," she recites, looking almost bored.

"Mikey Brown, sixteen, also fire," the red-haired boy next to her tells me.

I nod in approval, then glance at James to see how Jodie's doing. He gives me a subtle thumbs-up gesture, confirming that she did the pushups. Maybe I went too easy on her and should've given her twenty more. I really wanted to punish someone, to show them what happens when they disobey me or step out of line. Actions have consequences, and the sooner they learn that lesson, the better. They already know that real life out there can be brutal and cruel, but they need to see that they can avoid a lot of shit if only they learn how to control themselves.

That's where I come in.

For some reason, their parents didn't want to send them to the Academy where they could be taught all that. In the last couple of decades, there were movements within our communities that formed groups of our people that had different beliefs than us. I'm starting to suspect that the survivors belonged to them whether they wanted to or not. Until they're of age, their upbringing and education were in the hands of their parents. I'll have to talk to some of the older kids to get a clearer picture.

"Five laps around the manor, group A," I say. "With every complaint that reaches my ears or any sound that I don't like, I'm assigning you an extra lap. Go and remember that I have heightened hearing."

Quiet as mice, the shifters follow the path of the younger kids and start their run around the manor. James walks up to me, his notebook in hand.

"What do you think?" I ask him, wanting to hear his opinion.

"First of all, I wouldn't worry too much about Olivia for not shifting yet. I'm not much older than her and my ability still hasn't manifested itself yet," he tells me with a shrug.

"Yeah, but you've been through a trauma," I reply, remembering the state he was in when I found him on the streets.

"So was she," he says without missing a beat. "Besides the attack, we don't know what else they've been through. I mean, you have to admit that there was something weird about their living situation."

"Do you think they could've been the targets because of their beliefs?" I ask, casually running one of my theories past him. "Could it be that they believed in equality between humans and wolves?"

"If that's so, then why didn't they live among them?" James asks, making a good point.

"Maybe they did once the kids got older," I reply and scratch my chin in thought, massaging my five o'clock shadow. "If we look at it closely, all the families living there had kids younger than eighteen. What are the chances of that? What's the possibility that every single family living in that town has kids that are minors?"

"Minors have a harder time controlling their abilities," James comments, catching my train of thought. "They're too unpredictable to be a fully integrated part of human society. The chances of discovery are too high."

"Let's run with that theory. Try finding out as much as you can about their families, the way they lived, and if they had any other relatives," I tell him, then pat his shoulder. "I'm sorry you're stuck here with them. I'm still figuring out who I can trust, and when I do, I'll give you a better assignment."

"Don't worry, Boss," he replies, genuinely unbothered by it. "I quite like being useful for once."

I give him a small smile and shake my head. "I should get back."

"Why do I have a feeling that you don't want to?" James asks, raising his brow in question. "What's going on? There are rumors going around about how King Lafayette threw King Grey out of the manor. Does it have anything to do with that? Are you okay?"

"I wish it was that, James," I say with a heavy sigh.

"Oh, I see what it is," James says, giving me a knowing look as he gestures with his head toward the manor. "Let's have a drink before you go. Something strong, yeah?"

"I don't see why not," I agree, only accepting it because it gives me an excuse not to return home just yet.

I follow James to a room that he's turned into an office of sorts. He gives me an apologetic look as he cleans up the desk, putting the files he started on kids into a drawer. From a cupboard behind him, he pulls out two glasses and a bottle of scotch.

"That's a good brand," I say in approval, then smile. "I must be paying you too much."

"You don't pay me at all," he replies easily. "But I do have your backup credit card to support my lifestyle."

"If you never develop your abilities, you could look for a career in comedy," I say, happily accepting a glass of scotch, then going to the sofa in the corner where the hierarchy between us won't be so obvious.

"Will you update me on the latest?" James asks when he joins me. He had a good thought of bringing the bottle with him.

"You already heard about the engagement dinner party, so there's nothing else to add about that," I reply with a shrug, clink my glass against his and take a sip, welcoming the familiar burn down my throat.

"How are the in-laws treating you?" James asks, then gives me an apologetic look. "I've been cooped up with teenagers for what seems like forever. I'm desperate for some grown-up talk."

"They've accepted me with open arms," I say, indulging him. "The truth is that the Lafayette's have been treating me better than my own family ever did. I'd never realized what I've been missing until now."

"I know what you mean," James says, turning his glass in his hands. "You're the one that has given me everything I have, and you're also the one that has made me into the person I am today. I still don't know what you saw in me that day, but I'm glad that I was the one you picked out of that crowd."

"So far, you haven't made me regret it... yet," I reply, then take another sip to hide my discomfort.

"Why don't you tell me what's really on your mind?" James pushes, determined to get to the root of it all. "You've been distracted all day and not as ruthless as you usually are. The punishment that you gave to Jodie was half-assed, which is so unlike you. I expected you to force darkness down her throat until she vomited, or to torture her shadow a bit. You've never used physical exercise as a form of punishment."

"They're just kids," I say, trying and failing to use it as a proper excuse.

"I was a kid once," he replies without missing a beat. "You had no problem using those techniques on me. So, tell me, what's up?"

"Fine," I groan and roll my eyes. "I kissed Leia."

James raises his brows, his face a picture of surprise. He refills our glasses, then leans back into the sofa and furrows his brows in confusion.

"Isn't that what's expected of you?" he asks. Tilting his head to the side as gives me a questioning look. "I mean, she's your fiancée and all that, so aren't you supposed to kiss her."

"I wish it could be that simple," I reply and empty the contents of the glass before I dive in. "Leia and I are together because of a mutually beneficial agreement. I get to rule a kingdom while she can go around and do her thing with her charities."

"A lot of royal marriages are arranged, but I've never gotten the feeling that you two are one of those couples," James says, his brows furrowing. "I could've sworn that you were in love with each other."

"What makes you say that?" I ask and chuckle as I shake my head, trying to hide just how interested I am in hearing his answer.

"It's the way you two look at each other and how protective you are of her," he replies easily. "You can't fake those things. You two clearly care deeply for one another, even if you're not ready to admit it yet."

I give him a small, almost mocking smile. "I think you're delusional."

"Think whatever you want, but I've lived on the streets for most of my life. That shit teaches you to read people and do it well. One mistake out there and you're toast," James replies with a shrug, then offers to refill my glass.

"No, thanks," I politely decline and get up. "I should go."

James also stands up and gestures at the door. "Do you want me to drive you?"

"I need to clear my head a bit, so I think I'll run back," I say and grab one of the bags in the corner to stash my clothes in.

James leaves his office to give me privacy. My wolf inside me howls with excitement, eager to stretch his legs. The shift is instantaneous as the animal immediately responds to my summons.

When I leave the manor in my wolf form, some of the kids get scared and cry out. It occurs to me that their attackers must've been wearing wolf's skin. I don't have the time nor the energy to deal with them. I'll leave it up to James to settle the matter.

My heart is calling me somewhere and my body is being pulled toward a certain direction like a magnetic pull. I've shifted into a wolf more times than I can count, the animal being a part of me since I was born, and yet, I've never felt anything like this before. It's like a part of me is missing and, by following my senses, I'll be able to reunite the two pieces.

Not wanting to feel that weird feeling of emptiness, I do just that.

With the use of my ability, I travel through the populated parts without being seen. When needed, I summon the shadows for me to step through as one, using the mimicry to become one with them.

Interestingly enough, the unknown force is pulling me toward the Lafayette Manor. I follow it with new-found vigor, eager to reveal the secret. With my abilities, slipping unseen through the Lafayette security is way too easy. Definitely something that I'll have to bring up the next time I talk to Lucas. If our enemies are wolves, we need to be able to learn how to protect ourselves from all kinds of elements.

The scent of fresh snow gets stronger when I reach the second floor, my senses pulling me straight toward it. My heart speeds up in anticipation, my whole body tingling with electricity as if I'm getting close to a massive power source.

With the silent skills of a predator, I open the door of the room and slip in unnoticed. It's then that I see the reason for my senses going out of control.

Leia has her back turned toward me as she sits behind the desk, hunched over a pile of documents. Her brows furrow as she reads through them and absentmindedly puts the end of her pen into her mouth, nibbling on the cap. Her plump lips vibrate and move every time she gently buries her teeth in the pen. Some part of the text must've gotten her attention because she leans forward to re-read it, her lips silently moving as she follows the words. A stray ashen-white curl falls on her face, obscuring her vision. Without thinking, she automatically pulls her hair up into a messy bun and puts a pen through it to hold it in place.

Could it be? my wolf asks, wondering the exact same thing I am.

It can't be. We've spent a lot of time together and even share the same bed. It's normal that she's on my mind, I reply, refusing to believe that she's been in front of my eyes the whole time and I haven't seen it before now.

But that kiss, my wolf insists, conjuring up the memory of how her soft plump lips felt against mine, how perfect and right kissing her was.

She's a beautiful woman and I'm a man with needs, I shoot back with a tone of finality. *There's nothing strange about that.*

My wolf makes a sound that I can't quite decipher but suspect that he doesn't agree with me. Not wanting her to see me, I slip out of the room and go into one of the bathrooms to change and dress myself.

Sooner or later, I'll have to face her and these weird sensations I'm getting about her, but right now, I need to focus on other things, such as figuring out who was behind the attacks.

CHAPTER 12

LEIA

"Princess Leia! Princess Leia!"

The call comes from outside the room, carrying down the hallway as one of the servants comes to get me. Something must've happened because I've never known them to be so blatantly loud.

Without a moment of hesitation, I push myself away from the desk I had set up in my room a long time ago to deal with the paperwork related to charity fundraisers in peace. Although lately, I've been using it to bring myself up to speed with the affairs of the kingdom. The royal matters proved to be more complex and interconnected than I anticipated. I'm glad that Gavin's aware of the behind-the-scenes dealings and the scandals that have been seemingly successfully kept under wraps. The wolf-on-wolf attacks are only one of the latest atrocities, but not even the worst one in this last century alone.

I open the door and meet the servant halfway, catching the older woman before she can collapse on the floor with exhaustion. She's pushed herself too hard to get to me so fast, and now she's gasping for air, trying to push out the messages she's been entrusted to relay.

"Your...brother and...sister," she forces out between gasps.

"Levi and Lily?" I ask in bewilderment. "What about them? Are they okay?"

"The Academy..." the woman continues, gasping hard. "Attacked."

"What?!" I exclaim, struggling to stay patient and compassionate with the old servant.

"The conference room..." she continues, ignoring my questions. "Go now."

I pause only long enough to make sure she's sitting safely on the floor with her back against the wall before I go running down the hallway, retracing the path she took to get to me. I jump two or three stairs at a time, grateful that my stilettos are of the highest quality otherwise a heel would break off ten times over.

Without bothering to knock to announce my presence, I rush through the door, the momentum making it impossible for me to stop on time as I crash into a tall, muscular figure. His strong arms steady me, wrapping themselves around me and pressing me against his chest.

"Take a breath," a voice that I recognize as Gavin's tells me.

Identifying his arms as my safe haven, my muscles immediately relax. I melt into him, relying on him to protect me from the outside dangers.

When I'm calm and collected, he loosens his grip on me and leans back to look at me. The crease between his brows ignites the anxiety in me, but the confidence in his eyes prevents it from spreading like wildfire.

"What happened?" I ask, my voice coming out as a weak tremble.

Gavin steps to the side, revealing my father, my mother, and the four royal advisors standing around the conference table with a pile of papers on it. While he's not holding me anymore, he also doesn't leave my side, holding a hand on the small of my back at all times. I'm grateful for the constant reminder of his presence, and the confident stability he offers me.

"What happened?" I repeat, this time louder and firmer, determined to get the answer. "Are the twins okay?"

"The Academy's been attacked," my father tells me and while his tone is cold and indifferent, his eyes are shining with a mix of fear and anger.

"What?!" I exclaim yet again, unable to comprehend it. "How's that possible? It's literally the most protected and sacred place in the whole world. The interkingdom law assures that all the pups on the hallowed school grounds are safe, no matter their kingdom or beliefs."

"The law is failing. Wolves are attacking wolves. This very manor has been attacked and no one was held accountable for the burning down of the grand salon. If we don't punish the offenders, the crime rate will skyrocket," Countess Bailey says with a voice of reason, indirectly calling for justice.

"Nothing happened to Felix?" Gavin asks, raising his brow in surprise.

"He's a member of the Farrell royal family and our relations are already abysmal," my father replies with a heavy sigh. "We couldn't afford to punish him without risking them challenging us head-on. The consequences of a war between two royal families could be catastrophic."

"And because of that, the royal bastards can walk around, doing whatever they want without even getting a slap on the wrist," Gavin concludes with a low growl.

"I'm afraid so," my father confirms, letting the growl slide.

"What does that mean for the twins? Are they okay?" I ask, desperate to get some real answers.

"We don't know!" my mother cries out, catching everyone by surprise for breaking her usual regal control. Her cheeks are covered with tears, her pupils dilated with fear.

Gavin takes my hand into his and turns me to him. I tear my eyes away from my mother's broken image and focus on him, absorbing his strength and calmness.

"There's not much news, but here's what we know," Gavin says with a measured voice, his eyes fixed on mine. "The Academy's been attacked by an unknown group of people. They had to be wolves because the safety measures keep humans away from the grounds. We don't know the details of what happened, nor do we know if Levi and Lily are okay. That's all we have so far."

I nod, taking his words in and mulling them around. Our next step seems obvious, but the orders escape me. My father and mother are just as affected as I am, reacting to the whole disaster slowly and awkwardly. Fortunately, Gavin isn't a stranger to working under pressure and steps into the role of a leader, which is exactly what we need right now.

"We have to organize an envoy and prepare to extract the twins from the Academy," Gavin says, his voice full of the authority that comes with years of being a skilled commander.

All eyes turn to him, the royal advisors grabbing pens and making notes. My father gives him a nod, a silent permission to continue, letting Gavin take the lead while he takes care of his wife, who's in more distress than ever.

"We need to make a strong statement by sending the best pack you have," Gavin continues, his eyes darting from one royal advisor to the other. "I believe that's the Lafayette Pack, isn't it?"

"That's correct, Your Highness," Duke Green confirms. "Alpha Jenkins has already been put on alert, preparing the pack for a possible altercation."

"Good," Gavin says with a nod in approval. "Get the jet ready. We're going to parachute to the outskirts of the grounds to avoid possible air forces, then we'll shift into wolf form and run to the heart of the Academy."

"Right away, Your Highness," Duke Green agrees, then gestures to Marquess Wilson to do Gavin's bidding.

"What do you mean 'we'?" I ask more for confirmation than anything else.

"I'm leading the envoy," Gavin replies as a matter of fact. "The Lafayette Pack is strong, but they don't have any real battlefield experience. They'll need my instincts, my skills, and my knowledge to get through the mission with the highest probability of success."

"You can't go," I insist, and when Gavin opens his mouth to argue. "I forbid you from going. That's an order."

Gavin's eyes flash with black anger, his face darkening. He clenches his jaw, gritting his teeth with such force that I half expect them to break.

"Whether you know it or not, I'm the best and most powerful soldier in your whole kingdom," Gavin states, and despite the cold fire radiating from him, his voice is calm and collected.

"You're also next in line to be the king," I reply as a matter of fact. "You're too valuable now to be sent out on missions, no matter how important they are, and trust me, this one is of the highest priority."

"Leia's right," my father says, agreeing with me. "We appreciate your willingness to help, but in the grand scale of things, your life is currently more important than the twins'."

My mother whimpers when he says it, and even my father's face crumbles, pained to admit it. Gavin's tensed muscles relax ever so slightly as he finally nods.

"Send Alpha Jenkins and the Lafayette pack on their way now," Gavin says to Duke Green. "We've already lost enough time arguing and discussing the things that should already be set in security protocols."

He's right, my wolf tells me. Out of the whole mess, she chooses to react to this part.

"Don't we have the simulations of kidnappings, hostage situations, and attacks such as the one right now?" I ask, looking at the three remaining royal advisors.

"We should have them, but Duke Green claimed that no one from within would dare to directly threaten the royal family," Countess Bailey replies, throwing Duke Green under the bus.

"Wolves on wolves attacks are unprecedented, and all our protocols focus on humans and witches," Duke Green says in his meek defense.

"Update them now!" my father snaps, raising his voice, letting out a wave of power that drops the temperature in the room to a freezing level.

The royal advisors begin to bicker amongst themselves, trying to put the blame on one another. I can't bring myself to listen to them even a moment longer. If I stay in the conference room, I might accidentally give my control over to my wolf, letting her breathe the fury on them, freezing them into ice blocks.

Turning on my heels, I leave the conference room without a word, going back to the safety of my quarters. Unshed tears blur my vision, the rare solitary ones manage to trail a frozen path down my cheeks soon after turning to little drops of ice.

I forcefully shut the door, using an innocent way to release some of my frustration. The satisfying slam of wood against wood doesn't come, and I turn my head to inspect what stopped it.

Gavin's standing at the doorway, the previous darkness from his face now long gone and replaced by an unusual softness. His lips curl up into a tentative smile, his eyes silently asking for permission to enter, which he does when I don't argue against it.

"I'm sorry for pulling rank on you," I tell him after he gently closes the door behind him. "It wasn't right, and I shouldn't have done it. I should have found another way to explain it to you, but I took the easiest path."

"It's okay," Gavin says, sounding genuine and sincere. "I get why you did it, and I understand why you didn't have the time to handle me with kid gloves, which you don't need to. We have a lot to learn about running a kingdom, about our roles in it, and how to work as a team. What matters is that we don't take things personally and turn against each other."

His words hit home, getting me straight in the heart. I purse my lips together, but it doesn't keep them from trembling, doesn't keep my body from shivering for reasons that have nothing to do with the cold.

"What did I do to deserve you?" I wonder, realizing a bit too late that I've said it out loud.

Gavin doesn't seem to mind and gently puts his hand on my cheek, gazing down at me from his towering height. "You never judged me despite being next in line for the throne while I'm the fourth born. You were kind to me when others were mean. You were my friend when others tried to bully me and make an enemy out of me. You were loyal when I needed a confidant. You were thoughtful and attentive when I felt invisible. It's ironic that you're the future Ice Queen when you're nothing but warm. You have the biggest heart I've ever seen, and I'm hoping that one day, you'll give it to me because whether you know it or not, Leia, you've always had mine."

He loves you! my wolf exclaims, but I don't need her running commentary to process his words myself.

I throw my arms around him, wrapping them around his neck as I pull him down, crashing my mouth against his. His reaction is immediate, his lips moving against mine. He puts his hands around my waist, pressing me closer against him and sending my adrenaline through the roof. My body feels small compared to his, but it fits perfectly into his embrace.

My head is spinning with the realization that this is actually happening. I've been trying not to actively fantasize about this scenario ever since I had a sex dream about him. Real-life experience is so much better than anything my imagination tried to make me believe it'd feel like.

Gavin's grip on me is firm and secure, holding me close as we kiss. His lips are surprisingly soft and intuitive as they move against mine. He turns me to the side and presses me against the door, subtly showing me that he's in charge. My wolf purrs in excitement, allowing him, well, both of them, to dominate us.

His hand moves up my arm to my neck, caressing my skin. His own palms are covered with callouses, marking one more spot where he's hard. The butterflies in my belly dive into a chaotic flutter, bringing up my body temperature just at the thought of all the places he's hard.

His tongue invites mine to a soundless rhythm of a dance we both seem to be familiar with. It's like we've been waiting, practicing, and living for this very moment since the very first time we laid eyes on each other. Whenever his tongue brushes against mine, my knees buckle as the heat travels between my legs with such force like no one has ever made me feel before. His caress, his kiss, his taste...is pure ecstasy, speeding the beat of my heart to pump more lust and desire down my veins and into every part of my body.

If he's the drug, I don't ever want to stop.

Sign me up for an O.D., my wolf comments with a soft purr.

Without breaking the kiss, but needing him to do more, to go further, I give him not-so-subtle permission by putting my leg around him. A low, guttural groan comes out of Gavin, cut off by my kisses. He growls when I start grinding my pussy against his hard cock through our clothes.

Our breathing turns heavier and my moans mixe with his grunts. He presses me harder against the door, using it as a support to move with me in a perfect harmony of excitement and passion.

Gavin slides his hands lower and lifts me up into his arms, my legs hooked around his waist. We muffle the sounds we make with a kiss, but when he presses against me harder, my eyes roll to the back of my head. While Gavin uses the opportunity to kiss my jaw and my neck, all I can focus on is how his hardest parts push against my softest. With every movement he makes, no matter how small, his cock rubs against my pussy, driving me wild and insane with desire.

"Fuck me," I groan into his ear, giving him an order that he better not think about refusing.

He doesn't need to be told twice and carries me to the bed, holding me in his arms as if I weigh less than a feather. He gently sets me on the mattress, then trails a path of kisses lower down my neck, burying his face between my breasts. His hot breath wakes up every part of my body, sending shivers all down my spine, leaving goosebumps in its wake.

I slip my hands at the edge of his pants, grabbing for his shirt to pull it free. When it proves to be too slow, I move my hands to his chest, take a fistful of the fabric, then force it open with a resounding tear.

The corners of Gavin's mouth lift up, smiling against my skin. He has more control over himself as he undid the buttons rather than tear them open, but in my defense, his shirt had like ten of them while mine only two.

He's making his way toward my nipples, his tongue leaving a hot wet trail behind that even my ability can't freeze. My body temperature's too high, my lust and arousal obvious and unable to hide, not that I'd want to.

Running my fingers across his muscular chest and down his abdomen, I gently press my nails against his skin, enjoying when I make him groan. To return the favor, Gavin redoubles his efforts and goes straight for my nipple, catching it between his lips and gently sucking on it. My back arches, giving him even better access to it, and he slips his hands underneath me to hold me up.

Wanting to participate again and to drive him crazy, I go straight for his belt. His tongue distracts me, making me lose control over my fingers as they fumble around to unfasten one of the last things that stand between his hard cock and my wet pussy.

Gavin groans, the sound guttural and animalistic, when my fingers move around the belt and accidentally rub against his cock. He abandons my nipples and pulls up, straightening his back to do a faster and more efficient job on his belt. He pulls the whole thing out of its loops, then undoes the little button on his pants and pulls down the zipper.

I moan in anticipation, spreading my legs wide for him to slip between and under my dress. Before Gavin can do just that and before he can reach into his tight black boxers to pull out his cock, the loud knocking on the door gets our attention, interrupting us at the worst possible moment.

Our eyes meet, both of our expressions crazed with lust and desire. My ponytail has come undone, and his purposefully messy faux hawk is a complete disaster; both of our hair all over the place will be a clear indication of what we've been up to. If even his torn shirt or my exposed breasts weren't proof enough, then the large wet spot on my underwear and his hardened erection that's pointing out of his pants, no matter how he shifts, would definitely give us away.

"What is it?" I ask, reluctantly giving Gavin a gentle push to get off me, which might be one of the hardest things I've had to do.

I scramble to pull the top of my dress up to cover my breasts, then quickly check in the mirror to see that the wet spot can't be seen from the back. Gavin takes the new shirt from the closet and puts it on, then aligns the belt through the belt loops and zips up his pants.

"His Majesty is asking you both to come in the throne room," the servant announces through the closed door, the voice belonging to the same older woman who came to fetch me earlier. "The Lafayette Pack has returned with news."

Gavin and I exchange a look, the love and assurance in his eyes is exactly what I need right now. Whatever happens, at least I'll have him by my side.

Or inside, my wolf comments with a mix of frustration at being interrupted and a hint of longing to satisfy the burning need and desire for the handsome dark wolf.

Taking my hand into his, Gavin intertwines our fingers and guides me through the door toward the unknown fate of my two younger siblings.

CHAPTER 13

GAVIN

The throne room is on the other side of the manor. It's literally the farthest place they could pick to call us over, but still, we go rushing and running to get the latest news of the attack and the first verbal report of the events, describing exactly what, why, and how it happened.

Don't complain, my wolf tells me. *It's either that or showing up in front of your in-laws with an erection.*

He's right about that. The short but fast run definitely took care of the excess energy, channeling it out through other means. At least Leia's flushed cheeks have an easy and plausible explanation now.

I slow down ever so slightly to let her enter the throne room first. She never stops to take in the scene, never hesitates to approach the figure sitting on the floor.

Before my mind can connect the dots into recognition, Leia's arms are around him, pulling him into a hug.

"Levi," she cries, swaying them back and forth.

Her brother winces in pain but embraces his sister just as tightly. He looks the worse for wear, but apart from the still bleeding gash on his cheek, the other cuts and bruises seem mostly healed. His speedy abilities of recovery must've been working overtime ever since the attack. Chances are that he'd be dead without the wolf inside him to tend to his wounds in time to prevent him from bleeding out.

When Leia lets go of Levi, Valerie pulls him back toward her with the fierce protectiveness of a mama wolf. Lucas towers above them, his expression a mix of relief and anxiety. It's only when Leia says it that I realize something's wrong.

"Where's Lily?" Leia asks, her eyes darting from her brother to her mother and lastly at her father.

It's Levi who answers, "She's been taken."

"Alpha Jenkins," I call out, waiting for the Alpha to step forward from the back of the room. I'm taking charge of the situation, determined to get to the bottom of the story and help my new family deal with a situation that no one should ever be in.

"Your Highness," Alpha Jenkins makes his presence known, positioning himself with his back turned to the royal advisors to face me as he gives me a slight but respectful bow.

"Have one of your Betas escort the young prince to the infirmary," I say, gesturing at Levi. "He needs to be checked out before he tells us the whole story."

"I'm fine," Levi insists and tries to stand up, but wavers as his knees buckle under his weight.

"Gavin's right, son," Lucas tells him, giving him a small smile. "You need to be checked out, not only for your good but to be sure that there's no residue of other types of magic on you."

He doesn't need to say witches for us to know what he's talking about. Levi reluctantly agrees but makes us promise to come speak to him as soon as he's confirmed to be clean. His mother and one of the Betas go with him.

Once he's gone, I turn to Alpha Jenkins and fold my arms across my chest. "What happened out there? What did you see?"

"We didn't see any action," Alpha Jenkins replies. "Everything was quiet and the students were mostly unharmed. The attackers came there with purpose and intention, made their way straight to what they wanted, then left the school's grounds."

"What was their mission?" I ask, my eyes locked on Alpha's whose attention is fully on me, even though his king is standing beside me.

"We believe that their intention was to kidnap the young Princess Lily," Alpha Jenkins replies, his tone firm and sure. "His Royal Highness will be able to tell you more about it. He kept saying that he has a message for Your Highness, Prince Gavin, but he has also lost a lot of blood, so we can't be sure."

I struggle to keep a neutral, unreadable mask on my face, not wanting Alpha Jenkins to know just how surprised I am by this news. Someone out there is going through a lot of trouble to deliver a message to me, breaking a lot of laws and making a not-so-flattering point.

"You're dismissed, but stay close by," I tell him. Alpha Jenkins nods in acknowledgment before turning and leaving the throne room with his pack on his heels. My next words are to the royal advisors, "Same goes for you. Stay by but leave us alone."

"With all due respect, Your Highness, but I don't think you're in the position to dismiss us," Duke Green argues with forced politeness.

"Do as he says," Lucas tells him firmly, strengthening my authority.

The royal advisors exchange looks, but in the end, they do as their king tells them to. They'd be fools for trying to resist the orders. One after another, they file out of the throne room with sullen looks on their faces.

Once they're gone, I turn to Leia and Lucas, letting them see just how frustrating this situation is. I shake my head and run my fingers through my hair.

"What are your thoughts on this?" Lucas asks, his eyes studying me carefully.

"I'm not sure," I admit with a heavy sigh. "It's not a lie that I have a lot of enemies. I didn't get my reputation and respect by making them love me. Sometimes instilling fear deep into them was the only way for us to get out of certain battles alive. It's brutal out there, and we've all done things we're not proud of, but I've never thought any of them would stoop so low as to attack wolves. No,

I don't think so. We've all fought to protect them, so it wouldn't make sense to go around killing them for sport now."

"But why take Lily?" Leia asks, getting mine and her father's attention. "She has nothing to do with you."

"Maybe it's connected to both of our families," Lucas concludes, his expression thoughtful.

"I guess we better go see if Levi's been checked out," I tell them, then hold out my arm to Leia, silently offering her my unyielding support.

The infirmary is on the far side of the east wing, along with the servant's quarters. It's rare that a member of the royal family needs to go there, but in this case, it was better for Levi not to go to his own room just yet.

Valerie's voice carries down the hall, the anxiety and worry dripping heavily from every word as she fusses around her only son. Lucas picks up the pace slightly, reaching the infirmary moments before Leia and I do.

Levi's sitting on the edge of the examination bed, Valerie standing right behind him with one hand on his shoulder. Except for the doctor who's currently attending to the royals, the rest of the infirmary is empty. It's a good sign that all ten beds are unclaimed, and I'm hoping it will continue to stay that way.

"What's the prognosis, Doctor Patel?" Lucas asks the moment he joins his wife by their son's side.

"His Highness' physical wounds will be healed with the help of his inner wolf, but the psychological damage from witnessing the attack will have to be dealt with through a channel of professionals who are specifically trained for these types of traumas," Doctor Patel replies, lacking in the bedside manner area. "Other than that, he's fine. There are no residues of magic left on or around him."

"That's good to hear, Doctor. Thank you," Lucas says, then gestures for the doctor to leave, wordlessly dismissing him.

As soon as the doctor closes the door behind him, Levi jumps to his feet and grabs my hands. I suppress my primal instinct to react by beating him into submission. He gives me a wild look, his blue eyes wide and his pupils dilated.

Fear and anxiety linger about him like cheap perfume, my wolf comments with disgust.

"I have to give you a message," Levi says with a frantic voice. "He'll kill her if I don't."

"Who?" Leia asks, but her brother ignores her. She tries to push again more firmly, "Who will, Levi?"

"Go on," I tell him with a curt nod, letting him know that he has my full attention. It's clear that he won't be of much use to us until he gets this out of his system.

"He came in the middle of the day, unafraid and un-challenged," Levi says, suddenly jumping to the start of the story.

If before he looked like he had his shit together, now he's all over the place. His eyes glaze over, his mind taking him back to the moment of the attack.

"They wore their flames on them like a statement of power, their hair colors ranging from orange to red to gentle brown kissed by the sun," Levi continues, de-scribing his attackers. "I can't say for sure how many there were, but at some point, they all must have attend-ed the Academy because they seemed to know it pretty well."

Except that they're all fire users. That doesn't really bring down our pool of suspects much, my wolf comments, referring to the fact that all the wolves are welcomed to the Academy to learn the ins and outs of our abilities.

It's an important part of our education, highlighting the vital reasons to keep our species from being discovered and to integrate them into our communities, following the careers that have been listed for specific graduation years. The kingdoms tried not to have too many workers doing one job and none for the other. It was all about striking the right balance.

"Some of my friends got hurt," he continues with a shaky voice. "I'm not sure if they survived. I couldn't check. I had to find Lily."

"What did you do?" I ask when he falls silent for a second too long. I'm trying to be gentle and understanding, but Leia's younger sister has been taken, and in cases like this, time is of the essence.

"I shifted into my wolf form and ran across the campus, desperately following her scent," he replies, his eyes still staring blankly ahead. "I tried to reach her before they could, but I was too late. He already had her."

"Who?" Leia asks, the anxiety making her voice an octave higher than usual.

Levi's eyes suddenly focus as he lifts his gaze to look straight at me. His tone is eerie and heavy with emotion when he replies, "Prince Felix Farrell."

We should've killed him when we had the chance, my wolf growls, his anger momentarily getting the better of me and before I know it, my hands are clenched into fists, the shadows dancing around my ankles like lovers yearning for attention.

"That's impossible," Lucas says, then curses under his breath as he shakes his head left and right in disbelief. "If he attacked the Academy, that means that he..."

"He also killed all those innocent families," I finish for him when he trails off, unable to find the words for the atrocities committed by one of our own. "He and his followers are behind the massacre. They're the reason that the kids from my Pack of Survivors are orphans."

"But why would he do that?" Leia asks, finding herself unable to comprehend it just like her father before her.

"You both heard what he was saying at dinner," I tell them, not surprised at all that he's behind all that. "He wants to expose our species to humans, so he can take control over them and enslave them."

"But why would he kill our own kind?" Leia argues, her brows furrowed in confusion.

"It's not as much about killing our own kind as it is about getting rid of the sympathizers," I reply, slowly connecting the dots. "Just think about it for a second. I've been spending time with my new pack, and I've noticed certain things that made me look more into their little town."

"Such as?" Lucas asks, looking at me with a hint of intrigue in his eyes.

"For starters, all the families living on the block had kids and they were all minors," I reply, going through the data I've collected with James. "I've been led to believe that they stay there until young pups are in control of their abilities so they can't accidentally expose our kind to humans."

"What exactly are you saying?" Lucas asks, giving me the same confused look that's on his daughter's face right now.

"I'm saying that those wolves lived with humans as one of them. They chose to live in human society as opposed to being a part of our kingdoms," I reply, saying it as clearly as possible. "Those wolves would be one of the first to rise up and protect their human friends. If Felix was to convince the kingdoms to follow his plan, he couldn't afford to have such public protesters on an already highly sensitive topic."

"This is even worse than I imagined," Lucas breathes, visibly distressed by the new information I dumped in his lap.

"He has a message for you," Levi says, looking at me.

"What message?" I ask, my body on high alert. Taking a deep breath, I brace myself for whatever he has to tell me, gathering strength to keep my expression schooled into a carefully crafted mask of indifference.

"A letter will arrive where he'll challenge you to a duel, and you'll have to accept it or he'll kill Lily," Levi says, racking his brain to get every piece of information to us. "The duel will be in two weeks when the moon is full."

"He wants to fight me?" I ask, cocking my brows in surprise even though I've tried to keep a neutral expression. This was the last thing I expected, but it's also the best possible demand he could make.

It seems too easy, my wolf says with a thoughtful growl.

"You'll duel for Leia's hand," Levi continues, giving his sister an apologetic look as if it was his idea.

"Of course, he wants to marry you," I say with a scoff, locking my eyes with Leia's. "You're in the ideal position of power to carry on with his plan. He said so himself at dinner the other night."

"That's absurd!" Leia exclaims, her face turning red as the anger gets ahold of her. "I'm not a prize to be won. We're not in the fucking medieval ages anymore where a woman's wishes count for nothing."

"Why did he kidnap Lily to get you to fight him?" Levi asks, tilting his head to the side as he gives us a confused look. "Why not just attack you?"

They didn't get to the dueling part of the curriculum, my wolf says, realizing it at the same time as I do that Levi didn't get a chance to study that part of our history yet.

"A duel is an ancient tradition that both parties need to agree to verbally before the start and via signature, otherwise killing the losing party can be considered murder," Lucas explains with an aged and tired voice. "I think that the reason why Felix is doing it this way is because the winning party automatically gets everything and everyone that belonged to the losing party."

"I refuse to agree to that!" Leia snaps. "This was before women were accepted as equals to our male counterparts. Our opinion matters. Our rights are important. We're not doing this."

"But he has Lily," Levi says, his eyes darting around the room, trying to find someone to sympathize with him.

"Your brother's right," I say, focusing my attention mostly on Leia. "I have to accept the duel. I have to fight him."

"No, you don't, and you won't," she insists, shaking her head.

"I'm a better fighter than he is. I have the experience and skill like no one else in all of the kingdoms. I don't want to sound arrogant, but I'm hands down the strongest ability wielder with an incredibly dangerous and bloodthirsty wolf inside me," I continue, trying to get her to see reason. "Besides, if it makes you feel better, we still have two weeks until the next full moon, which means that I have plenty of time to practice and do some research on Felix and the Farrells."

"You're not fighting nor are you doing any research because it won't be necessary," Leia says stubbornly, narrowing her eyes at me. "We'll use those two weeks to track him down, treating them like criminals and murderers that they are. If we get other kingdoms to help us, we can make the world a very small place for him. We already know that he can't leave the country if he wants to fight you in two weeks."

"If Felix finds out that we're looking for him, he might kill your sister," I respond, the anger and frustration getting the best of me.

"Leia, please," Levi begs, grabbing his sister's arm. "Lily can't die. Please don't let her die."

"I won't let her die. Can't you see that I'm trying to save everyone?" Leia asks in exasperation.

"Here's what we'll do," Lucas says, finally stepping up to make an order. "Whenever Gavin goes to train the Pack of Survivors, Alpha Jenkins will join him as a practice buddy to make sure that his skills are up to date. In the meantime, we will put all our resources into locating Felix and finding Lily. We'll do everything in our power to keep the duel from happening, but if we fail, then we'll have to go forward with it. Is that clear?"

Leia purses her lips into a thin line to keep them from trembling. Her eyes are burning with cold anger, and I can only hope that she'll turn it on Felix instead of me.

We all nod, none of us happy about the situation we've been put in. Kidnapping Lily and holding her hostage to blackmail us is one of the highest forms of betrayal that the other royal family can make. Sooner or later, we're going to have to get in touch with the Farrells, hoping that we won't make matters worse by openly accusing Felix of committing those horrible crimes.

The peace between kingdoms is extremely fragile as of late. One wrong step will suck us all into a war with countless casualties on all sides and of all species. It's what we've been trying to avoid for the last decade, but it's becoming harder if not even impossible.

CHAPTER 14

LEIA

"Just listen to me, please!" Gavin calls after me when he stops the door from slamming into his face as I angrily enter the room.

"Listen to what? Huh?" I ask and turn to face him. "Your mind's already made up, so all you want to do now is to convince me to go along with your plan. Don't you realize how humiliating it is to be put up as a prize for the winner?"

"I hate it too, okay?!" Gavin exclaims, his face contorting with anger. "I hate it that that fucking bastard believes he can claim you through me. I hate that he's disrespecting you like that. It makes me want to murder him. It makes me want to make him suffer the same way he's making you suffer. I want to make him pay, Leia. I want to tear him apart, limb from limb. I want to see it in his eyes when I take his wolf away from him; when I leave him as an empty husk of the person he used to be. I fucking hate him."

Something in his eyes convinces me that he doesn't want to duel with Felix. While he doesn't mind fighting him, it's the rules of the duel that he seems to hate. It's all I needed to know. I needed him to confirm to me that I'm not some possession to be passed along or traded for.

"We'll find her," I say, trying to sound confident for both of our sakes.

Gavin takes my hands into his and turns me toward him. His eyes are soft and earnest, his brows slightly furrowed as he gives me a small smile.

"Yes, we will," he assures me and even though I know he's saying it to make me feel better, just hearing him utter those words helps a lot.

The sudden closeness puts my body on edge, every part of it wanting to press against him. Gavin must feel the same because he lowers his head and pulls me toward him, catching my lips between his in a passionate kiss. Our tongues dart in and out of each other's mouths in rapid succession as he absentmindedly lifts me off the floor. I wrap my legs around his torso and hold on to his upper body as he carries me to the bed. Without breaking the kiss, we collapse onto the bed.

I succeed in unbuttoning his shirt without tearing it open, and Gavin helps by quickly discarding it, throwing it across the room in the general direction of our bathroom. I take my time to run my hands over his toned bare chest before reaching further down his body. Gavin's cock is already hard and eager to finally get an intimate introduction to my pussy without any more interruptions. He pulls away to remove his shoes and socks, before giving me a straight path to take off the rest.

Hooking my fingers on the edge of Gavin's pants, I pull them down along with his black boxers. His cock happily stands to attention, his shaft hard and long. I lean forward on the bed, admiring my fiancé's manhood. I cup his balls, then let my mouth work its way down the length of his cock, leaving a trail of saliva in my path along his throbbing erection. Wanting to tease him, I suck one of his balls into my mouth and toy with it, running my tongue along the smooth skin, before moving back to the tip of Gavin's cock, passing the exquisite sensation along the sensitive edge of his cock head.

Gavin lets out a guttural growl, giving me the only warning before he pulled his cock away from my eager mouth. Kneeling down, he presses his mouth against mine again, starting another passionate dance of tongues. His clever fingers make quick work of un-zipping my dress, then help me slither out of the silk material as he lifts it from the hem up over my head before throwing it in the same direction that he threw his shirt.

Touched by the colder air, my nipples hardened and erected, growing even more tender. I didn't bother to wear a bra, the dress covering more than enough. Gavin firmly cups my breasts from behind, his erect cock press-ing into my back as I tilt my head up, my mouth looking for his to kiss me again.

When we shift positions on the bed, I'm lying on my back, enjoying the view of Gavin working his way down until he's kissing my navel. The small damp spot on my panties is a clear indication of just how much I want him. He gently grips my panties, and I obligingly lift my hips until my ass no longer touches the bed. Before I know it, my ass is bare as Gavin skillfully pulls my panties down, then applies slight pressure for me to lift my legs back up towards my head so he can completely get rid of them.

Gavin crawls between my legs as they lay wide open on the bed, gently kissing my thighs as he goes. When he gets closer to my pussy, he doesn't immediately move to the aching spot, but decides to torture me by prolonging the anticipation a little longer and working his way around my pussy by moving over it and onto my other inner thigh, then kissing his way down my ankle and back up my leg until he reaches my breast. He raises himself up onto his arms and gives me a deep, sensual kiss, his hard cock rubbing itself against my thigh. I lift my ass, trying to bring my pussy into contact with his member, but he breaks the kiss before I can do it, moving away from my mouth and slowly kissing his way back down my body to my breast and lower to my stomach until his tongue finally arrives at my soaking and silky smooth pussy.

Gavin tastes me, flicking his tongue across my pussy to lick my length, before moving the tongue in and out of my pussy, then onto my now exposed rosy-pink clit. His lips curl up into a small smile that I can feel against my sensitive skin milliseconds before he sucks on my little bud, then lavishes it with tongue strokes, alternating between gentle and firm, rapid and slow movement over the surface. He only stops when he spends a couple of moments sucking onto my clit, increasing the sensation of this delicate spot. At the same time, one arm snakes its way up my body while the other hand gently teases both entrances, one to my pussy and the other to my ass.

Gavin's tongue continues its unrelenting and un-yielding assault on my clit, coaxing out the heat from my pussy, replacing it with the usual cold temperature that everyone comes to associate with me. Mere moments later, my hips start to buck under the constant and stable teasing from Gavin's tongue and I moan in ecstasy as he fucks me with his tongue to a powerful orgasm, pushing me straight over the edge into an incredible climax, giving me the release that I've been yearning for ever since I had that sex dream about him.

He moves back up and kisses me, letting me taste my own juices while he gently positions himself behind me and spoons me until my orgasm subsides. His hands massage my breasts, playing with my nipples until my trembling stops. When I regain some semblance of my senses, I can feel his erect cock pressing against my ass. Wanting to feel him inside me, I raise my leg, then put it behind both of us as we continue to spoon. Without hesitation, Gavin gently thrusts his hips forward, his cock moving from my ass to my pussy. His groans mix with my moans as he enters me, finally doing the intimate introduction we've both so desperately wanted.

Gavin pulls back a little before pushing his cock back inside me, coaxing out another moan as his long erection fills my hot soaking pussy. We slowly do this again and again, until he buries his shaft deep in me, all up to the hilt, his balls pressing against my ass cheeks. I start to push back with my ass, trying to get him even deeper inside me, wanting and needing him to fill up all of me. We settle into a rhythmic lovemaking with his head buried into my neck, kissing and sucking on it, and his hands holding me tightly, closely, and possessively against him.

Gavin's breathing turns heavier and deeper, his grunts guttural and his thrusts harder, rougher even. Before he can come, he pulls out and rolls both of us over until I'm on all fours, my ass in the air. Without hesitation, he repositions his cock against my pussy, guiding the tip of his erection toward my hole before thrusting his hips forward, burying his shaft deeper and deeper into my expectant pussy. With every thrust, his balls slap against me, and with every pump, he hits the aching spot.

Before too long, neither one of us can hold back anymore. Together in a passionate embrace, we jump off the edge in unison. His throbbing cock pulsates and quivers as he shoots the stream of his hot load deep inside me, followed by another and another until he's empty.

My pussy contracts around him, my lower lips kissing his shaft as they contract and flex while I enjoy my second climax of the night. Reaching behind me, I grab hold of the base of Gavin's cock to make sure that he keeps it inside me as I flex my own muscles, eager to milk the very last drops of his load from his member.

When we're both done and empty, we roll over on the bed, me landing in his strong and protective arms. Our fingers absentmindedly trace gentle caresses across our naked bodies. My pussy is still quivering inside, sending echoes of my orgasm up my spine and making me shiver.

Our lips connect, our mouths melting into slow, deep kisses. Being here, right now with Gavin, is the best I've felt in my whole life. This is exactly where I'm supposed to be, and he's the only one who belongs by my side as I do by his.

The circumstances outside our little safe haven might be less than ideal, but that didn't keep him from making me feel like I'm the top priority in his mind. He took his time to satisfy me and make love to me. He did it all. He is all.

He's ours, my wolf growls possessively, staking a claim to him.

An answer comes back and although it can't be heard, it can most definitely be felt. As I lay in the crook of his arm, my cheek pressed against his chest, and his fingers playing with my hair, the missing pieces fall into place, connecting us as one.

Gavin's breath hitches and his heartbeat speeds up, giving me the only sign that I need to know that he felt it too. Slowly, I lift my head to look at him. His black eyes are filled with so much emotion, ranging from love to happiness. His lips are curled up in the most genuine and sincere smile that I've ever seen on his face.

Closing the distance, he gives me a sweet kiss, his tongue shyly introducing itself as if it's our first time, which it may very well be. It's not every day that we're lucky enough to have the bond slip into place, and we get to kiss our soulmate, our forever.

CHAPTER 15

GAVIN

Leia and I fell asleep in the exact same position that we ended up in after we had sex. It's like once the bond clicked, neither one of us wanted to move, afraid that something would break it.

I've never believed in soulmates, even though I grew up hearing stories about them. Finding one in our lifetime was so rare that it sounded more like a myth than anything else.

After Leia and I made love, everything felt right. For once in my life, everything was perfect. I was calm. She's my home and my heart. I'll do whatever needs to be done to protect her, to protect what we have. I'll fight whomever I need to, and I'll kill everyone that might threaten not just her, but the things that she believes in. If that means protecting humans, then that's what I'll do because I want her to be happy. The bond further intensifies her emotions, strengthening my already vast well of power whenever she's extra happy.

She's casually thrown her naked body over mine, her pussy pressed against my thigh. Just the thought of it already sends a fresh batch of blood straight to my cock, wakening it into hardness.

Her breathing is deep and slow, her body temperature surprisingly warm. I trace a line down her naked skin, taking in its softness and perfection.

We're so damn lucky, my wolf comments, giving voice to my own sentiments.

I must've done something right in this life for the wolf gods to reward me with her. Her natural beauty takes my breath away, her plump lips and gentle muscles make my heart skip a beat, and the softness of her pussy turns my cock harder than a fucking stone.

Leia's own fingers twitch on my abdomen, her mind slowly waking up. I listen for the changes in her breathing and watch as the soft edges of her face harden under the not-so-subtle pressure of the situation we've been forced into.

I turn my head toward her and kiss her forehead. The corners of Leia's mouth lift up and she snuggles up closer to me, her pussy pressing even harder against my thigh. My hard cock is fully exposed for both of us to see, my erection clearly at its height and the balls in need of emptying.

"Good morning," she mumbles, her lips moving against my chest as if they're giving me small kisses with every word she says.

"Good morning, Princess," I say back, tightening my grip on her, not wanting for this moment to ever end.

Leia tilts her head up just enough to look me in the eyes. While hers are heavy with sleep, they're also shining with genuine happiness. I must look the same because it's the only way I can feel after last night.

"Is it true?" she asks even though she knows the answer.

"It is," I confirm, replying anyway, then add, "You are mine, and I am yours. Now and forever."

"Soulmates," she whispers, her eyes tearing up. "They really exist."

"We exist," I correct her, unable to wrap my head around it myself.

"Gavin," Leia whispers, then pauses, her brows furrowing.

"What is it?" I ask, gently encouraging her to share herself with me.

"Don't break my heart," she says, her eyes silently pleading with me.

I put my hand on her cheek and look her straight in the eyes, wanting her to feel the sincerity of my words.

"You're my soulmate, Leia Lafayette," I start, my voice both soft and firm at the same time. "You're who I've chosen as my lifetime partner and you're who my wolf has chosen as his lifetime partner. I'll never do anything to hurt you in any way. I'd rather cut my own heart out than break yours. You're it for me, Leia. You're the girl I love."

I close the distance and kiss her, my tongue tasting her soft lips. Unable to hold myself back any longer, I move my fingers down her body, trailing a path along her back and down to her ass cheeks. I playfully smack them, then leave my hand there, loving the feel of her firm, soft flesh.

Leia's high-pitched giggle encourages me to continue my exploration, so I move my hand to the front, quickly finding her warm, smooth lower lips. As I gently finger them with one hand, I use the other to reach for her breast, feeling its weight and firmness.

Leia doesn't hesitate to spread her legs for me, giving me a teasing smile and a wordless invitation. I move both of my hands to her breasts, nuzzling her neck and then surprising her by lightly twisting her stiffening nipples, coaxing a low moan out of her.

I inhale deeply, savoring the scent of fresh snow that always lingers around her. Leaning forward, my cock rests between Leia's thighs, further hardening at the closeness of her warm pussy.

Our mouths engage in a passionate embrace, exchanging kisses as our tongues dance in the synchronicity of soulmates. The wetness from Leia's pussy starts dripping onto my cock, driving me wild with desire.

I hold the head of my cock right between her lower lips, splitting them apart with just the tip of it. Before she can get used to me, I surprise her by pushing my member as deep inside her as it can go, burying the whole length of my shaft into her soaking hot pussy. Her soft gasp is the most beautiful sound I've ever heard.

My intention wasn't to fuck her yet. First, I want to feel her and enjoy being inside her. My cock remains buried all the way to my balls, the heat from her pussy radiating all through me. Impatient, Leia begins grinding against me, desperately trying to make me start fucking her.

Realizing that she can't get me to do anything I'm not ready to yet, Leia stops and closes her eyes, letting herself enjoy the feeling of our connection. I kiss her neck, silently savoring being enveloped by my soulmate's tightness. A low moan escapes Leia's lips, the small sound precious enough to bring me to my knees if she wanted to. Unable to deny her anything, I do what she asks me for.

I slowly pull back, enjoying the feeling of my cock gradually pulling through my soulmate's lower lips. I can only exercise so much control until there's none left at all. Just as I pump forward, Leia thrusts her hips, meeting me halfway. My cock buries into her pussy all the way to the hilt again. Leia locks her eyes on mine, her expression wordlessly begging me to fuck her.

My inner wolf lets out a roaring growl so strong that the sound manifests itself as a guttural groan, demanding that I give our soulmate everything we are and everything we have. Happily obeying both of them, I start fucking her hard, pounding my aching cock in and out.

My left hand cups one of her breasts, gently squeezing it, my fingers playing with the nipple, feeling it bounce and shake as I pump my erection in and out of her. My right hand is at the back of her head, my fingers buried into her ashen-white hair, holding her beautiful face up, so I can watch her bright blue eyes rolling back into her head with pleasure. Her expression is one of blind lust and desire, her plump lips part open to let out low moans as I fuck her again and again, burying my whole length deep into her.

Leia lets one of her hands drop between her legs to play with her clit as I continue fucking her. She's so close to climaxing, her breathing turning heavier and deeper, her moans and cries filling the room along with the smell of sex that's mixing with her scent of freshly fallen snow.

A long, low-pitched moan comes from deep inside her as she starts to tremble and shake, until she suddenly stiffens, her back rigid. She took a leap off the edge, experiencing the climaxing orgasm, but that doesn't stop me from fucking her. I groan into her ear, feeling my throbbing cock getting ready to follow her into the abyss.

In a moment frozen in time, our eyes met, establishing a connection so pure and invigorating, highlighting the bond as unique as it is rare. Leia looks just as sexy as ever, cool sweat covering her body, her hair disheveled, and a delirious expression filled with satisfaction on her face.

With one last deep thrust into her pussy, I let out a guttural growl, giving her the only warning I can before I shoot the entirety of my load inside her.

We collapse into each other's arms, both breathless and satisfied. It's the best way to start the day.

"Good morning," I say teasingly, kissing her forehead.

Leia chuckles against my chest, the vibrations traveling all the way down to my cock again. It's impossible. I've just climaxed and want to go another round. It's like I can't get enough of her.

Aren't you glad for that soulmate bond? my wolf says happily, enjoying the intimacy as much as I am. While mine and Leia's is on the physical level, that doesn't mean that nothing happens on the magical side of the bond. Our wolves have a dance of their own, their feelings and emotions further intensifying ours.

"I need a shower," Leia says and gently pushes herself off me.

My eyes never leave her naked body as she walks toward the bathroom. Before she enters, she turns around and gives me a questioning look.

"Aren't you coming?" she asks suggestively, her lips curled up into a small, seductive smile.

I don't need to be asked twice. Jumping off the bed with newfound vigor, I run after her with a wicked smile. Leia giggles and escapes inside the bathroom, jumping straight into the shower, turning the water on. The cold stream doesn't bother her, but it definitely stops my attack, freezing me on the spot. She gives me a triumphant smile before turning the water to a warmer setting.

I come toward the shower, my hardening cock bobbing and swaying with every step I take. Stepping behind her, I hold her tight, pressing my erection against her firm ass as I cup her breasts and nuzzle her neck.

Leia turns around and guides my cock between her thighs, rubbing the head up and down the length of her pussy. Her smooth and warm juices mix with the hot water from the shower, dripping all over my erection. Her pussy's already opening up, eager to invite me inside. Needing it just as much as she does, I gently thrust forward, pushing my cock into her. Her hands slip around my neck, holding herself up as she shivers in pleasure against me.

The hot water splashes against her back as we slowly move together. If yesterday we fucked and this morning we made love, then now we're exchanging the most intimate hugs and caresses. Our movements are slow and lazy, even as our bodies cling together but not too tight. It's more like leaning on each other, enjoying the closeness and everything else we have to offer. Her head rests on my shoulder, her piercing blue eyes glazed over with a mixture of contentment and the passion we're igniting.

"Wait," I mumble, stopping us long enough to be able to focus. Her brows furrow in confusion, her eyes wide and pupils dilated with lust.

Momentarily ignoring her and the feeling of my cock still inside her, I do my best to concentrate on the small chair on the other side of the bathroom. I even lift my hand toward it to help me with summoning the thick, shadowy tentacles that could slide the chair to us. The floor around it turns into what resembles a moving shadow belt of sorts, bringing it closer. My brows furrow in concentration, the whole thing taking longer than I would've liked. Usually, I'm in great control of my power, and this would be as easy as taking a breath, but it doesn't help that Leia's body is pressed against mine, my cock buried deep inside her pussy and her lowers lips are eagerly clenching and unclenching around it, preparing to milk me for all I'm worth.

Just as the chair is almost within my reach, Leia shifts her weight from one foot to the other, subsequentially rubbing herself on me and moving my cock inside her. I lose the fragile control I had and accidentally yank the tentacles forward, causing the chair to fly straight at us. My wolf is too entranced with her wolf, for once in my life being utterly unhelpful and unreachable. Fortunately, my physical reflexes are just as quick, and I manage to catch the chair before it can hit us.

Leia chuckles and leans her forehead against my chest, tucking it right under my chin. I wrap my other arm around her, enjoying the feeling of our invisible but unbreakable bond.

When we stop laughing, I put the chair inside the shower stall and sit on it. Leia doesn't hesitate and straddles my legs, then climbs up to guide my cock back toward her entrance before lowering herself down, welcoming my whole length into her pussy. She wraps her arms around my neck, firmly holding on while I grab her ass to lift her up and down on my shaft. Her face is pressed against my neck, nibbling and sucking on it in between her moans.

Her hot pussy's grabbing and squeezing my cock as I lift her up and down my erection in long strokes. Her breathing turns erratic, her breath tickling my ear as her plump lips nibble on my earlobe, driving me wild. I can't hold it any longer and start thrusting harder and harder into her. My hands hold her ass tight, lifting her up before pulling her down on me hard while I thrust my hips up, giving my cock an extra push deep inside her pussy, hitting the spot that makes her eyes roll back into her head. I repeat the movement again and again. My knees buckle with weakness and my whole body's shaking, but not for being cold. Her temperature is surprisingly high, the arousal clearly making her icy blood boil. A familiar burning feeling wells inside me, my throbbing cock pulsating with sensitivity. It's like an itch that I can't stop scratching, loving the release that follows after its satisfaction.

To expose her swollen breasts to my hungry mouth, I have to lean her back a bit and move one of my hands behind her to make sure she doesn't fall. My other hand is still on her ass, helping me pump my cock in and out of her pussy harder and harder.

My cock swells up, the throbbing intensifies and the pulsing feeling speeds up until I shoot another full load deep into her pussy, with more force than usual. My erection vibrates and shakes inside her as it keeps filling her up with my juices. I'm still pumping in and out of her, but there's much less friction as my juices mix with hers, flooding the entrance of her pussy.

I let her slip away just enough for my cock to slide out and the refreshing warm water splashes around our intimate areas. She slides a finger inside her pussy, holding my gaze as she plays with herself. I lean over and kiss her cheek, then pull her earlobe with my lips, softly nibbling on it before moving lower to her breasts and running my tongue all over her nipples, gently sucking them into erection.

We exchange places except that as she sits on the chair, I kneel down in front of her. The gesture is so intimate and humbling while at the same time one of the highest forms of love and respect between us.

I spread her legs, then go straight for her pussy, my tongue diving right into her sweetness, tasting her delicious juices. When I clean her up, I start playing with her swollen clit, flicking my tongue all over it. Leia's body starts to tremble when I begin sucking on it. I reach up and play with her breasts with one hand while I use the other to help my tongue satisfy her through her clit, pushing my fingers in and out, then side to side.

After a bit of this, I take both hands and grab her thighs to slide her down even more, wanting her closer to me so I can bury my face in her pussy. My lips taste everything she has to offer as my tongue darts in and out of her, occasionally teasing her clit.

When she's ready, on the verge of impatience, I press my tongue firmly against her clit and curl it around, catching the whole area with the tip of it, then unwrap it only to start all over. I do it until she gives me more of her juices for me to drink on. Leia's holding onto my head for dear life, her fingers buried into my thick black hair. At some point, she even tries to push me away from her, the pleasure I'm giving her proving to be too intense, but

I don't yield an inch. Her loud moans and cries make it clear that she's getting closer to her climax.

Leia puts her legs behind me, getting a nice grip around my neck, and pulls me further into her pussy, eager to get the release of her life. This frees my hands to grab her ass cheeks, squeezing hard, which is just a cherry on top of her pleasure cake.

She grinds against my face, squeezing me harder with her legs. I reach up and fondle her breasts, cupping and massaging them. I'm holding her close as her body starts to shake with the orgasm, my mouth catching all of her juices. Everything she has is mine. She is mine. I'm not going to let even one drop go to waste.

Leia's eyes slowly return to focus, the bright blue color clearer than ever before. We exchange small smiles, before she pulls me up for a kiss. This time, when our lips meet, the moment isn't anything like our previous lust and desire. Those two things are momentarily satisfied, hopefully long enough for us to go through our day. No, this connection of our lips is gentle and sweet, a moment full of love and respect. It's a promise of everything that is to come.

Leia stands up, and I reach for the bar of soap to wash her. She just stands there, glowing as she soaks in the soapy massage that I give her. I take pride in making sure to get every part of her body, soaping her neck, shoulders, breasts, and stomach, until I need to lower myself into a crouch to clean her lower parts. Her ass cheeks require special attention as I run my hand along her perfect shape, down to her legs, then up on the front side until I'm cleaning her pussy, washing off the delicious blend of our juices.

Leia does the same for me, her soapy hand stroking my cock and fondling my balls. I give her a warning look, wordlessly letting her know what will happen if she continues that way. Her fingers trace my toned abdomen, her eyes admiring my muscled body.

When we're done, we wrap each other with soft towels. While mine is secured at my waist, hers is tucked around her breasts.

"What's the plan for today?" Leia asks me when we return to the bedroom, rummaging through the closet.

"I'm going to go ahead and check in with the Pack of Survivors," I tell her. I hope that I won't ruin the day and make her angry when I add, "I was thinking about asking Alpha Jenkins to join me, so I could sneak a quick training session in while showing the kids just how strong water wielders can be. So far, I have one water user, and he seems quite enthusiastic to learn, so Alpha Jenkins' presence could prove to be useful in more than one way."

"I think that's a good idea," Leia says, surprising me with her chill answer.

"Really?" I ask, unable to hold myself back from questioning it.

She turns my way and gives me a soft smile. "Yes, Gavin," she says with a small nod. "I trust you. I trust in your ability to make good decisions. You wouldn't have lasted that long on the frontlines if you hadn't known what you were doing. It's time I embrace every part of you, which isn't just as my fiancé and lover, but also a skilled commander and exceptional leader. We're soulmates, and we need to trust each other."

"An incredible lover, right?" I ask, reaching for her hand to pull her against me as I lean in and smile against her lips. "That's what you meant to call me, didn't you? If the answer is anything other than yes, I'm going to take you to bed again and again until you change your mind.

I'm willing to take all the time it takes to convince you otherwise."

"Yes, you're an incredible lover," Leia squeals when I grab her bare ass cheeks, possessively squeezing them and laying claim on her whole body.

I chuckle and pull back, curling my lips into a smirk as I wink at her. "Don't sound so surprised, Princess."

Leia rolls her eyes, her lips pulled up into a smile as we return to our respective closets to get dressed.

"What's on your agenda?" I ask, pulling my boxers up and over my cock, trapping it behind the expensive fabric before it can get a different idea.

"I'm going to check in on Levi then help my father call our contacts to try and track down Felix," she says, reaching behind her back to zip up her dress. "Someone has to know something."

"It's only a matter of time," I agree, then lean in for one last kiss before we go about our days.

CHAPTER 16

LEIA

"We can't go on like this," I say, pacing up and down the conference room. "It's been one week, and we have nothing to show for it. Did we even accomplish anything?"

"We're doing the best we can, Your Highness," Duke Green replies, sounding like he actually believes it.

"The best you can?" my brother echoes angrily and slams the palm of his hand against the table. "Your best isn't good enough. We didn't find even a single lead on my sister, and as far as we know, she could be dead!"

My mother bursts into tears at that, covering her face with an already overused tissue. She hasn't stopped crying since the day we found out that Felix has taken Lily hostage.

"Levi's right," my father says, siding with my brother. "What we're doing is not enough. We need to do more."

"Like what?" Duke Green challenges, momentarily forgetting himself. Then he quickly recovers and bows his head in apology as he humbly mutters, "Your Majesty."

"Maybe we should make it public," I suggest, then run with the idea when no one else says anything. "If we post Felix's picture everywhere, in all the newspapers, on all social media platforms, and news channels. We should spread his picture like an ad and even use fucking billboards if we have to. His face needs to be the most recognizable on the planet among all the species. I don't even care if the witches get him as long as he's found."

"We can't say that he kidnapped the young princess," Duke Green argues and shakes his head. "If he didn't already, he'll most definitely kill her if we turn him into the most wanted man on Earth."

My mother whimpers, her cries growing louder. She shouldn't be here listening to this. I don't have the authority to send her from the room to keep her from suffering even more than she already is, but then on the other hand, if I was in her position and my kid had been taken, I'd want to know everything that's happening. I understand why my father allows her to be a part of the meeting even if all she does is cry.

"We don't do it that way," I say, my reply getting everyone's attention. "What if we turn him into a celebrity of sorts? What if we set up a website and create a hashtag or something, then give people an incentive to post his picture on our website using that hashtag? For every viable photo, we pay them a little something, just enough to keep it going. That way we'll have eyes and ears everywhere, turning the whole population into our spies."

"That could work," Countess Bailey allows with a thoughtful nod.

"Those things in the clouds and the screens never work," old Duchess Crane complains. "We should do it the old-fashioned way and have His Highness Prince Gavin duel him. That way everything would get sorted fast and without a fuss."

"Maybe you should start considering retirement if you can't keep up with the times," I snap at the old duchess, momentarily forgetting myself.

We need somebody to conjure some ice stat! The cranky old duchess has a third-degree burn. My wolf chuckles, enjoying me losing control.

I hold my breath as I stare the old duchess down, her eyes wide in shock and her mouth open in surprise. I'm waiting for my father's reprimand, ordering me to apologize, but it doesn't come.

"The duel is too risky," my father says instead, ignoring the little spat between the duchess and I, probably chalking it up to the tension running so high. "While I have all the faith in Prince Gavin and his abilities, we can't afford to risk him losing. We have to believe that Prince Felix has some elaborate plan that justifies his reasons for challenging Gavin, even though on paper, our Prince is a lot more qualified and a hell of a lot stronger. Either way, the consequences of possible loss would be catastrophic. It wouldn't be just Gavin that would lose his life, but it'd be all of us that would end up paying for it."

"Why don't we wait for the bastard to show up to a duel and we corner him? He can't fight all of us," Levi suggests, but my father's already shaking his head.

"Felix is too smart for that," my father replies. "If he shows up, he'll come with the protection that falls on a dueler. He'll be untouchable. We must respect the rules."

"Let's go back to the photo idea that Her Highness mentioned," Countess Bailey says, successfully guiding us back on track.

"Should we run some possible scenarios that might happen in case we go through with it?" Marquess Wilson suggests, no doubt already calculating the odds of success with his analytical brain.

"It's simple," I say, taking point on this since it's my idea. "We create a team that sorts through the pictures. When we get a plausible hit, we send the Lafayette Pack to check it out. We give them a free-to-kill order on Felix."

"Sounds easy enough, but that's just the thing," Marquess Wilson says with a small shake of his head. "It's almost too easy."

"Maybe we're due for easy," I reply, tired of arguing the same old thing with the royal advisors. I turn to my father, silently begging him to interfere. It's his word that will count in the end, his order that will be followed.

"Whether we make it public or not, Felix already knows that we're looking for him," my father says at last, running his hand through his hair and brushing it back. "He revealed his identity when he showed himself to Levi, which means that he's not particularly worried about us finding him. Our contacts proved to be useless, other royal families hesitant to get between the growing tensions between us and the Farrells. Leia's idea could be our last chance, and if it doesn't work, then we have no other option but for Gavin to agree to a duel."

"Fine, let's say that we don't succeed, and Gavin has to duel him," I say through gritted teeth, forcing myself to talk through that possibility. "Let's say he wins, which means that Felix dies. What assurance will we have that his wild wolves won't kill Lily?"

"None that would be foolproof," my father replies, his face crumpling when my mother's sobs echo through the room.

"Or let's say that Gavin dies," I continue, my voice breaking at the last part. No one has figured out our bond yet, and even though it's something to celebrate, we agreed to postpone it until after we find my sister. "That means that Felix would ascend to his position as my fiancé and future husband. What will keep him from hurting any of us then?"

"Nothing," my father replies and shakes his head.

"I think that we all agree that Prince Felix shouldn't get anywhere near the throne," Duke Green says. When we all nod, he continues, "Therefore, I suggest that if we don't find Her Royal Highness Princess Lily before the full moon, we do nothing."

"What?!" my brother and I exclaim in unison.

"Are you suggesting we let her die?" I demand, narrowing my eyes at the duke.

"I'm sorry to say this, Your Highness, but if we have to choose between keeping the whole monarchy intact and safe, or saving Princess Lily's life, then I think we should pick the monarchy," Duke Green blatantly replies, unashamed by his answer.

"Thank you for your honest answer, Duke," I say with a low, cold voice. "I'll make sure that as soon as I ascend to the throne, you'll be one of the first people I release from duty."

"You can't do that!" the duke exclaims, his face eyes wide with shock.

"I can and most certainly will!" I snap back, not caring that my behavior is less than regal and not even close to what a princess should be like. "I want my royal advisors to keep my family and people close to me safe. I want them to do whatever they can for the good of our people. I want them to do better than what you're doing right now, which is basically shutting down any idea I have without providing any of yours in return. As far as I can tell, you're fucking useless!"

"Leia!" my father exclaims, raising his voice when I finally cross the line that shouldn't be walked over no matter how dire the circumstances.

"This is pointless," I say, looking at him and for once in my life, refusing to apologize for my beliefs, especially not to the old fuck who just suggested that we sacrifice my sister. "I need to get some air."

Without waiting to be dismissed, I turn on my heel and leave the conference room.

They're lucky that you're not freezing their asses, my wolf tries to console me.

Levi and my mother are the only ones who look at me with a hint of gratefulness in their eyes. None of them want to even think about sacrificing Lily. I hate that my father's even considering it, but some part of me understands that as a reigning monarch, he needs to weigh all the possibilities. It's what makes the job such a nightmare. We need to make decisions that no one else wants to.

Heavy is the head that wears the crown, my wolf quotes something that we read a long time ago.

We should see if Gavin's back, I tell her, desperately needing to see him. He's the only bright spot in this darkness, which is ironic because he's literally the Prince of Darkness while Felix is the one that wields fire.

My wolf in me picks up Gavin's scent when we get closer to our chambers. It's all it takes for me to pick up the pace and get to the room where I can throw myself in his arms. I need him to make me feel safe and protected, even if only for a moment.

He's here! my wolf exclaims, urging me to go faster then howls in excitement and anticipation as we run up the stairs.

I get to the door and nearly fall over because Gavin opens it at the same time that I reach for the handle. His eyes don't show any surprises, confirming that he felt me too. It's one of the advantages of the bond between us. We don't know much about it or the other things we can do because it was never really documented. The rare soulmates that found each other preferred to spend their time together as opposed to being studied like some lab rats. This just means that we'll have to figure it out as we go.

"I missed you," Gavin tells me, wrapping his arms around me.

I press my cheek against his chest and inhale his manly scent mixed with some expensive cologne that I haven't bothered to name yet. His body heat is enough to melt away my terrifying fears.

"It was horrible," I cry into his chest when he closes the door behind us. "They were talking about letting Lily die."

"What?!" Gavin exclaims and pulls away enough to look me in the eyes as if to check whether or not I'm joking.

"It was Duke Green," I say in between sobs. I've been trying to stay strong for so long, holding up a pretense of being as cold as the future Ice Queen should be. It didn't always work well because my emotions still seep through the cracks, especially towards the end.

"I've always fucking hated royal advisors. They're so full of themselves, pretending that they're doing what's best for us and the kingdom. When in reality they're just desperate to keep their little velvet chairs inside the manor," Gavin mutters, then caresses my cheek. "Don't worry, Princess. They aren't in the position to make decisions."

"That's not the worst part," I cry. "My father is actually considering their words. He is actively thinking about letting Felix kill Lily."

"Listen to me," Gavin says, applying slight pressure under my chin until I look him in the eyes. "It's your father's duty to take in everything that's happening around us. He doesn't have the privilege to shut it all out and follow his heart. Not like you and I still do. You know that once we ascend, we're going to have to look at the bigger picture too. But that time's not here yet, so our job is to do everything in our power to convince your father not to give up on your sister."

"They should've put a reward out on Felix's head when they tried to kill us by burning the grand salon down," I mutter, unable to comprehend that nothing's been done about it. "I can't believe I've never inquired about the matter. My father's right. I have been living in my own little world, trying to help humans when in reality, it's my own people that need just as much help if not even more."

"The world is a cruel and unfair place, Princess," Gavin agrees, tucking a stray curl behind my ear. "We need to take it one day at a time and do the best we can."

"Says the big bad wolf," I joke, his ability to make me feel better already working.

Gavin raises his brows and smiles. "I have no idea what you're talking about."

"Liar," I tease and poke him with my index finger. "I've heard about your new reputation long before the engagement dinner."

"Oh?" Gavin asks, giving me an amused look. "Care to elaborate?"

With the mood slightly lifted, we move to the sofa and sit down. Gavin opens an expensive-looking bottle of wine and fills up two glasses. It's the perfect way to finish the day while we update each other on our adventures, no matter how miserable they've been. If we don't slow down and take a moment for ourselves, we won't be of any use to anyone.

"There was a rumor that you took on a battalion of witches by yourself," I say, carefully studying his face for any changes in his expression.

"It wasn't a battalion," he replies with a small chuckle, then shakes his head, growing serious. "It was a married couple. A man and a wife. They've made it their career to hunt down wolves. They were good at it too, but their luck changed once I got a sniff of them."

"There was also a rumor that you organized a coup, overthrowing your own commander and seizing the power for yourself," I continue, sensing that he doesn't want to say more about the witches.

"Why am I not surprised that they didn't release the whole story?" Gavin muses with a roll of his eyes as he shakes his head. "The commander was a drug addict and an alcoholic. The only reason why he kept his position for so long was because his father was a high-ranking officer too. A general, I think. Once I joined the team, I quickly realized how things worked, but I kept my head down, determined to earn my way to the top through my own hard work. When his drunken decisions got one of my good friends killed, I couldn't take it anymore and went feral on him, letting my wolf off the leash."

"What happened then?" I ask, never having heard this part of the story.

"The other wolves chose me as their leader, and once I had them on my side, no one could touch me," Gavin replies with a nonchalant shrug. "If I had acted alone and without their support, the punishment would be death, and it wouldn't matter that I'm a king's son. But because I had so many wolves vouching for me and insisting that they'd abandon their military duties if anything were to happen to me, the leadership had no other choice but to assign me as the new commander."

"They could've killed you!" I exclaim, unable to suppress the look of horror on my face.

"It was a risk I had to take in order to save a lot of good wolves," he replies in a tone that makes it clear he's not regretting a thing. "I have a reputation of being ruthless and for a good reason too, but that doesn't mean I'm not fair. I'll fight for what I believe in, no matter the consequences."

"That explains it," I say, nodding to myself.

"Explains what?" he asks, his brows furrowing.

"Why you're respected by half of the wolves and feared by the other," I say with a small smile. "In a relatively short amount of time, you've made yourself a lot of enemies."

"That human Churchill made a good point when he said that if you don't have enemies, you haven't stood up for something in your life," Gavin says, then sighs. "There are a lot of things I'd like to change, but proper progress takes a long time."

"And you're way too impatient for that," I tease.

"Definitely," he agrees. "But at least now I'll be in a position to make things better, to balance the unfairness and open our kingdom to the wolves that don't belong anywhere. I learned a long time ago that if you help people when they're at their lowest, they'll feel forever indebted to you. The loyalty of that kind is unmeasured."

"Why would you need that? Is it about power?" I ask, not quite understanding whether he wants to help them or rule them.

"It's a bit about everything," he replies honestly, giving me a peek into what will happen once we get married. "There will always be people in power, and I'll make damn sure that it's us. There will always be people looking to overthrow us, which is why we need to surround ourselves with wolves that we can trust with our lives.

Only when we're not fearing for our lives every step of the way can we make changes."

"What kind of changes are you talking about?" I ask, trying to get a clearer view of the reforms he's thinking of making.

"Let's take my brother, Garren, for example. He's fucking around, leaving young pups in the bellies of both our species as well as humankind. Those pups will be abandoned and rejected as if we're still in medieval times. James was one of those, and he'd still be on the streets if I hadn't found him," Gavin says, his voice raising as he grows more passionate about the topic. "The fathers of those pups need to be punished, not the wolves. They can be tracked down, relieved of their positions, and forced to pay for abandoning their kids to a fate worse than being a proper orphan."

"Those laws are quite outdated, aren't they?" I agree, finding it quite difficult to think about it, much less talk, but it's clear that Gavin's spent a lot of time thinking about it.

"It would be one of the first things I'd like to change, but we'd face a lot of pushback because the majority of those so-called fathers are wolves in positions of power," he tells me. "We'd take our time tearing them down. First, we'd need to take care of the abandoned young pups."

I nod in agreement, then ask, "What did you have in mind?"

"An orphanage of sorts, kind of like the Academy," Gavin replies without missing a beat. He really did spend a lot of time thinking about it. "The Academy would never accept bastard pups, but we can create a safe space for them and bring the best teachers to guide them through the shifts as well as make them comfortable with their abilities."

"That's not all, is it?" I ask, doubting that Gavin would do that out of the goodness of his heart.

"No," he admits, giving me a small, almost shy smile. "Once they reach a certain age, they'd be given a choice of their careers, which would mostly be military oriented, although it would really depend on what the kingdom needed at the time. Their options would heavily depend on their ability. Do you want to know the best part about t his?"

I narrow my eyes at him, not sure if that counts as enslavement or not, but I suppose in many ways we'd still be saving their lives, so I let myself indulge him a moment longer. It's something I'm going to have to give a lot of thought to in the future.

"The best part is that the kingdoms all over the world are desperate to get rid of bastard pups. We can actually take them in from all over the world, which yeah, at the beginning would cost us a lot of money, but in time, we'd grow as the strongest kingdom with the highest number of soldiers," Gavin continues, his smile turning feral. "If the other kingdoms don't agree with the changes that come with a new world order, we could push them into submission. We could rule them all."

I love it! my wolf exclaims, clearly as ambitious as our soulmate, but I'm not so sure I'm entirely agreeing with that crazy plan of his.

"Let's first focus on getting my sister back, and we'll think about changing the world once we're actually on the throne," I say, not wanting to get into it now, but I do make a mental note to be present at every meeting to make sure to freeze his darkness before it takes us all. Deep down, Gavin has a good heart, but the lack of patience is what would push him into violence.

"You're right," he says, giving me an apologetic look. "I'm sorry, this isn't something we should even be talking about now."

"I'm glad we are," I tell him quickly, not wanting him to feel bad for opening up to me. "But speaking of Lily, what are we going to do?"

Gavin lets out a heavy, defeated sigh and leans back into the sofa. He shakes his head as he says in resignation, "I guess I'm going to have to go pay my family a visit."

CHAPTER 17

GAVIN

I didn't think I'd be back here so soon after I finally got a way out. My family won't be openly helpful or even kind, especially not after Lucas kicked them out of the Lafayette Manor. It's no secret that my father and my brothers hate me. My mother is my only ally here, but I won't do anything to make her choose sides. I'm the one who can leave whenever I want, while she needs to stay and live with those monsters long after I'm gone.

"Stop right there," a woman's voice orders when I enter the manor.

I turn toward her, taking in the familiar claw scar across her face. She seems a lot meaner than before.

"Tiana," I say in a way of greeting. "Fancy seeing you here. I heard you've been warming my brother's bed lately."

"What's between Garren and I is no concern of yours, Gavin," she replies sharply.

"*Prince* Gavin," I correct her. "I might not be a part of the Grey family anymore, but I'm still a prince. I'm still above you, now even more than ever, and I'm not referring to the fact that I'll be the king one day. I'm talking about how low you've fallen, spreading your legs for that disgusting leech."

"You left us," she says through gritted teeth, narrowing her eyes in accusation. "You were our Alpha, and you left. You abandoned your pack. You have no right to insult me when what you did is so much worse."

I nod my head left and right as if balancing our actions, then scoff. "Nope, yours definitely takes the cake. I mean, Garren? Really?"

I make a mock-vomit sound, then laugh in her face, enjoying watching it turn the darkest shade of red. Her breathing turns heavier as she struggles to keep control over her wolf.

"Come out to play, Tiana," I say with a teasing tone. "I'm sure we're both eager to finish our last fight. I can promise you that while I'll make it quick, it won't be any less painful."

"I can't believe we ever respected you. I'm disgusted with myself for ever following you," she says through gritted teeth, spit flying out as she struggles to take deep breaths.

"You never respected me. You feared me, which is a lot more effective," I tell her, lifting my chin ever so slightly, even though I tower over her, but it gives it the extra insulting effect when I look down on her. "Garren doesn't even have that. He will never have anything. Since the moment that I stopped being a Grey, this family's reputation has plummeted. It's only a matter of time before their fall from grace will be publicly confirmed, but I promise you that when it happens, I'll be the first in line to claim what should've been mine to begin with."

"That will never happen," she insists, her hands clenched into fists, her knuckles turning white.

"You and I were sort of friends once, so for the sake of those old times, I'll give you a piece of advice," I say and lean forward, although not without making sure that my shields are in place. "Find another backup plan because this one won't work."

Tiana's eyes turn darker, a slight hint of her channeling her power. Before she can openly challenge me, attacking a foreign prince and breaking the protection law, Graham enters the manor. Tiana recoils, her eyes wide as she realizes what she almost did.

I smirk and wink, then turn to my brother, refusing to give Tiana another moment of my time. As far as I'm concerned, she's dead.

We should've killed her when we had the chance, my wolf growls, proving that we're both more hurt by her betrayal than we're willing to admit. *We should've snuffed her wolf out, leaving her alive and forever alone, feeling the emptiness.*

"Everything okay here?" Graham asks, his eyes darting from me to Tiana and then back at me.

"All good, brother," I tell him and lift up my hand, shaking his while we awkwardly embrace each other.

"Leave us," Graham orders Tiana without taking his eyes off me, making it clear that even though she's sleeping with Garren, she's still no one. Once Tiana's gone, Graham seems to relax and even gives me a smile. "It's nice to see you, Brother."

What is he playing at? my wolf asks, suspiciously sniffing at Graham's kind reception.

"You too," I say, deciding to play along. I'm going to need his help after all. "How's everything?"

"Honestly?" Graham asks and when I nod, he sighs. "I didn't know it was possible, but ever since you left, things around here have been insufferable. Father's always angry, Garren's more or less ascended to the throne and he's taken over most of the duties, and Grayden turned into Garren two point oh. Not as bad as the original, but well on his way."

That sounds bad, my wolf comments, and I have to agree, reminding me once again how glad I am to not be a part of this family anymore.

"What about you?" I ask, wondering what he's been up to.

Graham looks around as if to make sure that we can't be overheard. When he's satisfied that we're alone, he leans forward and lowers his voice, "I've been working with some people on a computer program that could turn out to be really big."

"Are you serious?" I ask, raising my brows in surprise. "Why didn't you ever mention it to me before?"

"Because you've been under Father's influence and would do anything to get on his good side," Graham replies as a matter of fact.

He's not wrong, my wolf agrees with my brother. *You'd do anything to get a chance at a throne.*

"I'm sorry," I tell him, realizing how bad of a brother I've been. He shakes his head, both dismissing and accepting my apology at the same time. "Will you tell me more about it?"

"One day," he promises. "I'm guessing that there's something a lot more pressing to deal with, otherwise you wouldn't grace us with your presence."

Damn, you really suck. Big time, my wolf scoffs.

I put a hand on Graham's shoulder. He might be one year older than me, but in so many ways, he's a lot younger than me, lacking real-world experience that can't be taught through a computer screen.

"When all this is over, I want you to come over to the Lafayette Manor, so we can talk without interruption while emptying a strong bottle of scotch," I tell him and smile when he nods. "Can you take me to see Father?"

"They're in the throne room," Graham informs me. Then he lowers his tone in warning, "As I've said before, things are a lot different than they were before you left. Be careful what you say and how you say it. Garren's reign of tyranny has already started."

"Thanks for the heads up," I say, appreciating it more than the words could tell. It's nice to know that I have more than one ally between the cold dark walls of Grey Manor. When things settle down a bit, I'd love to have a proper chat with Graham to learn what he's been up to and hear the story of what's been happening with the Shadow Pack.

"Wait here," Graham tells me, stopping me in front of the entrance to the throne room.

Even though it annoys me because those are the very same doors I've walked through thousands of times, I understand that we have different roles now, so I give him a small nod in confirmation. My eyes stay on him as he goes in to inform our father of my arrival.

It takes longer than I would've liked before they call me in. In any other circumstance, I would've turned on my heel, showing them exactly how I feel about being disrespected like that. But this isn't my home anymore, and I'm not the Dark Prince of this manor.

"Well, well, well. Look what the cat dragged in," Garren sneers when I walk up to the throne. He's occupying our father's usual place, which means that the ascension has progressed more than I expected. It's bad news for me because now I'm not going to be appealing to my father, but to my brother instead.

"The prodigal son returns." Father smirks, leaning against the side of the throne.

While Grayden is right up there with them with the exact same sneer on his face, my mother stays on the sidelines with Graham, looking at me with warm and loving eyes.

"Thank you for taking the time to hear me out," I say as a way of greeting, unsure of who to address first.

"Of course, little brother," Garren says with a cruel smile. "I'd never miss out on an opportunity to hear you beg."

You should force a thick tentacle of shadow down their throats until they choke on it and when their vision blurs, you should squeeze harder until the light in their eyes shuts down, my wolf says with a low growl, going into way too much detail.

It's clear that my brother won't offer me a seat and instead will leave me standing in front of the throne as I ask for assistance. Knowing that I have no other choice but to swallow my pride, I take a deep breath and ignore my wolf's complaints.

"Before I tell you what I came here to ask you, I'm going to quickly summarize some things that happened, so you'll be better informed when making a decision," I say, hoping that I sound more helpful than arrogant.

"Go on," Garren says.

Even though the insufferable smirk is still plastered on his face, I'm taking it as a win that he's allowing me to continue.

"I'm sure that you've heard about the incident that happened during the engagement dinner where Princess Leia chose me as her future king," I say, then pause to let them fill in the gaps.

"If you're talking about our cousin trying to light up your sorry ass, then yeah, I've heard all about it," Garren confirms with a chuckle.

My body tenses when he calls Felix our cousin. I don't want anything to do with that wolf killer. He's bringing even more shame to both of our families than Garren's fucking around ever could.

"Suffice it to say that he's a sore loser," I continue, pushing past the anger that's starting to build inside me. "I suppose it's also safe to assume that you've heard about the attacks in the suburban communities of wolves?"

"Yes, we did," Garren says, his previously amused expression now changing into one of boredom. "Where are you going with this? Just get to the point because I don't have all day. There's a certain shadow Alpha in my bed waiting for me."

"I personally visited the crime scene and came to the conclusion that the attack was perpetrated by wolves," I say, then pause, waiting for them to react in surprise, but they don't. They've already had this information, and I'm not sure whether or not this works to my advantage. Either way, I continue before I lose whatever little attention my brother's giving me, "Soon after, the Academy was also attacked."

"Yes, yes, we know all that," Garren says, his voice heavy with boredom. "The beautiful twin was taken before I could introduce her to the Claw, and now she's in the hands of the big bad fire wolf, waiting for you to save her before the full moon."

I bite the insides of my cheeks, the sudden pain the only way to keep me from gawking in surprise. Garren's better informed than I expected. I've been hoping to play upon the new information, gently guiding him toward the correct decision, which would turn out to be what I needed him to do. But since he already knew everything beforehand, it's safe to assume that he's had plenty of time to talk it through with our father and the royal advisors. Either they decided not to help at all, or they're waiting for me to beg them for it.

Don't you dare, my wolf warns me. Neither one of us wants to humiliate ourselves in front of this backstabbing pack of vultures.

"What exactly is it that you need, boy?" my father asks, putting a mocking emphasis on the last word.

Careful, my wolf warns with a low, guttural growl.

"We're trying to track down Felix," I tell him, confirming what he already knew. "Time's running out, and we need help."

"You're going to have to be clearer than that," my father tells me, the corners of his lips lifted up into the smallest of smiles. "What exactly do you want us to do?"

"Don't forget to say please," Garren adds with a low snicker that's being echoed by Grayden.

Let me have a go at them, my wolf snarls.

"I was hoping that you'll be able to tell me if Felix was spotted in our...your kingdom," I say, catching my mistake at the right time. "Without your permission, we can't start an open search for him and cross the borders when we locate him. I need you to grant me all that and maybe even aid us by adding a couple of boots on the ground."

"You're forgetting something," Garren reminds me as soon as I finish.

I clench my jaw so hard that I'm afraid it might break. With a deep breath, I calm myself enough to force out that one word that my brother wants to hear. "Please."

Garren's smile widens, his eyes shining with insanity. There's something very wrong with him, and I really hope that Father realizes it before it's too late. While I'm not on the best terms with my family, I also don't want to see them hurt.

"I heard your request, and I will consider it," Garren says, and I let out a relieved breath, offering my brother a small smile.

"Thank you, Garren," I tell him, grateful that he's a bigger person than I ever gave him credit to be. "I really appreciate it."

"Not so fast, little brother," Garren says, his words having an immediate effect on me as they efficiently wipe the smile off my face. "I want you to lower yourself on both of your knees and bow down until your forehead touches the floor."

Let me out! my wolf howls. *I'm going to murder him!*

I swallow my anger and ignore my wolf's pleas to be unleashed. Garren's smirk is mirrored on our father and Grayden's faces. I don't need to look in my mother's direction to know that she and Graham are just as appalled by Garren as I am.

I lift my chin higher in defiance and give him a ghost of a smile as I cock one of my brows, then channel just enough power from within to turn my eyes into an impenetrable black color, making it clear to everyone that out of all of us, I'm the most powerful wolf in the throne room. While they're also wielders of the darkness, none of them has a sliver of experience that I do. Not even my father. If I wanted to, I could've had them on their knees in front of me, begging me for mercy. They wouldn't even have the time to call for help, much less wait for the reinforcements to arrive.

"If you think that I'd ever stoop so low as to bow to your whoring ass, you're sorely mistaken, Brother," I say with a cold and emotionless voice. "Enjoy playing with your kingdom, but keep in mind that every successful monarch needs friends. You've just burned the strongest bridge that you could've had. In fact, I'd strongly advise you to sleep with one eye open and watch your back at all times, because when you least expect it, I'll come back and claim what should've been mine in the first place. I'll make you regret not helping me. I'll destroy you and leave you out on the street like all the young pups you've fathered throughout the years."

"How dare you?!" Garren exclaims, jumping to his feet, the shadow dancing around him as he clenches his fists. They're not nearly as dark as mine, the years of alcohol and drug abuse further weakening him.

"I dare because it's true," I calmly reply, never taking my eyes off him. "If the throne had been handed to the strongest member of the family, you wouldn't even stand a chance of ever being king. Grayden has more power in his little finger than you have in your whole fucking body. Do you even remember how to shift?"

"Guards!" Garren calls, clearly done with taking my crap.

Predictably, Tiana's the first one to walk through the door, the rest of my old pack of Shadows close on her heels. I give them a mocking smile and shake my head.

"I can't believe how low you've all fallen," I say, talking to the whole pack. "Since when are you glorified guards? Since Tiana started fucking your future king? You're better than this. I trained you to be better than this. You belong out there, protecting our own on the streets, in the frontlines, killing witches. You're nobody's butler."

"This is your one and only chance to leave on your own two feet," my father says, speaking with the authority of a king. "From here on out, you're not welcome here anymore. You're lucky that we won't punish you for your threats and insults. You better crawl back into your hole and high up the Lafayette's ass."

"Are you jealous that I'm not up your ass anymore, Father?" I snap, momentarily locking my eyes with him.

I lift my arms as if in mock-surrender and do a little turn, making sure to meet everyone's eyes as I pass them. "The only reason why you've so politely offered for me to leave of my own volition is because you know that I'm able to take down every single wolf in this throne room."

"Don't push it, boy," my father growls, but doesn't acknowledge what I said.

"Don't worry," I tell him with a sneer. "I can see now that there's nothing worth fighting for here. I couldn't have chosen a better time to jump ship because Garren isn't a king that I'd ever be able to respect, much less blindly follow. I'm too disgusted by his weaknesses and the eagerness to stick his cock into any hole, no matter how full of disease it is."

Not waiting for anyone's reply, I turn on my heel and walk past the Shadow Pack, roughly crashing my shoulder against Tiana as I pass her. I wish things would've gone differently. I wish my old family and my new one could work together as a team. I wish Garren wouldn't be such an asshole and would help us find Lily. Most importantly, I wish I didn't need to leave my mother and Graham behind.

CHAPTER 18

LEIA

Tomorrow's the full moon. Time's up. We've lost.

We've gotten a lot of pictures with possible sightings of Felix, but after tracking them down, none of them turned out to be a solid lead. None of the other royal families wanted to have anything to do with this, ignoring our pleas for help as they preferred to stay neutral.

My mother hasn't left the room in days and even refused to eat. Levi's not much better, but while our mother's starving herself, he went down another path and is drowning himself in alcohol.

"I really think we should consider it or at least talk about it without you shutting it down and rushing out of the room," Gavin says as he walks up behind me and wraps his arms around me, gently pulling me towards him until my back's pressed against his chest.

His towering height allows him to rest his chin on the top of my head as he meets my eyes in the mirror. The bags under his eyes are twins to mine, neither of us have been able to get more than two hours of sleep per night.

"I can't," I tell him, my voice breaking. "I can't talk about the possibility of you dueling Felix. I can't talk about what will happen if you die, and I can't talk about Lily dying."

"But we have to," he urges softly but firmly. "The full moon is tomorrow, which means that the possibility of me dueling Felix is more real than ever. We need to talk and make a decision. Together."

He needs you, my wolf tells me. She's better at reading the subtext of what's not being said.

With a heavy sigh, I nod and turn to Gavin. He takes my hand into his and guides us to the sofa. I put my legs up and wrap my arms around my knees, pressing them close to my chest and making myself as small as possible.

"I don't want you to take what I'm about to say personally," Gavin starts and while his voice is serious, his eyes are soft and sad. "Time's up, and we need to talk about our next steps without ignoring the gravity of our situation."

"Okay," I say, trying to pull myself together because he's right.

"I think that by now we all know that we won't find Lily," Gavin says with a sigh. "Our only chance to save her is for me to accept Felix's challenge and meet him in a duel."

"We can't know for sure that he'll respect his promises," I argue a point that we've been through hundreds of times in the last two weeks.

"That's true, but what we do know for sure is that if I don't fight him, Lily's dead," he replies, making his case so much stronger with the certain outcome of my sister's death.

"Okay, but what if he wins?" I ask, my voice rising an octave higher as the fear sinks its claws into me. "What will happen to me when you're gone? We're soulmates, Gavin. Without you, I'm as good as dead. If you and your wolf die, my wolf dies of heartbreak, which means that soon after, I'm also dead. Is that really our best option? Our only option?"

"No, it's not," Gavin says, locking his eyes on mine. "Our best and only option is me winning. Let's face it,

Princess, we both know that I'm the clear favorite to win this battle. Why are we even discussing this?"

"Because we don't know Felix's reasons for challenging you," I insist. "What if he has some plan that we don't know about? What if he's actually an incredibly skilled fighter and a hardcore fire wielder? What is he's some type of a super wolf that's been laying low this whole time, waiting for the best opportunity to strike and take over the world?"

"I think you're overreacting and that your imagination is running a little wild," Gavin says with a small smile. "On the firepower, Felix falls on a scale of being a slightly above average wielder. As far as fighting's concerned, he never got real-life experience, and trust me when I say, that the skills you learn in the gym are nothing compared to what you face out there."

"Do you really think so?" I ask, a wave of hope washing over me.

"I do," Gavin confirms. "We've done some research, and we haven't found any anomalies in relation to the Fire Prince."

"Then why would he challenge you?" I ask, my brows furrowing in confusion when I can't find the answer to the one question that eludes me and would explain it all.

"Because, while he has nothing to lose, he has absolutely everything to gain," Gavin replies with a nonchalant shrug. It's clear that he's also given this a lot of thought. "He's ambitious, which I can respect. He'll never get his family throne, which means he has to shop around for one. That's where you come in, and that's why he needs to get rid of me. The problem is that if he gets rid of me by hiring an assassin or something, he has no assurances that you'll pick him as your future husband."

"If that's true," I allow, running along with his idea, "wouldn't it be better for him to get rid of you through a proxy and then challenge my next pick who wouldn't be half as strong and formidable as you are?"

"It would, but blind ambition and greed make us do crazy things," Gavin replies. "It may not seem that way, but this actually works to our advantage. When Felix is dead, we'll have definite proof of the atrocities he committed and strong leverage on some royal families that might've helped him. You know what they say, what doesn't kill you makes you stronger."

"You're such a dork," I say, but his words do help me relax a bit and even bring a smile to my face.

"There she is," Gavin says, gently putting his hand on my cheek. "You've no idea just how beautiful you are, do you? And when you smile...Man, I'm addicted to that little spark in your eyes. You have it all, Leia. Inside and out, to me and for me, you're perfect."

I push myself upward and into his arms, closing the distance between us. As I wrap my arms around his neck and lean my forehead against his, I inhale, taking in his scent and burning it into my memory.

"Can you promise me something?" I whisper, our faces so close that our hot breaths mix.

"Anything," he replies with just as low of a voice.

"Promise me that when you fight Felix, you'll give it your best. Promise me that you'll do everything to win. Promise me that you'll come back to me and never leave me," I say, the words coming out in one quick burst.

"I promise," he breathes, giving me all the assurance that I need.

Not wanting to lose any more time that we might not have, I press my lips against his. The kiss starts as gentle and sweet at first, but the underlying sense of what's to come and the very possible chance of us dying, quickly urges us to breathe each other in with desperation and passion like no other.

Next thing I know, we're tearing our clothes off each other, wanting to feel each other's skin without any pieces of fabric between us. While this time I'm more careful with Gavin's shirt and pants, he doesn't show any restraint and even shifts his nails into claws, literally cutting me out of the dress.

His erection is already hard and ready, eager to fill up my pussy that's just as open and needy for him. With our mouths locked in a passionate kiss and our arms wrapped around one another in an embrace, Gavin somehow still manages to get us to bed.

When he sets me down, he also shifts me around so I'm lying on my belly. He grabs one pillow to support my hips and the other to put under my head. His face is contorted with lust and his eyes shining with desire. I must look the same because I feel the same.

His strong hands grab each of my ankles, forcing my legs apart. This is the opposite of how we did it before. Our pure animalistic instincts are coming through and taking over us. We both want this, our wolves want this. The gentleness is replaced with roughness as the fire within us burns brighter, the unsatisfied itch, aching to be scratched in a way that only a soulmate can. The bond between us amazingly intensifies all the little sensations and feelings, making us a better team outside, and inside, the bedroom.

Gavin doesn't hesitate and goes right ahead, sliding his fingers straight into my wet and eager pussy, smearing my juices all the way up to my ass. I push hard against his hand, softly moaning as his finger slips in and out of my pussy. He eases another finger inside me and works his hand to the rhythm of me pumping against him. My breathing's turning shorter and louder, my cries of pleasure matching our rhythm.

Gavin moves one hand onto my hip and lifts me up on my knees. I bury my face further into the pillow, letting it swallow my moans. I blindly reach behind me, searching for his fully erect cock. When my fingers find it, I play with his member, stroking him up and down before I guide him to my lower lips. I slide it up and down inside the walls of my wet and warm pussy, touching lightly the entrance of the hole.

"Fuck me," I growl with a wolfish authority, giving him a clear and direct order.

A surprised chuckle escapes Gavin, the low sound full of delight. Gently but firmly, he pushes his cock into my tight hole, coaxing out a small gasp from me. He slowly eases himself back out, and then in again, each time burying his shaft further inside me.

I move my fingers to my clit, rubbing them around the swollen bud. With my firm grip around the sensitive bud and his cock securely wedged into my pussy, we began to rhythmically thrust and fuck back and forth against each other.

The noise that comes out of us is one of pure animalistic pleasure. The skin-on-skin contact of our sticky, sweaty bodies smacking against each other, our loud moans and guttural groans further adding to our sexy melody. Cries of pleasure and need replace the heavy tension in the air.

Soon, my moans grow more lustful, my need for him only getting bigger and more insatiable. Giving him my all meant losing some part of the control that I had. With a moan that turns into a growl, I put my hands up on each side of my head and bury my fingers into the sheets only to accidentally tear them apart with my claws.

"Fuck me," I growl, sounding half human, half wolf. "Faster. Harder. Deeper. Fuck me!"

Tightening his grip on my waist, Gavin tips his head back and roars with the force of a pureblooded Alpha. By giving into our wolf sides, the enhancements came out, and soon enough, he's pumping his cock into me deeper, faster, and much, much harder. His balls clap against my ass cheeks every time he buries his shaft to the hilt into me, hitting that exact spot that makes my eyes roll back.

Wanting to give him the semblance of what he's giving me, I meet his pumps with thrusts of my own. It only takes a couple of mismatched attempts before we move in a perfectly synchronized rhythm, our naked bodies drenched with sweat.

Gavin moves his hands onto my shoulders and pulls me into him, ramming his throbbing hard cock into me deeper than ever before. I cry out again and again, feeling the familiar burning starting at the bottom part of my belly and moving lower with so much force that I'm sure I'm going to explode.

Unable to hold it back even a moment longer, I go rigid against his thrusting, giving him the only warning before my whole body starts convulsing in a fit of shudders. My pussy sucks onto his cock, the muscles clenching hard around his shaft. He doesn't stop fucking me, the movement of his cock inside me, rubbing against my sensitive parts, bringing me even more pleasure as I jump off the edge and into my favorite abyss. I bury my fangs into the pillow, unsure of when my teeth shifted, suppressing my scream of pleasure as much as I can, not wanting anyone to interrupt my soulmate from giving me my much-needed release.

The muscles of my pussy throb and pulsate, gripping his cock harder than ever before. It's like my pussy is a clenching fist. Gavin keeps on fucking and thrusting into me as hard as he can, his balls smacking against my ass. With every pump, he brings me a new wave of orgasm, making me climax like never before.

As I feel his cock slipping in and out, his balls slapping up hard against me, his member starts throbbing and pulsating inside me. With a guttural groan, he lets me know that he's getting close.

Making sure that my claws have shifted back to normal nails, I reach back to grab a hold of his cock, squeezing his balls and pull at them as he further swells under my touch. With a roar, Gavin thrusts his hips forward in rough motion, burying the whole length of his shaft up to his hilt into my pussy and shooting up his load deep, deep inside me.

With each remaining thrust and pump, he shoots a hot and sticky load into my pussy, filling it up so much that the excess begins overflowing out of it. As it mixes with my own juices, they coat the length of his cock, which he uses as lube to keep pushing himself inside me, returning the juices back to where they belong.

It seems as though it would never end, but eventually, it does. With my pussy pleasantly aching and his empty cock now softly resting inside me in satisfaction, we collapse on the bed in exhaustion.

This was a special moment caught in time that neither one of us will forget. Breathing hard from the best fuck we've ever had, we lay in each other's arms, surrounded by drenched and torn-up sheets. The smell of sex fills the air, flowing from our every pore.

We rest in comfortable silence until Gavin shifts beneath me, lighting up the lustful spark, demanding round two. Our bodies instantly respond to each other and we are soon locked in a tight embrace, our lips tied up in a passionate rhythm as our tongues dance around to the choreography that only we know.

I push him onto his back and climb on top of him to straddle him. Without breaking the kiss, I reach down for his cock to guide him to my pussy.

Let's go for a fucking ride! my wolf howls just as I sit on Gavin's cock and the knock on the door interrupts our second bout of passionate fucking.

"What is it?" I growl, sounding a bit breathless. I don't bother suppressing my annoyance. The slightest bit of focus that I managed to gather is fully concentrated on getting the intruder away as quickly as possible.

"A letter has arrived for His Royal Highness Prince Gavin," the servant says.

"Leave it at the door," I snap back, well-aware of Gavin's cock buried deep inside me. With every word that I say, my body moves slightly, my hips gently rolling back and forth, Gavin's cock further massaging my sensitive spots.

"I'm afraid it's important," the servant says a bit timidly. "It has the fire crest of the Farrell's on it."

"That piece of shit just gave me another reason for wanting him dead," I mutter under my breath as I climb off Gavin's cock.

The absence of his member in my pussy is achingly obvious, every part of me wishing we could continue right where we left off, but our little break has come to an end as reality came knocking on our door.

"Slip it under the door," I call to the servant, eager to see the contents of the letter while, at the same time, not having the patience to find an appropriate outfit to throw on to open the door.

The servant does as I've asked, then finally leaves us alone, her steps echoing down the long corridor. Gavin's already on his feet, his cock safely confined behind the luxurious fabric of his black boxers. He crosses the distance to the door, his muscles flexing as he picks up the letter.

"What is it?" I ask, studying his face while he reads the letter. Apart from the slight crease on his forehead, his expression doesn't betray anything.

"It's an official challenge to a duel," Gavin replies when he finally looks away from the letter. "What should we do, Princess?"

He's not asking me because he wouldn't know what to do, but because he wants to give me the option of choosing. By asking me about our next step, he's showing me the respect that comes with my higher rank.

"We'll call a press conference where we'll reveal the contents of the letter, expose Felix's crimes to the general public of wolves, and then you'll accept the challenge, vowing in front of everyone to bring the criminal to justice," I reply, the confidence in us growing with every word.

"Sounds like a good plan," Gavin says, the corners of his lips curling up into a small smile. "Don't worry, Princess. I have every intention of finishing up what we've started."

A strong wave of heat spreads over my body and while it leaves my bottom part soaked, my face turns a dark shade of red that doesn't complement my pale skin at all.

I seriously need to cool down before we step in front of the cameras. Good thing that I'm the ice wielder because I doubt that a cold shower would be of much help. Not when Gavin's always around, his cock within reach and always ready to do my bidding.

"Fuck," I mutter under my breath and return to the closet to look for the outfit that will make me shine on camera.

Garner public sympathy by telling the truth, my wolf tells me, and I nod in agreement, glad that she's finally helping. Of course, I reacted to fast because my wolf adds, *The fuck-fest comes later. I'm down to pump that marathon until his stick bends.*

CHAPTER 19

GAVIN

"When are they coming?" I ask Lafayette's royal advisors as I pace up and down the conference room.

"We're not sure, Your Highness," Duke Green replies, still salty about the fact that Leia and I have decided to go ahead with the duel.

It's the full moon tonight," I comment, trying to remind myself that we're all being extra on edge because of its subtle but strong influences. "He should be here already."

"Our channels are playing your press conference on repeat," Lucas says, sitting next to a just as impatient Leia. "It's impossible that he doesn't know you've accepted the duel. He'll be here."

"Remember not to touch him when he comes," I remind them, knowing just how much they want the bastard dead for all the pain he caused so many people. "He can't be hurt in any way."

James comes rushing through the door, his eyes immediately on me. He doesn't need to speak for me to know what he wants to say.

He's here, my wolf says with a solemn voice, his mood just as somber as everyone else's.

I hope you're ready because I'm going to need your help, I tell him.

I was born ready, he growls back.

"Where is he?" I ask James, ignoring every other person in the room.

"Just outside the manor," he replies. "He didn't want to come in."

I nod in acknowledgment, then turn to Leia and hold out my hand for her. She reaches for me, allowing me to pull her to her feet and toward me. I lean my forehead against hers, taking in her signature scent of freshly fallen snow.

"I love you," I whisper, those three words carrying more meaning than anything else that I could've said ever would.

"I love you, too," she breathes back, sounding emotional and scared.

The look that she gives me when I pull away clearly reminds me not to forget the promise that I've given her. I'm going to win, save her sister's life, and then return to her for our happily ever after. Together, we're going to make the world a better place and fill it up with young pups of our own.

We will have that, the wolf says with stubborn determination. *We deserve it.*

Leia hooks her arm through mine, walking by my side as we go to meet Felix. Lucas and Valerie are close behind us, followed by James and Levi, and then the rest of the royal advisors.

"There's quite a crowd out there," James warns me when he catches up, rushing ahead of the reigning monarchs who are more worried about getting their daughter back than the royal protocol.

"I suppose they'll want to livestream the duel for everyone to see," I reply, not surprised at all. "We can use it to our advantage, once I win. It will also help to prove that Felix wasn't murdered but lost fair and square. I don't want any beef with the Farrells for it."

"I took the liberty of pairing up the members of the Lafayette Pack with wolves from the Pack of Survivors," James says, giving me the information that makes me raise my brows in surprise. "I figured they deserve to see their parents' murderer being brought to justice in person."

"Just make sure that they'll be okay with violence," I reply. "I don't want anyone interrupting the duel. The win needs to be fair and square, or it will leave us with the mark that we'll never be able to shake."

When we exit the manor, my eyes immediately go to Felix, who's standing in the middle of the large driveway. The large crowd of reporters, spectators, and guards have made a circle around him, turning the whole area into a makeshift court. The pack wolves will be responsible for keeping the shields up to make sure that no innocent bystander gets hurt by our abilities. It's not foolproof safety, but it's the best we can do. Attendance doesn't come without its risks.

The crowd parts, giving me plenty of space to walk in the middle of the ring while Leia stays on the outside with others.

"I'm so glad you could make it," Felix says as a way of greeting, giving me a big smile as if we're friends.

"Where's Lily?" I ask, determined to make sure that Leia's little sister is safe.

"What? No hello?" Felix teases, tilting his head to the side as he fakes a face of disappointment.

"Where is she?" I ask again and even though my voice is low, it carries forward with the strength of my shadows.

The crowd holds their breath, anxiously watching our interaction. Behind me, Leia's mother silently cries, wanting to see her missing daughter.

"Relax, man," Felix says with a lazy smile. "She's right here."

He gestures with his hand behind him at the group of wolves that must've come with him and are probably the same ones that participated in the attacks. The wolves step aside, revealing a disoriented-looking Lily. She looks a bit worse for wear, but besides that, she doesn't appear to be hurt.

"Let her go," I order, ever so slightly lifting my chin up to make sure he understands that this is not negotiable.

"Are you insinuating that my wolves will kill her if I lose the duel?" Felix mocks, voicing our exact fears. "Do you really think so low of me? Do you think me without honor?"

"I think you're the worst of the worst!" I snap back, rising to his bait. If he wants to play, then I'll make sure that the news cameras catch it all. "I think it takes the lowest of our kind to kill our own. I think you're a wannabe who will never accomplish anything in his life. I think that your parents made a mistake by not suffocating you with a pillow when you were still in a crib."

"And you think yourself so much better than me, don't you?" Felix asks, giving me an arrogant smirk. "Your brothers hate you. Your own father hates you. You had to leave your home to find a sliver of happiness in your life."

"At least I found it. You're still living a dark and miserable life, reaching for something that will never be yours," I reply without missing a beat, ignoring my suspicions that he might've been in touch with my family. For their sake, I hope that Felix is lying.

"And I think you're—"

"How about we get this duel started, huh?" I ask, enjoying how his face turns red with anger at my interruption.

More moves like this will throw him out of balance, my wolf says in approval. *The angrier he gets, the more impulsive he'll be.*

"Fine, but first let's go over the rules," he replies, then continues summing them up for the sake of the cameras. "The duel isn't to be interrupted in any way. The duelists have to fight until death. The winning party gets everything and everyone that belongs to the losing party. Don't worry, Leia. I can make you very happy."

I clench my hands into fists, holding back the anger that's not my friend right now. I need to keep a cool and level head, staying one step ahead of him. He doesn't make it easy on me, especially when he talks directly to Leia and even blows her an air kiss.

"You named the rules, now let Lily go, so she can be reunited with her family," I say, wanting to give Leia at least a little bit of comfort before she's forced to watch us fight to the death.

"Very well," Felix agrees to everyone's relief and waves his hand at his group of wolves.

Lily's free, but she's too weak to walk. Levi wants to run toward her, but the shields don't let him enter. I don't want the young princess to stay on the wrong side of the ring, so I walk up to her, passing Felix. Even though I pointedly turn my back on him, I'm aware of every single thing that's happening around us. I'm conscious of every movement he makes, keeping my senses open to feel if he's calling on his ability.

Lily takes one step forward before her knees buckle under her weight. She collapses but doesn't hit the ground because I jump forward on time, painfully landing on my knee as I catch her.

Let's hope Felix didn't notice that, my wolf says with an inner frown.

I hold back a grimace and suppress a wince. It wasn't my smartest move, but I couldn't let Lily fall on the ground. Putting one arm under her knees and the other behind her back, I lift her up in my arms, holding her tiny body against my chest.

With my head high and protective, an almost feral expression on my face, I return to the other side where Leia and her family are. Felix grins when I pass him, giving me plenty of space to go around him.

"Lily!" Levi calls, his voice a mix of hope and desperation.

"My baby," Valerie cries, too weak to hold herself up. The lack of food was bound to take its toll and now's really the worst time for it to happen. Lucas supports her and whispers something to Levi.

"Take her to the infirmary and make sure she's okay," I say to James, handing Lily over to him.

"I'll take her," Levi insists, pushing forward, but I quiet him down with one look.

"Clean yourself up," I tell him with a low voice, making sure that neither the cameras nor the microphones catch anything. "Your sister would be ashamed if she'd seen you that way."

Levi's eyes widen, the last bit of blood draining off his face. He purses his lips into a thin line, but not because he's angry. It's because he doesn't want anyone to see him quiver and tremble.

"It will be okay," I tell him, then turn to Leia and wink.

"Enough of the chit chat," Felix calls, clapping his hands together. "Let's fight."

I nod and step back toward the middle of the ring to face him, making a big show of untying my tie, then throwing it to the side. I walk around the circle, taking its measurements as I shake off my jacket, also throwing it to the side. Next, I slowly undo my buttons, my nimble fingers dealing with them one by one, my eyes never leaving Felix's. I shrug the shirt off my shoulders, revealing my strong, muscled torso.

"I didn't know we're fighting half-naked, but I suppose it does make a better show," Felix says with a grin, following my lead and taking off the top part of his clothes. "Here's a little treat for all the ladies out there."

When Felix is done, he gives me a long look, waiting for my next move. I turn my head left and right, loudly cracking my neck before tipping my head back ever so slightly and pointedly opening my mouth to show my teeth shifting into impressive, long fangs. Next, I clench my hands into fists, then slowly open them, exposing my sharp claws. That's all the shift I'll do for now, embracing wolf's strong points while combining them with my own.

I can't rely on the full moon because we're both wolves. Felix gets just as much of a boost as I do, but maybe, his fiery temper will be harder to keep under control if I rile him up.

"It's just you and me now, Grey," Felix says, his lips curled up into a snarl.

"How about you stop talking and show me what you got," I reply with a low growl, showcasing my sharp fangs.

Felix doesn't need to be told twice as he starts moving and turning his hands in hypnotic movements. My eyes are locked on him, my inner wolf on high alert.

A ring of fire comes out of nothing, surrounding both of us. While the flame is yellow instead of blue, it's just as hot and dangerous as the flames he wielded that night in the salon.

He'll manipulate the ring's power as opposed to creating a new spark from the start, my wolf warns me.

Smart, I admit in approval. *He's saving his energy.*

"Come on!" Felix roars, tipping his head back to look into the sky. His mouth's wide open, and from the darkness, a glimmer of light comes from his throat, growing in size and brightness.

Duck! my wolf orders.

Without thinking, I do as he says, relying on his sharp instincts more than on my own. At the last moment, I jump out of the way of Felix's fire breath. These flames are a mix of blue and white, which means that while he prepared the fire ring to keep him going for a longer time, he's starting strong in hopes of finishing me before his spark dies out.

I roll and land on my feet, my balance just as strong and unwavering as before. Felix played his hand and missed, but now it's my turn.

The next few movements I do as fast as I can, trying to have it done before Felix realizes how open and vulnerable I am. It's a big risk, but one that I have no choice but to take.

Raising myself up to a standing position, I pull myself to my full height and open my arms wide as if offering to give someone a hug. Felix furrows his brows in confusion and tilts his head to the side, watching me with interest. It's my lucky day because every seasoned warrior would know better than to give me a moment of peace, which is exactly what the untrained Felix does.

With wide, open arms, I welcome inside me the light from the surrounding areas. I absorb the light from the full moon and the billions of dead stars. While light absorption can't smother the flames, it can take away its brightness. Not always though, but I'm the strongest wielder of darkness in centuries plus the full moon's extra boost and the light's out. They still emanate the heat, though, and they're just as dangerous as before, although invisible to anyone who doesn't have night vision like I do.

He'll still be able to wield them, my wolf tells me, confirming my suspicions that, as a fire wielder, he doesn't need to see them as long as he can feel them within his reach.

"What is this?" Felix calls, trying to mock me, but there's a clear underlying tone of fear in his words. "Are you scared that everyone would see me kick your ass?"

I keep quiet, not wanting to reveal my position. While I see him as clear as day, he's blind and forced to rely on his other senses. If I were fighting with a fellow wielder of darkness, I would have considered camouflaging myself with shadows, but there's no need for that.

Let's end this, my wolf agrees and growls.

I move through the darkness, careful to keep my steps silent. There are many ways I could've ended him with the use of my abilities, but I want the death blow to be a physical one. I want to feel his pulse slow down until his heart stops beating altogether. He's already had too much time in the spotlight, and I don't plan on giving him even another second more. When I'm done with him, I'll go after his followers. They'll all pay for the crimes they committed against our own kind.

With my claws at the ready, I'm inches away from getting in the reach of Felix's neck. Raising my right arm, I pull it back ever so slightly to gain the momentum I need to finish him fast.

It's then that something eerie happened. Felix's amber eyes lock on mine and he gives me a wicked smile.

Impossible! my wolf exclaims.

We're too far in, the momentum too strong to stop, making it easy for Felix to dodge under my arm, running his claws along my side as he passes. A guttural groan escapes me as I stumble forward, pressing my left hand against my bleeding ribs.

It's just a flesh wound, my wolf tells me and although he tries to calm me, he sounds just as shocked as I am. *It will heal in no time.*

"Neat trick, isn't it?" Felix asks, the eerie wicked smile still on his face. His eyes track my every movement, making it clear that he can see in the dark.

"How can that be?" I ask, unable to hide my surprise.

"When you make a deal with the devil, everything's possible," he tells me with a smirk. "Did you really think that I'd kill all those poor wolves with no good reason? What do you think I am? A monster?"

He shakes his head and makes a tsking sound with his tongue. My eyes widen in disbelief when he clenches his hands into fists, then slowly opens them, holding a ball of light that's nothing like fire.

"I met a certain young witch who's been open to rewarding me for doing her little favors every now and again," he says, sounding as nonchalant as if he's talking about what he had for dinner the night before. "It took a very complicated mix of ingredients for her to make an incredibly rare concoction that gave me these powers."

"What powers?" I ask, wanting to keep him talking to learn as much as I can about him. It's the only way I can defeat him without putting myself too much at risk.

"I'm already a fire elemental, but ever since you stole my princess from me, and I've decided to fight you, I realized that I needed a bit of your own ability as well as the one that falls on the other side of the scale," Felix says, openly admitting that he also has control over darkness and light.

"This is treason," I tell him, disgusted by the fact that he's my family on my mother's side. "You betrayed your own kind in the worst possible way. I'll be honored to kill you, and I'll proudly describe the moment you went down to anyone who shows the slightest bit of interest."

Felix laughs, pure amusement in the melodic tones. He shakes his head and opens his mouth to continue speaking, but I've had enough. I don't want to hear more about his betrayal.

I leap forward, catching him off guard as I land on him with a force that throws us against the ground. Felix roars, calling on the full moon's light to dispel the shadows. I have his body pinned underneath my weight, my claws dangerously close to his face, but somehow, he has enough strength to keep me at bay.

With a groan, I push myself forward, trying to close the distance between my claws and his throat. Felix's eyes widen, a spark of fear in them that's soon replaced by the bright blue flame as his hands catch on fire. With a cry in pain, I jump away from him and snuff out the fire on my hands. The smell of burning flesh fills my nostrils, further fueling my anger.

Felix is on his feet, cautiously looking at me. While he's eager to kill me, he's also not an idiot. His fiery temper must be buried under the blanket of darkness that he bought off the witch for a horrible price.

"Come on!" he yells, banging his fists against his chest as he roars.

I pull myself up, the residue of his fire still burning through my skin, sending waves of pain to my brain.

We've been through worse than that, my wolf reminds me. *Embrace the pain. It's our friend.*

My wolf's right. While I'm powerful by birth, I would never be able to tap all that potential if my father hadn't beaten me for every ridiculous mistake every kid makes. It was then that I promised myself that no one would touch me ever again.

With the light also comes the shadow, my wolf says, bringing my attention to Felix's.

My lips curl up into a small smile, mostly to try to make him believe just how unaffected I am by his sudden reveal. I reach my hand out and wiggle my fingers toward his shadow, getting it to dance to my will.

Felix's eyes widen and his hands fly to his throat as his invisible shadow starts to choke him. My eyes narrow as I intently watch him, not wanting to miss a single detail as his face slowly turns blue.

With a sudden circled movement of his arm, a bright beam of light appears around Felix. The radius of its brightness is wide enough that it erases any kind of shadow his body might throw. My hold on his shadow puppet disappears with it, and the pressure on his throat disappears, allowing him to gasp for breath and refill his lungs.

Without the shadows, I have no ability to rely on. I can try to fight his power head on, but it's clear that there's nothing natural about his abilities. This will come down to a physical fight, but I won't participate in my weaker form. With a roar, I call on my wolf, inviting him out to shed my weak body, replacing it with his much superior one.

On all fours, I look through my wolf's eyes at my opponent. Suddenly, he doesn't seem so formidable anymore. My vision sharpens, catching little beads of sweat gathering at the edge of his hairline. My ears prickle, taking in the rapid beating of his heart as he struggles to keep the panic at bay.

In the next moment, Felix does the same, softly landing on his gigantic paws as an orange-brown wolf appears before me.

You look like Garfield, I snicker, telepathically communicating through our wolf-like abilities.

Felix lets out an angry growl and springs forward. Something about my comment must've set him off because he's running at me with no apparent plan. I flex my muscles and slightly lean down, bracing myself for impact.

Felix crashes toward me, but I'm ready and quickly maneuver my strong body to the side and out of his way, sinking my fangs deep into his neck. He howls in pain and thrashes around, but my grip on him is too strong.

With an unexpected roll toward me, he catches me by surprise as he slips underneath me. Turning on his back, he kicks my wolf's exposed belly with all four paws, throwing me off him.

I land awkwardly on my shoulder, ignoring the loud crack that I'm hoping is just a dislocation. Gritting my teeth, I somehow manage to pull myself up and stand on all four paws again. My eyes never leave Felix's. Neither I nor my wolf will pay the ultimate price for underestimating him.

His amber eyes shine with the same determination that I share with my wolf. The fight is nearing the end. Our next move will be our final one.

Ignoring the pain in my shoulder, I start running toward him at the same time as he races at me. Pushing my paws hard, I leap high off the ground, my fangs and claws ready to strike. Felix does the same and our powerful bodies collide against each other nearly twelve feet from the ground.

The flying momentum makes it impossible for either one of us to influence our trajectory or change our minds. We're both fully committed to this move, to ending the enemy once and for all, and going home with the princess.

Felix misses my face by mere inches but buries his fangs into my hurt shoulder. Embracing the pain as my friend that helped me defeat many opponents in the past by tricking them into thinking that I'm vulnerable, when in reality, they're the ones that have exposed themselves to me.

With brute force, I sink my fangs deep into Felix's neck then yank my head back, taking a chunk of his flesh with me. Felix howls and whimpers, but the sound soon dies off as we land on the ground, only one of us still standing.

My muzzle is covered with Felix's blood, his flesh still between my teeth. I wait the longest of moments, my eyes never leaving the fallen wolf's body.

He's dead, my own wolf tells me, confirming it after he can't hear his heartbeat nor see any movements of his torso that would indicate breathing.

With a deep breath, we prepare ourselves to announce our victory with a roar that would've made even a T-Rex piss himself.

The battle might be over, and I've won the duel, but Felix revealed to me that there's a bigger enemy waiting for us in the shadows. A species so cruel and cunning that managed to turn our own kind against each other, making brothers kill brothers while they stayed in the background and watched the show. Not for long, because they're next on my list. It's time to exterminate the witches like the pests they are.

CHAPTER 20

LEIA

"Can you lay still for one fucking moment?" I snap, my patience wearing thin.

"There's no time," Gavin growls back. "We need to bring in Felix's followers. They've been working with the witches."

"My father and the advisors are on it. There's nothing you can do about it right now," I tell him, then continue with a softer tone, willing him to listen to me. "You need to heal first. Our enemies can wait another day."

Something in my voice must've convinced him because he lays back down, the weight of his body sinking into the mattress. He seems to relax enough for me to wash off the blood from the mostly healed claw mark that Felix left on his side. If it was any other wolf, he'd have the scar there for the rest of his life. But this is Gavin, and his strength is unimaginable, so there's barely any mark visible.

"For a moment there, I thought you were going to die," I tell him with a low voice, trying to keep my lip from quivering. "I was so scared for you and there was nothing I could do to help you. I never felt more helpless, and I don't ever want to feel that way again."

"Hey, hey, hey," he says quickly and takes my hand into his, ignoring the wet sponge in my grip. "It's over, okay? It's finished. The good guys have won and I'm okay. We're okay, Lily's okay, your brother's okay, and your parents are okay. We're all okay."

I nod, swallowing back my tears. Now that it's over, and he's safe, the adrenaline's side effects are gone from my body, leaving behind an emotional mess.

Gavin puts his hands on my cheeks and makes me look at him. His beautiful black eyes stare into mine, his face radiating with so many different emotions, but there's one that clearly stands out.

"I love you, Leia Lafayette," he whispers, his eyes softening. "I am in love with you, my soulmate, my princess, my queen. I love you with everything I am, everything I have and everything I will be. You and I are forever, and nothing and no one will stand in the way of that."

"I love you, too," I breathe, before pushing myself forward to close the distance between our mouths.

I want him so much it hurts, but the memory of him tearing Felix's neck wide open is still too fresh in my mind. Fighting my own urges, I put a hand on his chest to keep him from coming after me as I break the kiss.

"W-what's wrong?" Gavin stammers, his eyes glazed with lust and desire. His naked body is covered with a small towel that does nothing to hide his growing erection.

"I'll prepare a bath," I tell him, giving him a seductive smile. "Wait five minutes, then come."

Without waiting for his reply, I slip into the bathroom and get the water going in the luxurious hot tub. We mostly use the shower because our days are too busy, which is a shame because in the other corner is a perfectly good and extremely comfortable tub.

I grab a bunch of candles from the cupboard underneath the sink and light them around the tub. Whether Gavin knows it or not, today is a special day. He saved my sister, defeated our enemy, and looked sexier than ever while doing all that.

Gavin gently knocks before entering the bathroom, his eyes holding a happy shine in them. I glance at his grown member and smirk, my own body waking up to his call.

"It's beautiful," he says, his voice sincere and full of emotion.

"Get in," I tell him, gesturing with my head toward the tub.

He does as I say and as he submerges himself in the water, its levels rise several inches. I walk over to the tub and watch his eyes as he takes in my every move. Reaching back, I slowly undo the zipper of my dress, then shimmy my arms out, exposing my breasts to him. My nipples immediately react to the fresh air, hardening and waking as a result of exposure.

Before stepping up on the hot tub's step, I let the dress fall on the floor, quickly followed by my bra and panties. Stepping into the tub, I let out a low gasp as the warm water surrounds my body. I walk over to where he's sitting and kneel right at his feet. Pushing his legs apart, I nestle right in and lay my head against his chest, listening to the steady drumming of his heartbeat.

When I slightly turn my head, my lips fall on his chest. With light and gentle kisses, I work my way over to his nipple, finding it already hard as I close my lips around it and suck on it. He puts his hands on my head, pressing my mouth against him harder. I kiss my way to the other nipple, gently sucking it into my mouth, flicking, licking, and teasing, all the while, his cock steadily grows against my belly, hardening with my every suck and lick.

"Hold still," I tell him with a low, seductive voice as I bring my lips up to his mouth.

With my tongue, I gently trace his bottom lip, enjoying the growing hardness between us. My tongue glides across his top lip, then smoothly slips inside, softly doing circles as I taste his mouth. Feeling his tongue slowly but eagerly reach out to touch mine, I draw him into my mouth by sucking on it.

"Sit on the edge," I tell him after we exchange gentle kisses for a while.

Gavin's lips curl up into a small smile, his eyes shining with curiosity. I'll do everything I can to help my man relax and unwind after the battle he had. Watching him stand, I see just how hard he is as his cock grows to its full length and size. When he sits on the edge, I push his legs apart and catch his eyes for the shortest second, drinking in the expression on his face when he realizes what I'm about to do.

Wrapping my fingers around his shaft, I gently lower my mouth to him. I start by kissing the tip, then slowly run my tongue against him, pricking my ears when he lets out a guttural groan. My tongue slides back and forth across the tip, cleaning off his pre-cum. I tilt my head to the side and kiss my way down his shaft, sucking on his length, leaving marks in my wake. My fingers trace his balls as I suck my way down. Cupping his balls in my hand, my lips slide to them and tease them with flickering licks. Sucking softly on his balls, he tips his head back and closes his eyes, his hard cock throbbing and pulsating against me. Holding him up, I lick and suck underneath, then work my way back to the tip of its h ead.

As my tongue slides across the rim, I linger there, teasing and sucking the tip into my mouth, swirling my tongue back and forth across it. Hearing him groan, I suck my lips onto him harder and stronger. My hand's at the base of his shaft, beginning to stroke him up and down as I pull my head back, enjoying the view of me pumping his cock. I lower my head and lick off the small drop of juice that I coaxed out, tasting my wolf's manliness. Gavin arches his hips to me just as I open my mouth around the tip and let him push his way in. His cock fucks me deep into my throat, making me moan. The vibrations from the guttural sound I made travel the whole length of Gavin's shaft, bringing a low growl out of him.

Sliding him in and out of my mouth, I'm not sure whether he's fucking me or I'm the one giving him a blowjob. He's thrusting and pumping his hips, burying his cock in my mouth, but I'm also eagerly and actively participating, lifting, and lowering my head, taking him as deep as I can before coming up for air.

I slide his cock out to the tip and suck the head, drawing more juices out of him drop by drop. When I take my mouth away from him, he makes a small sound, complaining about the absence of my heat. I move back up and kiss him lightly on his neck, then gently nibble on his earlobe.

"I'm not done with you yet," I tell him, my words carrying the weight of a promise. "This is only the beginning."

Gavin sits back and lowers himself down in the water. Under the surface, I take his hand in mine and guide it to my parted legs. As his fingers trace my swollen lower lips, I leave my hand on his to feel what he's feeling from the moment he slowly caresses my pussy to the part where he slips between my lower lips and strokes his thumb against my clit, sending chills throughout my body and all the way down my spine. Removing my hand from his, I shut my eyes and let him play.

Long slow strokes between my lower lips make me burn even hotter under his fingers. Stroking back to the entrance of my pussy, I whimper as he slips one finger in, then gasp with pleasure when a second one joins it. When he pulls them out, taking them from me, I open my eyes and shoot him a dirty look.

"It's my turn," he purrs and smirks. "Sit up."

I go into the same position as he was in before and immediately open my legs, exposing my most intimate area to him. He doesn't hesitate to shower me with kisses, his lips nearing my clit and making me shudder as he licks up, almost touching it.

The next thing I know, he closes his lips around my clit and begins to suck on it with gentle force, making me swell harder in his mouth. His fingers trace my smooth lower lips, teasing them open. As he sucks on my clit, he pushes two fingers inside me, filling my pussy with him.

"Fuck, I can't," I moan, then make inaudible sounds as my pussy squeezes his fingers. My grip on the edge of the tub tightens as if I'm holding on for dear life as my body shudders under his touches and kisses.

When I recover, Gavin pulls his fingers out of my pussy, leaving behind a phantom feeling of their presence. His mouth is on my pussy next as he sucks on my pussy, coaxing every drop out of me and drinking it in.

When he's done, I slide back into the water and immediately reach for his hard, throbbing cock. His eyes lock on mine, the unspoken communication exchanged, and our next step decided without the need to use any words.

We position ourselves so he can take me from behind. I turn and bend over the edge of the tub, legs apart and waiting patiently as he nears me. Taking himself in his hand, he guides his cock toward my pussy and begins to rub the tip of its head against my swollen lower lips, playing with them by parting them open and then leaving them to close again. Reaching down between us, I pull him firmly toward my opening, needing, and wanting in right this very moment. He sets his hands on my hips for balance and thrusts forward, plunging deep into my pussy. I gasp as he pulls back out to the tip of his cock, then thrusts forward, taking me deeply again.

With every pump, he buries his cock in me up to the hilt. His balls slap against my ass cheeks every time he plunges back in. Moving faster and faster, he slowly but steadily begins to throb and pulsate inside me.

Gavin puts his hands on my shoulders to hold me in place as he wildly pumps into me, thrusting his hips back and forth like a maniac. Squeezing his cock with my pussy, he groans and grunts. I push back against him, matching his thrusts with my own, we fuck each other harder and deeper. Gavin roars, his eyes glazed over with lust and desire as he takes me, possessively burying his cock into me as if there's no tomorrow. His hands move down to my hips again as he plunges himself into me one last time, slamming the whole length of his shaft into me, his balls smacking against my ass cheeks.

He jerks violently and wildly, his cock shaking and throbbing inside my pussy as he shoots his hot load deep into me, filling me with his juices and mixing them with plenty of my own. I clench my lower muscles, milk him for every last drop, wanting him to give me everything he has.

Pulling away and turning to him, I give him a smile that only he can get out of me. "I love you," I tell him, meaning it more than ever before.

CHAPTER 21

GAVIN

It's been weeks since my duel with Felix, but there's still so much to be done. The main thing that I need to address is what I've been trying to avoid for so long but can't anymore. Not even I can run from my responsibilities, no matter how horrible they are, which right now, they're pretty damn terrible.

I find myself sitting in the back seat of the car as James drives me up to my father's court again. Once again, I need to enter the manor that used to be my home where I've spent most of my life surrounded by wolves whose favorite pastime was to try to humiliate me. The same thing happened last time and when I swore that I wouldn't return, I meant it. Unfortunately, duty came calling, and I had to suppress my personal preferences.

"Do you want me to come with you?" James asks, catching my eye in the rearview mirror.

"I wish," I reply, then sigh. "Unfortunately, it would only make matters worse. I'm not sure if they're aware that you followed me to the Lafayette's, but if they don't, now's not the right time for them to find out."

"Whatever you say, Boss," James replies. "But call me if you need me, okay?"

I offer him a wry smile and tilt my head to the side. "Are you going soft on me, James?"

"Me?" he asks with a scoff. "Don't forget that I've been shadowing you for almost ten years now. I've seen what you can do. There are things that a young pup can't forget no matter how many times he sees them."

"Am I really that bad?" I ask, raising my brows in question.

"Much, much worse," James replies and gives me a small smile.

"Flatterer," I mutter under my breath but loud enough that his enhanced wolf hearing can catch it.

We fall silent as he drives up to the Grey Manor, stopping as close to the front entrance as he can. I give him a small nod, a silent signal for him to get out of here for the time being, which he does as soon as I climb out of the car.

"Gavin," my mother calls out as she rounds the corner on the side of the manor where her gardens are.

I open my arms wide, ready to embrace her as she comes running to me, pulling me into the kind of hug that only a mother can give.

"I heard about your duel," she whispers into my ear, holding me close. "I was so worried. I begged your father to let me go, but he wouldn't. I'm so glad you're okay. My baby boy."

"Don't worry, Mother," I reply, taking in her warmth and motherly love. "I'm not as easy to get rid of as many might've hoped."

"You have no idea how glad I am about that," she tells me, giving me one more hug before pulling away and locking her eyes on mine. "Why did you come back here, Gavin? It's not safe for you here."

"I know, Mother," I reply, understanding the amount of danger I'm voluntarily walking into. "There are some things that I learned from Felix during our duel, and I have to at least try to keep my father's court from imploding into itself. I'm trying to save Garren from himself."

"Garren and your father are in the conference room," my mother says at last. "I'll take you there and make sure that Tiana stays in her place. Ever since Garren took her to his bed, she's been acting as if she's the next queen in the making. The poor girl has no idea that she'll be back on the street as soon as your brother tires of her."

"He's only interested in her because he thinks it bothers me," I tell her. "As soon as he realizes that I couldn't care less, he'll find someone else."

"Fingers crossed that when that happens, she won't have a pup in the belly," my mother whispers conspiratorially.

"That's cold-blooded," I say with a chuckle and shake my head.

"Hey, your father didn't let me get a word in on how you were raised, so I'm putting Garren's fuck ups entirely on him," she replies with a sharp look. "You're the only one who learned to navigate the dark corridors of monarchy without creating public scandals. You're my pride and joy. Your brothers have a lot to learn, but lately, I'm seeing some potential improvements with Graham, although I'm afraid that the same can't be said for Grayden."

"I want you to know that I'm mostly doing this for you and Graham," I tell her. "I'm also starting to realize that I've terribly misjudged Graham. There's something about him that I can't quite put my finger on, but at the same time, I can say with certainty that it's not bad."

"I'm glad to hear you say that because, sooner or later, he might need your help," my mother tells me, then hooks her arm through mine. "Let's find your father and brother before they dig themselves into an even deeper shithole than they already did."

"Fingers crossed that they accept the ladder I'm offering," I reply, building on her metaphor.

My mother shakes her head and gently squeezes my arm. It doesn't take long for us to come upon the very first obstacle on the way to the conference room.

"State your business," Tiana growls, defiantly staring me down as she folds her arms across her chest.

She's not even trying to be on guard, my wolf mutters in annoyance.

She knows we won't attack her here. Not without a good reason, I reply, pushing down his anger before it can show on my face.

"Nice to see you too, Tiana," I tell her, surprising myself by actually meaning it. My words must've caught her off guard because the hatred on her expression momentarily wavers.

"Why are you here, Gavin?" she asks, but this time with a much softer voice.

How dare she refer to you like that? my wolf growls. *You're a prince. Soon to be king. She should be on her knees, doing circles around you.*

"I came to see my father and Garren," I tell her, ignoring my wolf as I lift my hands up in mock surrender. "I come in peace."

Tiana glances at my mother, who gives her a curt nod. At last, my old Beta steps aside, giving me plenty of space to walk past her. I offer her a small smile, hoping that she won't take it the wrong way. The last thing I need right now is for her to think that I'm mocking her.

My mother escorts me all the way to the conference room but refuses to enter with me. It's better this way because I don't want to put her in the middle of a possible argument. She's the one who suffers whenever our family fights, and I hate that most of the time is because of me.

"Don't be a stranger," my mother tells me and gives me a quick kiss on my cheek. "I'm very proud of you and of my wolf that you've become. Leia is a lucky girl. You two will be very happy together. I can feel it."

"Thank you, Mother," I say in a low voice. Then I pull her into a quick but meaningful hug as I whisper into her ear, "I love you."

She leaves me to my business, giving me one last wave before rounding the corner. Not wanting to start my visit with disrespect, I lift my hand and gently tap my knuckles against the hardwood. The sound of my knock echoes down the hall, quieting the voices inside the room.

"Enter," my father's powerful voice booms from the other side of the door.

I turn the knob, letting myself into the room. A small part of me is relieved to see that my father and Garren are alone. I have a much better chance of reaching an agreement with them without an audience. They might be more open to listening to me without feeling the need to keep up the pretense for any outsiders.

"Gavin," my father breathes in surprise at the same time my brother snarls, "What are you doing here?"

I go through the same play I used with Tiana. With my hands raised in mock surrender, I say, "I come in peace."

"What part of 'you're not welcome here' you don't understand?" my brother asks with hatred in his voice. "Get the fuck out."

"Stand down, Garren," my father orders, then he gestures to one of the empty chairs behind the long conference room table. "Please sit down."

Smells like a trap, my wolf says, also surprised by my father's polite reception.

He's not stupid, I tell my wolf. *He knows that there's a war brewing, and he'll need all the allies he can get.*

"What can we do for you, Gavin?" my father asks when I sit down on his left side, which is also the chair opposite Garren's.

"As I said before, I come in peace," I repeat my previous words. When he nods, giving me a gesture to go on, I continue, "I'm sure you've heard all about my duel with Prince Felix Farrell."

"We heard that you almost got your ass kicked." My brother chuckles.

"Garren," Father warns him, shooting him a look before turning back to me. "What about it?"

"Some troubling information came to light," I start, then take a deep breath before diving into the story. "We have plenty of wolves on the matter, thoroughly investigating it, but the gist is that Felix and his followers have been working with witches."

"Impossible!" Father exclaims and shakes his head in disbelief. "No wolf would ever work with those foul creatures. They're much, much worse than even humans."

"I'm afraid that times are changing," I say with a heavy sigh. "Felix was a fire wielder, but apparently, he made a deal with the witches. I don't know the details except that he massacred a town full of wolves and young pups, and in return, one young witch in particular, helped him gain two more abilities. When I fought him, he was in control of darkness and light as well as fire."

"Blasphemy!" Father breathes, his eyes wide with horror. "This can't be happening. We're not strong enough to keep the witches at bay while at the same time fighting our own. It's too much. It's too dangerous."

"I actually think that cousin was onto something good here," Garren says, his brows furrowed as he's lost in thought so much that he doesn't even notice how disgusted Father and I are by his statement. "Imagine the possibilities if our family could wield all the elements. We could take over all the kingdoms and unite them under one name, the Grey name."

"While I admire your ambition, this is not the way," Father says to Garren with a reprimanding voice. "There's a reason why we have so many kingdoms. The important thing is that the wolves in our territories are well taken care of. If our kingdom gets too big, we can't provide for them."

My father's words serve as a reminder that, while he's horrible to me, he was once a good man, who deeply cares about his wolves. If he manages to keep Garren in check, maybe this family isn't as doomed as I'd thought.

"I'm fairly certain that this isn't the end," I continue, not wanting to get in the middle of their argument, which will surely follow if Garren's face can be judged.

"The witches might either try to find another wolf to do their bidding, or they'll try to kill us off, once and for all."

"It's been a long time coming," my father confirms, his face pensive. "I was sort of hoping that we wouldn't be the generation to deal with it, but it's not up to us. If it comes, we'll have to stand up and face it."

"The war is brewing," I agree. "I don't think it will take long. The witches have been attacking with fierce determination, testing our frontlines. I believe that they have a new leader, probably the same young witch that gave Felix the abilities that he should never be able to wield. While we might be able to use her youth and inexperience to our advantage, we shouldn't assume that she's not willing to listen to her elders."

"What do you suggest?" my father asks me, momentarily catching me by surprise for listening to me and wanting my advice.

"The most important thing is that our species doesn't get discovered," I reply, suppressing any kind of reaction and keeping my expression just as indifferent as ever. "All royal families need to stand together and present a unified front. It's extremely important that we keep a low profile until we know more. Once we do, we'll talk about our next step and discuss whether or not it's time to strike at the witches."

"And so the prey becomes the predator once again," my father comments with a ghost of a smile playing on his lips.

"That's bullshit!" Garren exclaims and slams his fist against the table. "You're not a part of our family anymore, Brother. I'm the one who'll decide what we'll do."

"Stand down, Garren," my father repeats his earlier order, but my brother is too focused on me to hear him.

"You have no right to come here and tell us what to do. You're lucky that I'm not demanding your head," Garren snarls. "You'll do well to remember that I'm the king and you're nothing but a piece of trash."

Fucking bastard, my wolf growls, sending a blast of anger through my body that forces me to clench my hands into fists to keep a wave of power from escaping me.

"That's enough, Garren!" Father yells and stands up, slamming a fist of his own against the table.

He doesn't bother suppressing the blast that sends Garren flying into his chair until it flips backward. His power doesn't do anything to my shield, thanks to the force of my darkness being too strong and impenetrable.

"First of all, you're not the king and with that kind of behavior, you might never even become one. I'm sick and tired of listening to you bickering with your brothers," Father says, his voice sharp and firm. "You either stop with the jealous games and help us come up with a way for our species to fly above witches' radar, or I'll be forced to teach you a lesson that you won't soon forget."

Garren awkwardly picks himself up and stares at our father with wide eyes. No one has ever talked to him that way, and it has been long overdue.

We should go, my wolf tells me, although I can tell that he'd prefer to stay and watch Garren's humiliation.

"I'll be in touch when we know more," I say, then get up and leave the conference room before Father can turn the full force of his attention onto me.

Garren says something to Father, but it's low enough that I can't hear through the door, and I don't really bother to strain my ears, using enhanced wolf hearing. Whatever argument they have, it's between them. My brother was right when he said that this family's matters weren't my business anymore.

"This is your last warning, Garren," my father says, his raised voice loud enough to echo down the hallway, following me as I leave the manor. "You'll either learn how to behave or I'll take all your privileges away and send you to live in the barracks. You'll train like a soldier, you'll act like a soldier, you'll eat like a soldier, and you'll shit like a soldier. I'll take your royal status away from you and force you to earn it back stripe by stripe, climbing up the very high ladder until you earn the right to be the Grey King."

Holy fuck! my wolf exclaims just as shocked as I am. *Papa Grey finally set his foot down.*

Better late than never, I agree, hoping that Garren will get his shit together. If anyone's the weak link in our chain, it's him.

I leave the manor with a lighter step, happy that I haven't only put this matter behind me, but I've also dealt with it in a successful and grownup manner. I shake my head, banishing the problems of tomorrow out of my head. Leia and I will deal with them together, but first, we have a wedding to plan.

EPILOGUE – LEIA

"You look beautiful," Lily tells me after she's done with the final touches on my hair and makeup.

"Thank you," I breathe, unable to come up with more words to express what I'm feeling.

I'm so grateful that this day has come and that my whole family is alive and well. When my father ordered me to marry, I'd never even in my wildest dreams thought that I'd find my soulmate at the end of this path. Gavin is everything I ever wanted but never dared to hope for because I believed it to be too good to be true, but he's real and he's mine.

"Are you ready?" Levi asks when he enters the room. "Father will meet us at the church to walk you to the altar. He and Mother are welcoming the guests."

"They're not worried that I'll get cold feet?" I tease with a small smile.

"Anyone who has spent some time with you two love-birds would know that you two are meant to be," Levi replies, but he raises his brow in suggestive question.

"It's almost as if you two are soulmates," Lily finishes her twin's thought, giving me the same questioning look as Levi.

"That would be something, wouldn't it?" I tease, not wanting to announce the big news without Gavin.

Levi and Lily exchange a look, having their silent-twin conversation that I'm not a part of. I don't mind it anymore because I've been doing the same thing with Gavin. Ever since the bond clicked into place, it was like we could not read exactly, but more like sense each other's minds. It's hard to explain or put into words. It's something that had to be felt and lived through. It's incredible, beautiful, and unique. It's us, two soulmates bonded for life.

"We should go," Levi says, tapping his watch several times to subtly express urgency.

The manor is mostly empty. We've invited the staff to the wedding ceremony, wanting to celebrate the special day with everyone that's in our lives. Neither one of us is too happy about all of the royal families attending, whether in full or at least sending one wolf to represent them.

Despite it being a public event, we're determined to make it our own in many other little ways such as instead of spending our first night as a married couple in the Lafayette Manor, we'll go to the most expensive and elite hotel in New York City's honeymoon suite. It's our way of showing our independence and setting our foot down by putting us first, without inadvertently risking other people's lives.

Lily helps me carefully stash the whole length of my wedding gown into the back of the car before joining Levi in the front. They are my escort to the church, and the only two people I want to have by my side as I stand in front of everyone and promise Gavin my eternal love.

My sister's phone rings and even before she answers it, I know who it is. I feel it deep in my gut.

"It's bad luck to see the bride before the wedding," Lily says by way of greeting.

"Which is why I called," Gavin replies. I don't even need to strain my ears to hear his voice because the volume setting on Lily's phone is up high. "Is she there? Can I talk to her?"

"You really shouldn't," Lily replies, but before she can say anything else, I already reach forward and yank the phone out of her hand.

"Hey!" she complains, shooting me a dirty look, but I don't care. It's Gavin.

"Hey, handsome," I coo into the phone, my smile brighter than the sun.

"Hey yourself, beautiful," he purrs. He pauses before continuing in a seductive voice, "What are you wearing?"

I chuckle and roll my eyes. "You'll see soon enough."

"I can't wait," he replies, and I can hear a smile in his voice. "I just saw my family enter."

"Yeah?" I ask, knowing that there was a reason for his call.

"Yeah," he confirms, the lightness gone from his tone. "To be honest, I didn't really expect them to come. I mean, I knew that someone would have to come as a representative, but I didn't expect all of them to be here."

"How do you feel about that?" I ask, not wanting to assume that it's a good thing even though I think it is.

"I'm not sure. I suppose I'm glad," he tells me with a soft chuckle. "Even Garren is here, and so far, I didn't hear any female screams, so I'm guessing that he put his claw away and is on his best behavior."

I laugh but Lily grimaces, no doubt remembering her own experience with Gavin's lovely brother. Nothing can rain on my parade tonight. Not even his family who doesn't deserve him.

"I can't wait to see you," I say into the phone, willing us to be there already.

"Me too," he replies, then asks, "When will you arrive?"

"In sixty seconds," Levi says loud enough for even Gavin to hear.

"Give me that phone," Lily orders and yanks it from my grip, hanging up without giving me a chance to say bye to him. "Time to go."

It's almost as if the twins have trained for this moment their whole lives. They both get out of the car at the same time and open the back door on Lily's side. I accept Levi's offered hand, letting him pull me out, and Lily immediately starts fussing around the back of my gown, smoothing the invisible car creases out.

My father comes down the church's stairs, a huge and proud smile on his face. His blue eyes shine with the gleam of a cloudless sky as opposed to cold ice.

"Are you ready?" my father asks me, taking over for my brother by my side.

"I am," I say, and nothing has ever been truer.

Lily and Levi position themselves in front of us and enter the church first. I listen to the music for our cue. Once the twins arrive at their places, the song changes, playing Richard Wagner's *Here Comes the Bride.*

"I'm proud of you, kiddo," my father tells me and gives my hand a comforting squeeze mere moments before the double doors open, revealing our path to the altar.

I'm glad that my father's at my side to guide me because my eyes are glued on Gavin from the second that I see him standing tall and proud. His usually schooled expression is open and radiating an amount of love that would be overwhelming if I hadn't felt the same.

My brain barely registers the many guests seated on the left and right sides as we walk past the rows. I don't care for anyone else but him. He's the whole reason I'm here, he's the reason for the smile that's playing on my lips for everyone to see, and he's the reason for me being truly happy for the first time in my whole life. I thought I was happy in the past, and that my life wasn't too bad, but I didn't even realize that there's a whole new level of that emotion that he helped me discover. I know he feels the same way because our expressions mirror each other and the love for one another gently sings through our bond.

When we finally reach Gavin, I'm so excited that I want to go ahead and yank my arm out of my father's grasp, but he holds onto me tightly and looks at my future husband.

"I'm entrusting my daughter to you, my most precious treasure," my father tells Gavin in a solemn voice. "Treat her well and with the respect she deserves, and you will always have a place in our family."

"I promise I'll always put her first," Gavin assures him, his eyes on my father's.

Whatever my father sees in him must be enough, because he turns to me and gives me a gentle kiss on the cheek before offering my hand to Gavin. Our fingers intertwine and our smiles brighten. Together as one, we turn toward the priest to promise each other in front of our wolf gods.

"Welcome, loved ones," the priest says, his booming voice reaching the farthest corners of the church. "We are gathered here today in the sight of Akkadian, Medeina, Fenrir, Skoll, Hati, Lupa, and other wolf gods that are just as important but too many to name, to join together His Royal Highness Prince Gavin Grey and Her Royal Highness Princess Leia Lafayette in the holiest matrimony of wolves that has also been blessed by the most sacred o f bonds."

Gavin and I smile as our guests gasp, the news about us being soulmates traveling like wildfire to the ears that didn't catch it. The priest goes through the usual wedding procedure, the readings, and exclamations. A part of me tells me that I should pay more attention, but it's very hard when Gavin's standing in front of me looking like a Greek god incarnate.

We've both decided to go with the classic vows, not wanting to share our deepest feelings and emotions in front of a crowd. We're already both out of our element for being somewhat exposed and vulnerable, especially in turbulent times such as these when you don't know who's your friend and who's planning on stabbing you in the back before the next full moon.

The priest looks at me, giving me a subtle nod, indicating that we have arrived at the part that I've been waiting for.

"Do you, Princess Leia Lafayette, take Prince Gavin Grey to be your lawfully wedded husband? Will you cherish him in love and loyalty? Will you share with him the joys and burdens of life? And together, will you face whatever challenges may come, in sickness and in health, from this day forward, for as long as you both shall live?"

Through the times of wars and peace, through the many sleepless nights as the baby pups scream their lungs out, my wolf teases, feeling just as joyful.

"I do," I say in a loud and powerful voice.

Gavin smiles, his black eyes sparkling with unspoken emotion that's only reserved for me. A wave of warmth spreads through my chest as if he sent a reminder of love my way.

The priest turns to Gavin now and clears his throat.

"Do you, Prince Gavin Grey, take Princess Leia Lafayette, to be your lawfully wedded wife? Will you cherish her in love and loyalty? Will you share with her the joys and burdens of life? And together, will you face whatever challenges may come, in sickness and in health, from this day forward, for as long as you both shall live??"

"I do," Gavin confirms, his voice never wavering.

We exchange rings, engraved with our initials and the date that our soulmate bond clicked into place because, at the end of the day, that's a lot more special and unique than the human-like wedding.

"By the power vested in me by our wolf gods, I now pronounce you husband and wife," the priest announces, and I think he continues by telling Gavin that he can kiss me, but I don't hear him at all because my husband's lips are already on mine, claiming me in the most intimate way.

The crowd erupts in applause and cheers. Gavin smiles against my lips, his body pressing against mine in the most perfect way. He has given me his heart just as I've given him mine. Our wolves have found each other, and at last, we'll be a family.

It might be a bigger one than you think, my wolf teases, but I'm too distracted by Gavin's presence to fully process her words or the meaning behind them.

Hand in hand, we walk past the rows of guests and toward our new life.

Thank you for reading **Alpha's Frost Bound Fate.**

Did you LOVE this book?

Then continue with the next book in the Fated Mates of the Royal Wolf Court Series!!

Shadow King's Redemption

A Prince's Journey of Redemption and Forbidden Love!

Sent to reform, Garren discovers his fated mate in Alyssa, the fierce Alpha of the Dark Hunters.

As a powerful witch coven threatens their bond, their love becomes the key to saving the kingdom.

Immerse yourself in Shadow King's Redemption TODAY, Read Free in Kindle Unlimited, or purchase the eBook or paperback on Amazon...

https://www.amazon.com/dp/B0CZ2D1M3S

Here's a quick snip it:

He was a prince, lost in self-destruction.

She was an Alpha, his fated mate.

Training under her, he found power and purpose.

But their love put them in the crosshairs of a witch coven.

Captured and facing mortality, he realized the depth of his love.

With treachery and danger surrounding them, can he
   prove himself worthy?

Can their bond survive the ultimate test?

**Find out what happens next in Shadow King's
Redemption!!**

**Read Free in Kindle Unlimited or purchase the
eBook or paperback on Amazon...**

   https://www.amazon.com/dp/B0CZ2D1M3S

Sneak Peek – Shadow King's Redemption

I was a reckless prince, addicted to pleasure and self-destruction.

Sent to a military camp to reform, I never expected to find my forbidden fated mate.

She is the fierce Alpha of the Dark Hunters pack.

I dream of claiming her, marking her as mine for all eternity.

Training under her, I discovered a rare power that I never knew I had.

But our bond made us targets of a witch coven, determined to destroy us.

Captured and facing our mortality, I realized the depth of my love for her.

I vow to become a man worthy of her heart.

With treachery in our midst and danger at every turn, can I be the man she deserves?

Can our love redeem my past and secure our future?

Shadow King's Redemption is a standalone royal paranormal romance with a happily ever after. No Cheating.

-Fated Mates

-Forbidden Romance

This is the second book in 3+ book series

Get your copy of Shadow King's Redemption now! – Free in Kindle Unlimited

https://www.amazon.com/dp/B0CZ2D1M3S

Chapter 1

Garren

I'm on top of the fucking world, and life couldn't be better.

Last night, I used my tongue, fingers, and everything else at my disposal to push three human women into orgasmic oblivion. Their naked bodies are sprawled around me, their minds lulled into satisfied sleep.

Another round, my wolf says, wanting to wake them up just as much as I do. Well, if they can't, I'll simply get my pack to bring me new ones. It's good to be king.

You're not one yet, my wolf reminds me. The ascension process hasn't finished yet.

Semantics, I reply with a roll of my eyes.

I'm aware that until the coronation, I only have as much power as my father allows me to have. The ancient rules state clearly that only the oldest son can ascend to the throne, which definitely works in my favor because everyone can see that stupid Saint Gavin is my father's favorite.

We're lucky that he married into another royal family, my wolf says. He's just as relieved as I am that we don't need to constantly watch our backs now that my overly ambitious younger brother is out of the picture.

I have used my newly found extra time well. My second-in-command, the Beta of my pack, and the wild wolf that I sometimes take to my bed, is very good at locating the pure and uncut drugs. Getting top-shelf alcohol was always easy because all I had to do was hold my no-limit credit card up in the air.

My cock's already waking, which means that one of the ladies should do because I won't take care of my needs alone. With my right foot, I lazily kick at the young blonde at my side. She jumps and whimpers at the contact, her sleepy eyes locking on me as she gives me a startled look.

"You have work to do," I order, then let my head slip into the pillow as I close my eyes and wait for her nimble fingers and her mouth to do their thing.

The other two sleeping beauties make small sounds in complaint as the young blonde pushes past them to get between my spread legs. The corners of my mouth lift as I brace myself for contact. It never comes because someone picked that very moment to knock on the door and interrupt my morning.

"What?!" I yell, not bothering to keep the anger out of my voice.

The door opens and though I'm expecting Tiana to walk in, the person that enters doesn't resemble my Beta one bit. I react even before I manage to properly process the newcomer, my reflexes automatic and quick.

I don't care that my knee connects with the young blonde's cheek when I get up. Everything else is secondary to the person standing in front of me.

"Father," I breathe, looking at him with my mouth open. "What are you doing here?"

"Grab the whores and take them to the doctor!" my father shouts the order to Tiana, who I'm only now noticing is standing behind him. "We need to make sure that they don't leave with bastard pups in their bellies."

"Right away, Your Grace," Tiana says with a submissive tone.

With a slight gesture of her head, the other members of the Pack of Shadows move ahead and pull the three women off my bed. No one offers them any clothes, and the women are too hungover to put up a fight.

"Stop," I order, looking at my pack. "Get your hands off them."

Not even one wolf obeys me, nor do they show any signs of hearing me. Gavin trained them well to listen to their superior, but it seems like they've forgotten that I'm their leader.

"Your Alpha is telling you to stop!" I command, putting as much authority into my voice as my high and drunken ass can manage.

"You're no one's Alpha," my father tells me, narrowing his eyes as he looks at me from head to toe with his lips curled in disgust. "For fuck's sake! Will you cover yourself up a bit? You're an embarrassment to our family's name."

"The Pack of Shadows is mine," I argue weakly, but to no avail.

"The Pack of Shadows will always be Gavin's," my father replies coldly after I wrap a blanket around my waist, his words hitting a sore spot. "You'll never be half the man that your brother is. Now that he's a Lafayette, Tiana's the only suitable option to lead the pack. She was Gavin's protégé after all."

"You're right," I say at last, figuring that it's best to agree with him. "Besides, I can't be both Alpha and a king at the same time. My life is too valuable, and I can't be expected to focus on ten people when I need to lead our whole kingdom."

My father's eyes darken, his look wiping the smile off my face. My intoxicated brain seems to have forgotten for a second that he found me in bed with not one, but three human women. While he's been hearing rumors about me fucking around for years, he never had any actual proof. At least until now.

"I'm freezing your ascension process," my father says, getting straight to the point.

"You can't!" I exclaim. I'm wracking my brain to find a way to convince him, but I can't think clearly through the fog and the headache that's beginning to pound behind my eyes. "Our laws make it clear that the firstborn son is the future king. So, unless I die, I'm the future Grey king."

He won't have us killed, will he? my wolf wonders as soon as I say those words.

"I know what the laws say," my father tells me, sounding far from happy. "I'm aware that you'll be the next king, which is why it's my duty to prepare you as best as I can so that you'll lead our family well."

"I'll make you proud, Father," I promise him with a determined nod. If I wasn't half-naked with only a blanket around my waist, I'd probably sound a lot more convincing.

"It's not your fault, Son," my father says with a heavy sigh. "I should've put an end to your playtime years ago, but I chose to ignore it. Even after I was warned about your disgusting ways, I still didn't want to see the truth."

"This is nothing," I tell him with a nonchalant wave of my hand. "It's just some harmless fun."

"You're the Grey heir, and you should hold yourself to higher standards," my father says in a firm voice. "If you want others to follow you, you have to lead by example. Right now, I don't see anything I like, but don't worry because I have a plan that will fix everything."

It seems like not everything's lost, my wolf says, finding a sliver of hope in this otherwise dark conversation.

"I'll do anything," I tell him, knowing it's the quickest way to get out of this predicament. "Just name it."

"I'll order a coffee to be brought while you put on some clothes," my father tells me, and the fact that he's planning on us sitting down further confirms to me that I won't like what he has to say.

I nod, then grab my clothes off the pile in the corner and go to the bathroom for some privacy. My head spins when I lean down to put on my boxers.

Can't you heal us already? I ask my wolf, needing a clear head to talk to my father.

I would if it was only alcohol, my wolf complains, feeling just as beat as I do. Fucking drugs are too hard on us. I told you not to mix so many of them.

I grunt in response and throw some cold water on my face before I continue dressing myself. The healing process is too fast when using only one drug, making it nearly impossible to feel its effects. But when mixed in a neat and pure cocktail, then either sniffed or washed down with a potent liquor, I'm on top of the world.

When I'm all dressed and the buttons of my shirt are somewhat buttoned up correctly, I return to the hotel suite that I have permanently rented. Even I wouldn't dare to bring humans back to the Grey Manor.

I walk past the bed to my father, who's already sitting at the table by the window and sipping out of his cup. His eyes carefully observe me as I reach for my own cup and mix in two little bags of sugar before topping it off with cold milk.

"What would you like me to do?" I ask him when I finish prepping my coffee and lean back into the comfortable chair. "A diplomatic mission to the Farrells? I'm sure they're quite upset with the mess Felix and Gavin created. Or should I travel to the Middle East to check on our new rig? I'll be happy to make rounds to confirm that all our businesses are bringing in the most money they can."

"I'm afraid that I have different plans in mind for you," my father says, a small smile playing on his lips.

I don't like this, my wolf tells me, and I have to agree with him.

"As I said before, I haven't paid enough attention to you. Now that we've started the ascension process, we're in a rush to turn you into a king," my father tells me. He pauses long enough to take a sip of coffee and let his words sink in. "The best and fastest way to do that is to send you off to a military camp where they'll make a proper man out of you."

I tip my head back and laugh. It's the best joke I've heard all day, and for a moment, I was actually worried that he was being serious. When I realize that he didn't join in, my laughter slowly dies down.

"Please tell me that you're kidding," I say, looking at him in disbelief.

"I'm afraid not," my father says, his previous smiling face now turning grim. "You'll be sent there undercover, and you'll be forbidden to tell anyone who you really are."

"Or what, huh?" I challenge, clenching my jaw in defiance. "You can't force me."

"I can, and I will," he tells me with a nonchalant shrug. "Should you dare to tell anyone about who you are, I'll kill them, their family, and everyone that person might've come in contact with. Be careful what you do, otherwise all those lives will be on you."

"You can't do this," I insist, calling his bluff.

My father takes his time and finishes his cup of coffee before replying. When he's done, he sets it on the table, locking his eyes on mine.

"You seem to forget that I'm the king, Garren," he reminds me. "I may not be willing to punish you directly just yet, but push me far enough, and I will have you removed from the royal line. Until then, people around you will pay for your shortcomings. Tread carefully."

Our eyes are locked in a battle of wills, but it's very clear who's the dominant one. He doesn't even need to use his powers to make me submit. Clenching my jaw so hard that it hurts, I bow my head at the neck, wordlessly agreeing to his plan.

Seemingly satisfied, my father nods and gets up. He looks around the room, his nose scrunching up in disgust. Lucky for me, he doesn't bother to comment any further. He'd made his position clear enough.

"Tiana should return soon to take you to the military encampment. I've assigned you to a pack called Dark Hunter," my father says, his words making my eyes widen to comical proportions as I realize that I'm supposed to leave right now. "The Alpha is from a prominent military family. All her siblings are Alphas of their own packs, and her mother is the Alpha Captain. Her father died on the frontlines, but he was also the Alpha Captain, leading ten packs, the same as her mother is doing now."

"Is that supposed to impress me?" I growl and roll my eyes.

"Yes, it should," my father tells me, narrowing his eyes at me. "It should also show you that I'm putting you in the best pack with an opening. They recently lost their tenth member, which makes this a perfect opportunity for you to get in. I might possibly be sending you to fight on the frontlines, but at least I'm making sure that you're surrounded by capable wolves."

"Come on, Father, don't make me do this. It's bullshit," I say, not even caring that I sound like I'm whining. "I promise I'll get better by myself. From now on, I'm cut off from the alcohol and drugs."

"You're right about that because you won't have any of it in the encampment," my father says with a smile. "The best we can hope for is that this experience turns you into at least half of the man that your brother is. If that happens, we'll consider it a win."

It's over, my wolf tells me, making me face the truth. You'll have to let it go for now.

"Yes, Father," I say, forcing the words out through gritted teeth.

With a curt nod, my father turns on his heels and leaves me behind in the hotel suite that smells like sex, alcohol, and stale cigarettes. On any other occasion, I'd consider the night to be a fucking success, but right now, I don't feel like smiling and patting my shoulder for a good fuck fest.

When Tiana arrives, I'm still sitting in the same spot, holding my now cold coffee. Not even three hours ago,

I was on top of the world, and now I've fallen to the absolute bottom. I'm joining some random pack as a commoner, as a soldier with a lower standing. Following that theory, even Tiana has more power than I do.

We'll show them all, my wolf promises. They'll end up begging us for forgiveness.

You're right, I agree. Once we rise up the ranks, Father will have to eat his words. We'll even put Saint Gavin to shame.

My wolf makes a sound in agreement, channeling his motivation and confidence into me. It's potent enough that I lift my head high up and meet Tiana's eyes.

"Ready to go?" she asks, her usually playful behavior nowhere to be seen.

I don't think she was too happy to find us in bed with human women, my wolf speculates.

Good point, I allow, then force a smile on my face to hold up the pretense that nothing can shake me.

"What's the rush, sweetheart?" I ask as I set my coffee on the table and get up. I nod toward the bed, raise my brow, and smirk. "How about it? You in for a ride?"

Tiana's face darkens, and she steps aside, giving me a clear view of the door where I only now notice Jay standing. The second Beta, or well, now that Tiana is Alpha, I suppose he got promoted to her spot, is looking at me with an air of superiority.

Bloody commoner! my wolf hisses, his disgust heavily dripping from every word.

I'm the future Grey king and I won't be disrespected by trashy little nobodies like these two. It's important that I make it clear who's the real Alpha here in every sense of the word.

With a deep breath, I send a signal to my wolf to bring out the claws just as I jerk forward and roughly grab Tiana's neck, my fingers dangerously curling around it. I expect Jay to assist his Alpha, but Tiana holds up her hand, stopping him in his tracks. My lips curl up into a triumphant smile and I tighten my grip around Tiana's neck.

"Learn to respect your superiors or I'll add another scar across your beautiful face," I say with a low voice. "I'd hate for everyone to know that X marks the spot to punch."

Tiana's dark eyes are locked on mine as a slow grin spreads on her face. A guttural scream comes deep from within me before my brain even has the chance to realize that something's wrong. The hand that I had around Tiana's neck is broken in half, the bone protruding through the torn flesh.

I let go of her and cradle my injured hand close to my chest. My eyes dart to Tiana's, my vision blurring as the pain becomes too much.

"What did you do?" I force out, my voice hoarse and low.

"You should always keep an eye on your shadow," she replies with a nonchalant shrug. "The most painful backstabbing is the one you do to yourself."

She animated our shadow and used it as a puppet, my wolf growls, panting hard as he's doing his best to heal us through the drug and alcohol-induced fog of my own doing.

"You'll pay for this," I promise her through gritted teeth. "I'll make you regret the day that you used your powers on your future King."

"It's time to go," Tiana says coldly, not sounding worried at all. That's okay because it only means that she doesn't bother to keep her guard up around me. It will be easier to slip through the cracks and punish her.

The blinding pain makes me sway on my feet, my head feeling light, and my vision unclear. I shake off Jay's hand when he grabs my arm and weakly growls at him. It's the only sound I'm able to make, but at least I somehow manage to make my own way to the van.

I might hate what my father has planned for me, but he's right in one thing. I need to get clean, so I can get stronger. While my powers are nowhere near Gavin's, I'm not as weak as everyone else thinks. It's my own fault for consuming so much crap, which cut me off from my vast well of darkness.

I'll go to the military encampment, I'll climb my way up the ranks to shut my father's mouth, and then I'll return to sit on the throne. I'm the only legitimate future this family has, but before I make our kingdom stronger, I'll get rid of the traitors such as Tiana and Jay.

No one will ever laugh at me again.

Get your copy of Shadow King's Redemption now! – Free in Kindle Unlimited

https://www.amazon.com/dp/B0CZ2D1M3S

Get a Steamy Alpha Romance for FREE!

I write steamy paranormal romances centered around fated mates... wolves, witches and any other supernatural being that is in my imagination!

Do you want to be the first to know when I release new books, access to exclusive sneak peeks, and give-aways? Then join my newsletter and get Alpha Bound by Fate for Free for signing up!

An Enemies to Lovers Steamy Paranormal Romance

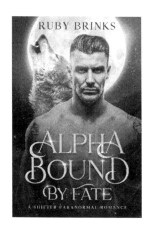

CLICK HERE-https://www.BookHip.com/BTX CMDS

Made in the USA
Columbia, SC
19 November 2024

46546172R00236